Southern
Exposure

Southern Exposure

KAREN KELLEY

BRAVA

KENSINGTON PUBLISHING CORP.
http://www.kensingtonbooks.com

BRAVA BOOKS are published by

Kensington Publishing Corp.
850 Third Avenue
New York, NY 10022

All Kensington titles, imprints and distributed lines are available at special quantity discounts for bulk purchases for sales promotion, premiums, fund-raising, educational or institutional use.

Special book excerpts or customized printings can also be created to fit specific needs. For details, write or phone the office of the Kensington Special Sales Manager: Kensington Publishing Corp., 850 Third Avenue, New York, NY 10022. Attn. Special Sales Department. Phone: 1-800-221-2647.

Brava and the B logo Reg. U.S. Pat. & TM Off.

ISBN 0-7582-0711-5

First Kensington Trade Paperback Printing: April 2005
10 9 8 7 6 5 4 3 2 1

Printed in the United States of America

This book is dedicated to my aunt, Christy Donahoo, who is teaching me the true meaning of perseverance. To the BG's: Sheila, Mary Beth, and Darese—thanks bunches! To Judy Elliot because she's known me a long time and still likes me, Kelley McMillion for making me laugh, and to Charlie who knows a good book when he reads one!

Everyone needs someone in their life who will be there to comfort them, encourage them, and be their best friend no matter what. For me that person is my husband, Karl Kelley. This book is especially dedicated to him.

Chapter 1

The charged air sizzled and snapped with an undercurrent of expectation. Somewhere, the steady thudding of a drum echoed. Moisture dotted Logan Hart's upper lip. He could almost see the saliva dripping from sharp teeth, hungry predators waiting to pounce on their next victim.

What the hell am I doing here?

He wiped his sweaty palms down the sides of his black leather pants . . . like that helped a whole hell of a lot, and let the curtain fall back into place. "How did I get myself into this mess," he muttered under his breath.

"I'll tell you." His brother spoke up. "You made a bet you could do any job for one shift. Then you promised the devoted readers of your newspaper column that you'd write a monthly update on your adventures." He didn't try to control his snicker of amusement.

"Thanks for reminding me." He frowned. "What's the old saying about blood being thicker than water? You're not lending much moral support. The least you could do is help me figure a way out of my predicament."

"And miss all this?" He swung his arm in a wide arc.

"Damn it, Kevin, you're not helping." He lowered his voice when one of the prop men glanced in their direction. "I've done everything the people of New Orleans have thrown at me. Sales at the newspaper have doubled since I started writing these articles." He ticked off the list on his fingers. "I've managed to jump out of a plane, get battered in a football game, dig ditches, tend bar, add figures until I was dizzy, package meat, work in an assembly line and lay brick. But this is ridiculous. I mean"—he waved his hand down his body—"look at this getup. I feel like an idiot."

Black leather pants and a vest. No shirt or shoes. And a blasted thong! He wanted to rip the strip of leather out of his ass. Whoever invented this instrument of irritation should have their head examined.

Kevin's eyes narrowed as he studied Logan. "I bet the women will think you look . . . sexy."

"I'm glad you find this whole thing amusing, *little brother.*" He could tell Kevin was biting the insides of his cheeks to keep from laughing. Logan would probably hear about this at the next several family gatherings. He inwardly groaned. One family member would tell another, and that one would tell another . . . Why did he have to be born into such a large family? And why did Kevin decide to visit him *this* week? Things couldn't get any worse.

Taking a deep breath, then expelling it in a whoosh of air, he peered from behind the heavy curtain again. Things certainly hadn't gotten any better. If anything, the crowd had swelled to alarming proportions.

"I can't do it." He started to turn away.

"Giving up? When you only have this project and one more before you complete your ten assignments?"

Kevin sidestepped two prop men carrying a fake palm tree. As soon as they were alone, or at least as alone as they could get backstage, he continued.

"If you don't supply the readers with a story everything you've done will be for nothing. Do you want that? Besides, you've been practicing this for weeks. All that hard work will go to waste." He straightened to his full height of six feet three inches. "And I might be two years younger, but in case

you haven't noticed, I'm as tall as you. I'm not that little anymore."

Damn it, Kevin was right—on both accounts. Kevin *was*
as tall as him, and Logan *was* almost finished with his chal-
lenges. It would be crazy to pull out now.

"The job of assistant editor isn't a shoe-in," he reminded
Kevin. "Don't forget about Hank. He's still in the running."

"But this will put you a step ahead of the competition."
He gave Logan a hard look. "Will it really be *that* bad?"

Logan took a deep breath and stared once more between
the curtains. Okay, so maybe all of it wasn't going to be a hard-
ship. The woman seated at the front table stood out from the
rest, grabbing his attention. The music had changed to a more
sensual beat. As she swayed to the rhythm, her straight, jet–
black hair brushed her shoulders. Her sultry movements had
him wanting to stride from behind the curtain and scoop her
into his arms like a warrior with his prize.

He groaned when her eyes closed, and her lips parted
slightly. He imagined her naked, lying beneath him, and
looking just like she did right now. A flash of heat stole over
him. The Velcro on his pants crackled.

This was all he needed.

"Okay," he growled. "Let's get it over with."

The music filled Jody, spinning around inside her head,
touching her, caressing her soul. She swayed to the sensuous
strains, losing herself in the swirling colors of erotic sounds.

She could almost touch each note, could almost feel the
beat of each drum. The tempo suddenly changed and the
haunting notes of a flute floated over her. She closed her eyes,
letting the melody sweep her into another realm.

Her reverie was unexplainably jarred. A different sensation
washed over her. Her eyes snapped open. Someone watched
her. She could feel his gaze . . . burning, caressing.

She glanced to her left. Her friend Andrea had struck up a

conversation with the woman next to her. The girl had never met a stranger. Slowly, she moved her gaze around the room, stopping at the heavy, black velvet curtains that ran across the middle of the low stage. The hairs on the back of her neck tickled.

The knowledge someone watched her grew stronger. Not the same as the intuitions she had when she worked her beat as a cop in the Big Easy. This time was different.

Goose bumps covered her arms. She leaned back in her chair and stared at the curtains, wondering what lay behind the velvety folds.

With a certainty born from experience, she knew something was going to happen tonight.

Andrea had said her life had become too routine . . . to the point of predictability. She had a feeling all that was about to change.

Her grandmother had once told her if she paid attention, Jody would be able to sense the changes in her life before they happened. Sometimes her grandmother would go into a deep meditative state for hours to interpret if it would be a good change, or a bad one.

Jody wasn't quite sure she believed *everything* her grandmother said or did, but sometimes *Mamere* was so accurate it made her ways more believable.

"So, did I surprise you, birthday girl?" Andrea asked, interrupting her thoughts.

Jody smiled. "You couldn't have given me a better present."

"I still want to get you a gift. You know, the kind you open. It's not a true birthday unless you can unwrap something."

They were an unlikely pair. Andrea, with her blonde hair curling wildly around her face, blue eyes and perky personality. Everything Jody wasn't. But on the inside, where it counted, they were the same. Two lost souls who came together and formed a bond of friendship. Two kids who'd grown up in the Louisiana bayou.

"You need to get out more," Andrea continued.

"I do. I patrolled the streets of New Orleans just last night."

Andrea crossed her arms and leaned back in her chair. "That's not what I meant and you know it."

A slight alteration in the music, a subtle difference in the sound, pulled Jody's attention back to the stage. She nodded toward the curtain. "The show's starting."

Andrea paused in reaching for her drink. A few seconds later, the curtain rose. "How do you know these things?"

"I'm paid to know. Remember, I'm a cop." Not that Jody thought that was the real reason. Being a cop helped, but again, her grandmother had taught her to use her five senses—really use them. Then she went a step further and taught her how to read signs, like when the weather was going to change. Anyone could do as much, if they only took the time to listen.

And she'd always had the ability to sense when something was about to happen . . . like now. Premonitions—everyone had them. It was no biggie.

Except she'd never had a premonition quite like this.

Excitement skittered up and down her spine, even though she wasn't as comfortable around people as Andrea. Which was odd, since they were both raised deep in the swamps where people were scarce. They hadn't even met until Andrea came to work at the police department. As different as night and day, Andrea seemed to crave people, whereas Jody could spend days by herself.

Multi-colored lights began flashing overhead. Jody concentrated on her surroundings, absorbing the deep reds, vibrant blues, and emerald greens that dazzled her eyes.

She strained to see onto the shadowy stage. A man melded with the darkness, head bowed, legs spread apart, arms at his sides.

The crowd grew silent. Jody held her breath. A deep voice blared over the intercom system.

"The Eighth Wonder of the World Casino and Hotel in fabulous New Orleans, Louisiana, welcomes Hot Southern Men! And to start off tonight's performance, please welcome our newest heartthrob . . . Logan Hart!"

Bursts of fire shot up from the floor around him. The boards beneath her feet vibrated as the roomful of women roared to life. Onstage, the lone male began gyrating his hips, slowly at first.

Lights bathed him in hues of cool yellows and hot reds.

Nice package. "I think I've decided what I want to unwrap for my birthday," Jody said close to Andrea's ear. Tonight she wanted her life to be different. She wanted more.

"I thought you'd like the show." Andrea grinned and began stomping her feet and whistling along with the rest of the women.

Jody reached for her drink, wrapping her fingers around the glass without taking her gaze off the performer. Logan Hart certainly affected her senses. Broad shoulders and lean, oiled muscles. The vest he wore didn't even come close to hiding his rock solid chest from her hungry eyes. Her gaze moved lower, to his taut stomach, to the leather pants riding low on his hips, hugging every sinewy muscle. She returned to his face, but it was hidden from view by a dark cowboy hat. She wondered what the shadows concealed, and if his face could be as mouth-watering as the rest of him.

Raising her glass, she drank the last of her tequila sunrise and set it back on the table. The alcohol did little to quench her sudden thirst.

Music blared across the room, women screamed and began waving different denominations of bills. He seemed oblivious to his surroundings as he continued to keep time with the music. A flash of light shot from the ceiling, illuminating his features as he raised his head and seemed to look straight at her. She drew in a sharp, ragged breath.

A five o'clock shadow outlined a strong jaw. Had not shaving been intentional? Probably. It worked. At least for her. She liked the slightly rough, less than perfect air about him.

She barely stayed focused as he danced toward their tiny table. Surely he wasn't coming toward her? She glanced toward her friend. Andrea oozed lush sex appeal. She had to be his target.

But when she looked up, her gaze collided with his. He didn't seem aware of Andrea. He danced closer, his body undulating with every pounding beat of the music. Raw, male magnetism emanated from every pore.

She tried to swallow and couldn't. She reached for her glass, remembered she'd finished her drink, and drew her hand back to her lap where she clasped her fingers in nothing less than a death grip.

His gaze slid down her body touching every part of her with a hot, melting look. Her face, her shoulders, her breasts. She licked dry lips and could almost taste the salt of his skin. The crowd faded. Andrea faded. It was just the two of them in the room. A man, a woman.

Her normally cautious nature fled, right along with her inhibitions. She tossed back her hair, challenging him. He cocked an eyebrow, then grinned, a slow, sideways smile. He accepted.

When he held out his hand for her to join him, she hesitated, a moment of panic washing over her. What was she doing? Andrea nudged her, but Jody couldn't go up on the stage.

Something in his eyes just before he turned away said he thought she'd have more courage.

Was she going to take that?

She watched him saunter away all of two seconds before she stood, her chin jutted out. The sudden whistles and yells of encouragement from the throng of people had him turning around, approval reflected in his eyes.

She walked up the two steps to the stage floor, an exaggerated sway to her hips as she sauntered past his outstretched hand with barely a glance in his direction. A few feet away, she whirled around and faced him. Their gazes locked.

She began to dance. For him. Her body melted into liquid heat as she moved to the music. Shoulders swaying, arms raised, the pulsating beat consuming her. Her eyes drifted shut as the music enveloped her. She fed off the sound, hips slowly rotating from side to side.

She didn't flinch when he came up behind her, sliding his hands down the sides of her body, past the contour of her breasts, fanning over her hips and down her thighs, then returning to her waist. She leaned against him, their bodies touching, moving as one to the beat. His hot breath scorched her neck where he'd pushed her hair to the side. Flames shot up around them, but it couldn't compare to the heat building inside her when his tongue slid up to her ear and he tugged the lobe with his teeth. She drew in a deep, shuddering breath.

He slid his arms up hers. Her back pressed intimately against his front. She felt his need. Taking her wrists, he spun her around to face him, his eyes heavy-lidded and filled with restrained passion. A surge of fire shot through her, flames licking . . . burning. Their breath mingled and fused. Her breasts were crushed against his chest, her nipples hard and sensitive.

Was she caught in a vivid dream? Would she wake any moment and discover this man only a ghost lover?

Her fingers splayed across his chest, feeling the thump of his heart. This was real. She moved her hands down his sides, gliding over the contours of his hard body.

Once more the music changed tempo. The wild drums slowed and were replaced with the haunting strains of violins. Logan tossed his hat and brought her hands to rest on his shoulders. He stared down into her eyes as he danced her around the stage. Suddenly she didn't want to be alone anymore. At least not tonight. She liked the way his arms enclosed her in a cocoon of sexual fantasy, and she didn't want it to end here.

"Who are you?" he asked.

Having freed her mind and body from restraints, she laughed up at him. A deep, throaty sound, but she didn't tell him what he wanted.

As they came to a stop, he rubbed his thumb across her lips. "Meet me later."

Careful what you wish for. It was almost like her grandmother whispered in her ear.

But isn't this what she wanted? No entanglements? A one-night stand?

He dragged her hands downward and hooked her fingers into the loops at the waistband of his pants. "Say yes." He nibbled her neck. "Right after this number is over. I want to know you better."

"Yes," she breathed.

A slow sideways smile appeared on his face. "Pull."

"What?"

Logan tugged on her fingers. "Jerk real hard."

She did and his pants came away in her hands, leaving him wearing only a black leather G-string. Her gaze moved back to the pants she held. With a swift kiss on her lips, he took them and strode offstage. The cheeks of his butt were just as tanned as the rest of him.

The applause behind her was deafening, but she barely heard it over the pounding of her heart. A desire to have this man take her in his arms again burned its way down her body, leaving in its wake a need to be satisfied.

She walked back to the table, said a quick good-bye to Andrea, grabbed her purse, and headed toward the door as the next act began.

Chapter 2

Logan hurried out the back entrance of the club, going around the outside of the building so he wouldn't have to wade through the crowd of women.

Two thoughts ran through his mind. Would she be waiting? And why should he really care? After all, he'd survived his night as a stripper, he had his story. That was all that mattered. Or so he tried to convince himself.

What was it about this woman that made him want to see her again? It might just be the assignment that had him on edge. Or the city. Since moving to New Orleans he'd felt an undercurrent of something unexplainable.

Whatever it was, when she'd been in his arms tonight, his instincts had come alive. There had been something lurking in the depths of her deep blue eyes. The reporter in him sensed a story with this woman, but the man knew there was a stronger reason for wanting to meet her.

Maybe it was the gutsy way she'd stood up in front of a crowd. Or maybe it was the way she'd turned the tables and begun a seduction all her own. He had a feeling it was the latter.

Probably because she did it so well.

He rounded the corner and all his expectations disintegrated. She wasn't there. Had he really thought someone who looked like her would meet him out front? Hell, she didn't even know him.

Well, he certainly couldn't go back inside. Kevin would have a field day. He started to turn, but caught a movement from the corner of his eye. As she stepped from the building, relief flooded him. He waited until she joined him, then he spoke. "I thought you'd decided not to meet me."

She let her gaze drift over him. "I almost didn't."

"What made you change your mind?"

She smiled and his breath caught in his throat. There was something damned alluring about her smile.

"You were disappointed when you saw I wasn't there. That hasn't happened very often in my life. It's a strange feeling. I guess I wanted to see why you would care."

Now there was a story he'd like to explore . . . later, when they knew each other a little better. "Want to go for a drink?"

She nodded. "My car is in the parking garage. I'll follow you."

Cautious. He liked that about her. Twenty minutes later they were sitting in a small bar. She ordered a tequila sunrise, but wouldn't let him pay for it.

Their drinks arrived. He raised the bottle to his mouth, but he didn't really taste the beer. Holding the bottle kept him from reaching across the table to touch her, to caress her face, to run his finger across the fullness of her lips. He shifted on the green vinyl, but changing positions didn't ease his ache.

"Have you been a stripper long, Logan Hart?" Amusement tinged her words.

Heat crawled up his neck. He cleared his throat, took a drink, and wondered what he should tell her.

People had a way of clamming up when they discovered he was a reporter. He guessed they were afraid their life story would end up on the front page. Most never realized what they could tell him would probably put the typical reader to sleep.

"Not long." It wasn't exactly a lie, he reasoned. Once he knew her better, and she him, then he would explain the situation. "You never told me your name," he changed the subject away from him.

A crowd of late-night revelers entered the bar, interrupting them. Their raucous laughter filled the small room.

She leaned across the table. "Do you want to go somewhere quieter?" she asked.

He nodded. "Do you know a place in all of New Orleans that would be open *and* quiet?" He yelled above the noise of the jukebox that had been resurrected with a quarter.

"There's a motel not far from here." Her gaze never wavered from his.

His heart pounded inside his chest almost as loud as the bass on the jukebox. "Are you sure?"

She did pause then.

He held his breath.

"Yeah, I'm sure."

On the drive to the motel she called herself nine kinds of a fool. She didn't know this man. He could be a serial killer for all she knew. She did know enough self-defense to extricate herself if things didn't work out. Not that she thought force would be necessary. Her premonition that this was meant to be was growing stronger.

She waited while he got a room, then followed him in her car to the back of the motel, parking next to him.

If you're going to do something, you might as well do it right.

Go away, Mamere, she told the little voice inside her head. *I plan on doing it right.* She cut the engine and climbed out of her car.

How long had it been since she'd been with a man? Six months? Yeah, somewhere around there.

She should never have let herself be seduced by a coworker. It made things messy when it ended. To save his ego, Paul had started a number of rumors. Hell, some people already thought she dabbled in the black arts. She'd been tempted to leave a voodoo doll in his locker, but she had a healthy respect for things she didn't fully understand. Maybe tonight would be a sort of cleansing of an old relationship that had gone sour. Maybe she needed that more than anything else.

He waited while she locked her car, then moved to the motel door, and inserted the key. Once inside, he tossed it on the night table and abruptly turned, taking her in his arms.

"God, I wanted to do this as soon as I laid eyes on you." He kicked the door shut before lowering his mouth to hers.

Jody melted against him as heat stole over her body. His tongue teased, while his hands glided up and down her back. When she moaned against his mouth, he pulled away.

"I'm sorry. I didn't mean to pounce as soon as the door was closed." He truly looked apologetic.

"*J'aime te faire l'amour avec toi,*" she spoke in a voice filled with barely restrained passion.

"French? Sexy."

Too many words ruined the moment, unless they were words of love. She didn't want to think . . . only feel.

And she didn't have to explain the words she'd spoken as she moved to the first button on her shirt and slipped it from the hole. Then the next. And the next until there were none left.

For the last few months she'd refused to date anyone, but as her blouse silently drifted to the floor, so did her misgivings. She needed this release, and she sensed he would be the man who could soothe her cravings. So what if he thought she was easy? He would be gone from her life after tonight, and only a memory would remain. She unfastened her bra and shrugged out of it.

She wanted it to be a damn good memory.

She kicked off her sandals, then unzipped her skirt. The loose, flowing white cotton material puddled at her feet. She stood before him wearing only a pair of white, lacy bikini panties.

He stared, then drew in a deep, shuddering breath. "You're beautiful."

She smiled. His expression had already told her before he said the words. She liked that about him.

"What's your name?" He pulled his T-shirt over his head and tossed it on a nearby chair.

"Does it matter?" Somehow exchanging names would make tonight too personal. She didn't want that, only liberation from the pent-up emotions she'd held at bay for much too long.

He paused, his hand on the zipper of his pants. She had a feeling it would end right here if she didn't give him what he asked.

A man with principles.

"Jody."

"Just Jody?" He raised an eyebrow.

"Just Jody."

He tugged the zipper down and kicked out of his jeans. He still wore the black leather G-string.

She reached forward to cup him, closing her eyes, and enjoying the moment. Her boldness surprised even her, but this was a night for surprises. She lightly squeezed, feeling him harden beneath her touch. The fluttering quickened inside her stomach. He sucked in a deep breath.

"Who are you?" he whispered, taking her hand in his and moving it away. "Are you a phantom of my imagination?"

"Didn't my touching you feel real?"

"I'm not complaining." He silently studied her for a moment. "Maybe you're a witch."

Paul had called her a witch, too. Every time she narrowed her eyes in his direction, he would quickly leave the room. Somehow, she didn't think Logan would move.

"Maybe I am. Would it bother you?"

"I think you've already cast a spell over me." He reached toward her, cupping one breast, brushing his thumb across the tender nipple. She arched toward him as heat spiraled downward to settle between her legs in a slow-burning fire. She wondered exactly who had cast the spell as a sweet ache began to grow inside her.

He lowered his head and kissed one breast, then the other, swirling his tongue around the taut nipple before taking it in his mouth and gently sucking. She held on to his shoulders to keep from swaying, but she couldn't stop her desire to touch him.

Locked in a hazy fantasy realm, she explored the sinewy muscles of his back while he sucked at her breast.

He was firm, still oily from his performance. She inwardly smiled knowing he hadn't taken the time to wipe off. Had he been that eager to meet her?

His mouth tugged at her nipple one last time before he moved to the other breast. She gasped as pleasure and pain washed over her. She'd never wanted a man more than she did Logan right now. The need to have him fill her body was almost overpowering.

Apparently their thoughts were the same. He guided her to the bed, easing down to the mattress. She ran her hands over his hard body, feeling the contour of each muscle. She cupped his butt, massaging. He groaned, but instead of drawing closer, he pulled away, and stood.

"I want you," she breathed. God, she wanted him. She'd never felt this strong a physical response to anyone. *"Cher,"* she whispered. "Make love to me, *cher."*

He hooked his fingers in her panties and pushed them downward. His G-string followed. She drew in a deep breath. It *had* been a long time if the sight of a male penis could make her damp so quickly. She got comfortable on the bed, while he slipped on a condom.

His gaze met hers. "Are you sure?"

More sure than she had been of anything in a very long time. She nodded and spread her legs in invitation. He stared down at her. Heat rose up her face as a moment of indecision swept over her. What was she doing here?

Before she could change her mind, he tentatively brushed his fingers across her mound. She gasped and arched her hips. All rational thought fled as he leaned down and kissed her curls, then scraped his tongue over her clit. She clutched his head. "Ah, *cher*," she moaned, writhing beneath what his mouth was doing to her. It felt so damn good.

"You taste sweet . . . and hot." He licked her, sucking and pulling on the sensitive flesh.

It had been too long that she'd denied her body this kind of gratification. She couldn't hold back the tremors racing up and down her body. Her thoughts were incoherent as pleasure flooded her body.

Before the orgasm ended, he'd entered her, filling her with his body. Slowly, he rose above her, then plunged downward. She gasped, wrapping her legs around him, drawing him deeper . . . closer, until their bodies melded as one with every thrust.

Tension began building inside her once more, like a tightly coiled spring. Each time he plunged inside her body, the spring tightened. When sweet release exploded over her, she cried out, her nails digging into his back.

His body jerked as he came, and he fell on top of her. Their breaths mingled. After only a moment, he rolled to his side, dragging her with him so he didn't lose the connection.

"Sweet Jesus, you are a witch," he said as he fought to draw air into his lungs.

Panic stole over her. It wasn't supposed to be like this. Not this good.

"Hey, why such a serious look?" he asked, brushing her hair to the side of her face.

Don't worry about it, she told herself as she quickly brushed her hair back in place, covering the scar above her right ear. *It's only for tonight. He means nothing to you. Laissez les bon temps rouler. Let the good times roll.* "Maybe you surprised me a little. I didn't expect it to be so fantastic."

He frowned. "I thought I looked pretty damned good on-stage tonight. How could you expect anything less?" he said in mock seriousness. "You've wounded me." He slapped a hand over his heart.

"Ah, I'm sorry." She lowered her eyes as she got caught up in his game. Then, in a sultry voice, she continued, "Tell you what, I'll make it up to you by scrubbing your back while you shower."

"Only if you'll join me."

"I wouldn't have it any other way."

"I'll turn the water on so it can get warm," he told her as he left the bed, grabbing a condom from his pants pocket before he sauntered into the bathroom.

She sighed, her gaze glued to this magnificent specimen of the male anatomy. He certainly wasn't wasting his talents stripping for a bunch of bored women. She shoved the cover to the side and stood. This was how life should be lived—one day at a time. Her night of pleasure would be like turning over a new leaf in her life. No guilt, no recriminations, no past . . . She drew in a sharp breath. No, she wouldn't forget her past, but neither would she let it intrude. Not tonight.

"The water's nice and hot," he drawled from the doorway.

She let her glance slide over him. Tonight she would only think about satisfying her needs. And he certainly had the tool for the job.

"You might want to turn the hot water off," she murmured. "I think we can steam the place pretty well all on our own." She sidled past him, brushing her hand across his already hard arousal. His moan made her smile.

She stepped into the shower, reached for the bar of soap, then turned to face him. He stood perfectly still while she lathered his chest, swirling the suds through the sprinkling of dark hair. "I'm glad you're not one of those dancers who shave their bodies. I like the way your hair tickles my breasts." She couldn't believe she'd spoken her thoughts aloud, but he didn't seem to mind as he took the soap from her hand and began to rub the flat side of the bar across her nipples.

"You're breasts are very sensitive," he said. "As soon as I touch the nubs, they tighten into hard little pebbles. I like sucking on them, pulling them between my teeth and flicking my tongue over them."

A quiver ran up the insides of her thighs. He ran the soap over her abdomen, then between her legs, applying firm pressure. She met his gaze as her breath came in small puffs.

"Do you like me rubbing you there?" He leaned forward and delved his tongue into her ear. "Do you like it?"

"God, yes." She bit down on her bottom lip, sucking in a deep breath.

He stopped his assault on her body, long enough to slip the condom on, then caught her waist and raised her off the shower floor. Automatically, her legs circled him as he entered her. She countered his thrust with a rocking movement of her hips. He plunged deeper. She closed her eyes tight as the tension coiled inside her.

"Ah, this feels good," he muttered.

She clenched her inner muscles and he groaned. When she thought she would die without release, spasms swept over her. Vaguely, she heard his cry and felt his body jerk.

She slowly unlocked her legs and eased them to the floor of the stall. If she hadn't held on to Logan, she would've collapsed to the tiles in a mindless heap.

"Yeah, I think maybe you just might be a witch," he rasped out.

Later, as they lay in bed, Jody listened to the sound of his breathing as he slept. What had happened tonight? They'd made some kind of connection. But she didn't want to bond with anyone else.

She reached up and lightly ran her finger across the scar above her right ear. The furrow the bullet had made was scarred over leaving only a vague memory. She squeezed her eyes closed as she pushed it from her mind. Nothing could change the past.

Logan mumbled something in his sleep and rolled to his side.

But she could damn well change the future. Her grandmother always said for each one of us there's a soul mate. That special someone who could make your life complete. She said Jody would know when she met that person.

She slipped from the bed, careful not to jar the mattress, and pulled her clothes on.

Who could say Logan might be that special man? She just knew she couldn't afford to find out. Before she slipped out of the room, she took one last, lingering look. A sigh of regret slipped from her lips before she silently closed the door.

Chapter 3

"You have that faraway look in your eyes again," Andrea said as she took a seat across from Jody in the break room of the police station.

Heat stole up her neck and to her face. "Daydreaming, I guess." She quickly raised her cup and took a sip of coffee then set it back on the table, absently rubbing her finger across the smooth rim.

"You've never been a good liar."

"I was thinking. Is that a crime?" She immediately regretted her harsh tone. "Sorry."

Andrea opened the pack of powdered doughnuts she'd brought with her to the table. "That's what I'm talking about. You act like you're PMSing really, really bad. Even though Paul is a real jerk, the poor guy has started looking over his shoulder like you're going to hex him any minute."

She frowned. "I haven't said two words to the man."

Andrea chuckled. "No, you've just been giving him the evil eye." She pushed the doughnuts toward Jody. "Help me eat these so I won't gain twenty pounds."

"Like twenty pounds would hurt you." Andrea's words sank in. Jody straightened. "And I haven't been giving Paul the evil eye. I just haven't felt well," she said as she took one of the doughnuts and bit into the soft pastry, then brushed the white powder off her shirt.

Andrea leaned back in her chair and studied her, the dough-nuts apparently forgotten for the moment.

Jody felt like a molecule under a microscope. "What?" she finally asked, knowing Andrea could outlast her on any stare-down.

"You've been acting odd since the night you ran out of the club to meet that stripper." Her eyes widened, and she slipped into her native Cajun. "It must've been some hot date if you still be thinking 'bout him, *chere*,"

"I'm not still *thinking* about him." The lie tangled on her tongue.

Paul opened the door and stepped inside the break room. Jody cast a glare in his direction. He quickly downed his head and stepped out, closing the door behind him.

"See, I be tellin' you. Everybody be scared you put the gris-gris on dem." Andrea gave her a knowing nod.

"Well, maybe I be puttin' a hex on them—and you too. Maybe I just be visitin' *Mamere* and be gettin' one of her evil potions." She shoved the rest of her doughnut in her mouth, then tried to chew around it with her cheeks stuffed full.

Nonplussed by Jody's threat, Andrea leaned forward, rest-ing her hands on the red Formica table. "It's worse than I thought, isn't it?"

Jody took a drink of coffee to rid herself of the powdery doughnut still stuck to the roof of her mouth. Andrea waited patiently. How could she lie to her friend? She sighed, her temper leaving as quickly as it had come. "He was the best lay I've ever had."

"That's all?" Andrea's eyebrows rose almost to her hair-line.

Jody didn't meet her eyes. "No. There was a . . . I don't know . . . a connection. It's hard to explain."

"You know I just happened to find out they'll be doing a show in Bossier City at one of the casinos. We could drive up. Maybe do a little gambling."

One eyebrow arched. "I'm not a groupie."

"Who said you were? I just thought we could get out of the city for a while."

Temptation came close to overriding good sense. For a moment she could almost feel Logan's arms wrapping around her, the warmth of his embrace enveloping her. Making love with him had been *so* sweet . . . and hot. She clamped her legs together. There had been lots and lots of heat.

A door slammed down the hall, but to Jody it almost sounded like a shot fired. Without conscious thought she rubbed the scar at her temple.

Steely determination washed over her. She squared her shoulders. "No, it was a one-night stand. That's all. I'm just feeling moody."

"Someday you're going to have to let go of the past." Andrea patted her hand.

Jody saw the sadness reflected in Andrea's eyes. She didn't want her pity. She didn't want anyone's pity. "Maybe I don't want to let go. Maybe I want to remember." She pulled her hand free and stood, going to the door.

"Why?" Andrea's brow furrowed.

"He took everything from me. Someday we'll meet again, but this time I'll be ready."

"That won't make anything better." She took a deep breath. "It only be making it worse, *chere*."

She closed her eyes tight. "It's the only way I can deal with it, though." She opened the door.

"Jody . . ."

She turned. "No more talk." She hated the look of worry on Andrea's face. She understood what her friend was trying to do, but Andrea couldn't fix her life.

"Okay, I'll let it go. I came in here to tell you the captain needs to see you." She hesitated. "You want to go for drinks after shift?"

"Sure." She smiled, her anger draining away. "We go have us a drink. Listen to a little music, maybe dance some if they have good-lookin' fellas."

"Let the good times roll, eh?"

A bittersweet feeling washed over her. *"Laissez les bon temps rouler."*

"You want me to do what?" Jody sat hard in the chair across from the captain.

He frowned, looking like a bulldog with a bone in his mouth . . . and he wasn't about to share. "You take him on your beat, show him the ropes enough so he can work one shift as your partner."

"No." She shook her head. "He's a civilian. What if he gets me killed?"

"Then you won't have to worry about him anymore if you're dead." He sighed. "Listen, this guy is doing a series of articles where he works different jobs, then writes a story about his experience." His eyes narrowed on her. "I'd like it to be a good one."

She crossed her legs and narrowed her eyes. "Why not send him with Paul? Or Joe?"

"Because they're men."

She could feel her hackles rise. "I beg your pardon?"

"That's not what I mean." He sat forward, leaning his elbows on his desk. "We've been getting a lot of bad publicity lately. You're the only one I trust enough to send him with."

"So you want to invite the alligator into your nest?"

He sighed. "You can show him the other side of law enforcement, Jody. Just keep it nice and quiet. Don't take any chances."

"You mean don't arrest anyone?"

He frowned. "I'm saying hang back. I'll add another unit on the street. You don't always have to be the first one on the scene."

"You're joking?" He wasn't.

"It's the safest thing to do. He should get what he's after, and if you're friendly, then maybe he'll write a better story."

"You want me to go to bed with him?" she asked with more than a touch of sarcasm.

"Do you think it would help?" He leaned forward. "No, I don't want you to go to bed with him. When I said friendly, that's all I meant. It's only for a month. Help me out here. He could give the department some good publicity, and heaven knows we could use more of that."

Damn, she really liked the captain. He'd only been here a few months, but he'd made an effort to clean up the department's image. He'd been trying really hard to improve conditions for everyone.

But she didn't want a reporter hanging around, watching her every move. He continued to stare her down. *And people thought she was the one who could put a hex on them.* She sighed. "When do I meet him?"

"I knew you'd see the importance of having good publicity." He glanced at the clock on his desk. "Actually, he's late." He frowned.

"I won't wait on him. If he doesn't hang on my shirttails, he'll get left behind. He'd better understand that right up front."

The captain looked toward the glass door. "Here he is now." Standing, he offered a welcoming smile. The door behind her opened as she came to her feet.

"Good, you made it. Logan Hart, I'd like to introduce you to your partner for the next month, Jody Dupree."

Oh, crap, this wasn't happening. She could feel the color draining from her face. Please, let there be more than one Logan Hart. The doughnut she'd eaten earlier threatened to come up.

Surely there had to be another Logan Hart. She hadn't felt anything. Not one little tingle that something would happen. But just in case, she sent a quick prayer upward. Please, please, please let it be a middle-aged man with thick glasses, three kids, and a wife.

Slowly, she turned. Her heart clunked to her feet, but shot

right back up on a flutter of excitement that she couldn't ignore. Right on excitement's heels came irritation.

What the hell was a reporter doing stripping in a club? Had he been moonlighting? No wait, the captain had mentioned a series of articles. His stripping had only been another story to him. Damn, damn, damn!

Logan watched the changing expressions on her face. Surprise, disbelief, and right now she didn't look at all happy. He wasn't exactly pleased himself. When he'd opened his eyes the next morning to find her gone, he couldn't have felt more used if she'd left money on the nightstand.

A couple of the male strippers had warned him most of the women only wanted the fantasy to become real for one night. After that, they'd sneak home to their unsuspecting husbands. The men at the club told him it worked out well for everyone concerned.

It hadn't worked well for him. Hell, he hadn't been able to get her—or the incredible sex they'd shared—out of his mind. But it'd been more than that. He'd felt something deep inside him. Something he'd wanted to explore. But she'd left.

How do you look for someone when you only know her first name?

"Mr. Hart."

She held out her hand. He didn't hesitate as he took her hand in his. Hers felt small and warm, the palm a little moist. Was she nervous? She should be. She returned his grip with a solid shake of her own.

Okay, so she wanted to pretend she didn't know him. That was fine with him. Two could play that game. "Let's not be so formal. You can call me Logan. And I hope it's not presumptuous of me if I call you Jody. Or would you prefer I use your *last* name?"

"Jody is fine." Her jaw twitched.

Suddenly, he saw the humor in the situation and smiled. "It will be a pleasure spending the month with you. *I'm sure* you'll show me a lot I hadn't planned on seeing."

Her smile could've chipped ice. "*I'm sure* you've seen more than I will ever show you."

She didn't have to add—*again*. He easily filled in the blank. "I don't know. I can be pretty persuasive, I'm told. I want to know everything . . . about law enforcement and the city, that is."

"And Jody will be the perfect guide. She knows this town backwards and forwards. And she's a damn fine cop." The captain looked quite pleased with himself.

Logan grinned as he followed Jody out of the room, and to the parking garage. She never said a word, not that he minded. He liked the sway of her hips. But the enticing movement didn't fool him. Her back was rigid, and her shoulders squared. She didn't want him within ten feet of her.

The other strippers were right, she'd only gone to the club for a one-night fantasy. He should be angry, feel used, but how could he when he'd never spent a sweeter night? Having her arms tangled with his, her legs wedged between his, had been as close to heaven as he would ever get in this lifetime.

And he didn't intend for it to be the last. She'd enjoyed their night together as much as he had.

She stopped next to a blue and white patrol car and whirled around to face him. Whatever she'd been about to say must have gotten hung in her throat. She stared at him without speaking until some officers walked past talking and laughing.

"Don't look at me like that." She frowned. "What happened between us is over."

A lazy grin lifted the corners of his mouth. "You enjoyed it as much as I did."

She jerked her keys from her pocket, almost dropping them as she strode to the driver's side and unlocked the door. "Did I say it hadn't been enjoyable?" She met his gaze across the top of the car. "I said there wouldn't be a repeat performance."

As she climbed in and unlocked his door, his smile grew

wider. So, she had enjoyed their night together. He hadn't been one hundred percent positive, only about eighty. The odds were in his favor there *would* be a repeat performance— whether she was ready to admit it or not.

"It won't happen," she told him as she started the car, apparently reading his expression.

She didn't sound at all convincing, though.

He leaned against the back of the seat, and for the first time since he'd awakened to realize she was gone, he relaxed.

But as the evening progressed, he came to the conclusion just because he was with Jody, it didn't mean she was with him. Not the way she ignored everything he said or answered with a clipped yes or no.

Then, when they arrived on scene too late to catch any action, he began to suspect she held back. Why? Did she want to ruin his career? No, he didn't think so, but before this night was over, he wanted a few answers.

Chapter 4

Logan leaned against the concrete wall. Where the hell was she? He glanced at his watch. Another ten minutes had passed as he waited in the parking garage. Jody was certainly taking her time putting away her gear.

He straightened when the door opened and she emerged from the station. He caught his breath when he saw she'd also changed out of her uniform. She sure packed a lot of sex appeal into a snug-fitting white T-shirt and a tight pair of jeans. He cleared his throat, and tried to remember why the hell he was pissed. When she cocked an eyebrow and tossed a bored expression in his direction, he remembered.

"Are you planning on giving me the silent treatment all month?" Logan asked. Her yes and no answers had already worn thin.

"Oh, I'm terribly sorry. I wasn't being a very attentive guide, was I?" she said as she strode past. "I suppose you would've preferred I point out the sights. Why, I could have shown you the French Market, and not far from . . ."

"That's not what I'm talking about and you know it," he growled. At the rate they were going, riding out with her for a month would be a fate worse than death.

"I'm off duty, Mr. Hart, and that means I don't owe you a damn thing—including an explanation," she tossed over her shoulder.

It was time they cleared the air. Hell, he didn't really know what reason she had to be angry. He was the one who woke up the next morning to find her gone.

He caught up to her. "Listen, about that night . . ."

She unlocked her car, but instead of getting inside, she whirled around to face him. "You could've told me you were a reporter!"

"Like you were so informative! You didn't even share your last name."

His anger boiled close to the surface. What right did she have to act the injured party? It was time he explained a few facts. Before she could do more than open her mouth again, he began speaking. "You left the room while I slept. That was pretty damn low. If anyone should be angry, it's me."

He'd rolled over in bed, expecting to snuggle with her, and all he got was a cold pillow and an indentation of where her head had been.

"But I wasn't supposed to ever see you again!" She waved her arm. "And now here you are."

Even though the dim lighting cast them in shadows, he could see her eyes flashed fire . . . and passion.

For a moment he couldn't breathe, he couldn't move. He could only stare. God, she was beautiful. Her lips . . . so full and pouting . . . and so damn tempting. A temptation he found too hard to resist.

He pulled her into his arms and lowered his mouth to hers. He'd dreamed of this for a week, lay in bed at night and fantasized about it, tossed and turned, yearning to have her wrapped in his arms once again—to feel the heat of her body crushed against his. He'd wondered all week if she'd actually been real, or just a figment of his imagination.

But this was real, she was real . . . and she wasn't pulling away. She returned his kiss with as much ardor as he felt, making the memory a reality. Damn, she tasted as hot and spicy as he remembered. It still wasn't enough, though. He ached for more.

He tested the smoothness of her cheek, running his knuckles across her soft skin before moving his hand downward and cupping her breast, rubbing his thumb across the hard pebble of her nipple. He caught her moan—it mingled with his. This was how he remembered her—soft and pliant in his arms, touching him as he touched her.

It took all his willpower to ease away from Jody's willing body. As he did, Logan noted her glazed eyes, her swollen lips . . . the need reflected on her face. It mirrored his own. He almost said to hell with trying to stay in control, but she looked too damn vulnerable right now, and he wouldn't take advantage of her. But he did want answers.

"Tell me you haven't thought about me, not even once?" His words rasped out.

What had she done to him? Bewitched him? Put a hex on him? He kept replaying each minute, each second in his mind. He hadn't even been able to look at another woman since their night together.

He tried to clear his mind, not an easy task. Her sultry beauty invaded his space. Closing his eyes, he drew in a deep breath and attempted to rein in his tattered emotions.

Dampness from recent rains hung heavy in the air. Logan had never lived where it rained quite this much. Dry heat and long periods of drought, that's what he was used to. This town, this state, had captured and held his interest for longer than he could remember. Just like the woman in front of him was doing now.

He opened his eyes and looked at her. "Tell me you haven't thought about me even once, and I'll walk away. I'll ask your captain for another partner. You won't have to be around me again." He held his breath. She could lie. He counted on her not to.

She met his gaze before looking away, her silhouette rigid. "Yeah, sure, I've thought about that night. Are you happy? But it won't happen again so don't get your hopes up."

Disappointment flooded him. He wanted to make love to

her. He wanted to feel her naked body pressed against his, her legs wrapping around his waist, drawing him in deeper and deeper. He wanted to feel the heat of passion again. He wanted to see if his memories were real, or if he'd only imagined sex with Jody was that damn good.

But now she was telling him she didn't want an intimate relationship? That hurt—in more ways than one. "Why? What are you afraid of?"

When she flinched, he knew he'd hit a sore spot.

"Not a damn thing, Mr. Hart, but touch me again, and I'll be the one going to the captain and asking him to put you with someone else." She crossed her arms in front of her. "You don't understand. I'm not interested in getting involved with anyone."

"Okay, I won't bother you if that's what you want."

"It is."

Her words might say one thing, but her body had already told him something different. She wanted him, but for some reason, she wasn't going to admit it.

Realization dawned. Damn, how could he be so stupid. Her fingers were bare of jewelry, but that didn't mean there wasn't someone in her life.

"Are you married? Engaged?"

"No. There's no one." She turned away and opened her door, sliding into the seat.

Maybe it was time she had someone in her life. He'd been right when he sensed there was more than met the eye when it came to Jody Dupree.

The reporter inside him mentally took notes. Why didn't she want to let him get close? What secrets did she harbor? He didn't know, but he intended to find out.

The bars on Bourbon Street spilled jazz, country, rock and zydeco music into the crowded street. The rich aroma of gumbo, beans and rice, and the exotic blend of Creole and Cajun spices filled the air along with a hint of musky incense from shops proclaiming they had the perfect potion to take away all your problems. It was the wee hours of the morning; Jody's shift had ended just over an hour ago.

Usually, Jody could lose herself in the essence of the French Quarter. Whether it was in the middle of a swarm of laughing people on Bourbon Street, or walking down one of the quieter streets absorbing the history, wondering if maybe Jean Lafitte had also strolled down the same street. There was something about the French Quarter that pulled at her. *Mamere* said it was the spirits. They loved the French Quarter too much to stay away for long. Maybe her grandmother was right.

But tonight she wasn't in the mood for gaiety, or the jostling crowds, lingering spirits or absorbing anything. She wanted to go home and sleep. But she knew exactly what she'd do once her eyes closed: think about Logan. That was the last thing she wanted to do. Besides, she'd promised Andrea she'd have a drink with her after their shift.

"So let me get this straight." Andrea sidestepped a rain puddle. "The stripper isn't really a stripper. He's a reporter."

"And I'm stuck with him for the rest of the month." Jody complained.

"But is that *really* a bad thing? I mean, at least you don't look all moon-eyed. In fact, I haven't seen you this revved in a long time."

Jody frowned. "You couldn't be farther from the truth." Irritated might be a better description than revved. He should've told her he was a reporter. She didn't like being wrong about someone. Besides the fact it was damned hard concentrating on her job when he was sitting so close to her. She kept re-membering their night together. The way he'd held her in his arms, the way he'd filled her body. A thrill of excitement shiv-ered down her spine.

Damn it! He was making her crazy.

"So, you're saying you're *not* glad he's here?"

She waved her arms. "*Merde!* Can we please talk about

something else?" She was tired of talking about Logan. She was tired of thinking about the man. She was tired of him period. And she had twenty-one more days in his company, and that was subtracting the days she wouldn't be at work. Twenty-one long, torturous days.

She closed her eyes for a moment to regroup, but in those few seconds she could almost feel his arms pulling her close. She quickly opened her eyes, refusing to let herself remember the way his mouth felt against hers, but she couldn't stop the slow-burning heat that spread through her.

No, she wouldn't let him get to her! She'd been plagued all week remembering how his hands had caressed her, touching . . . stroking. A shudder swept over her trembling body.

"So if you don't want to talk about your new *partner,* what do you want to talk about?" Andrea broke into her thoughts as she glanced around. "Nice rain we had. Everything got fucking wet. There, is that better conversation? Or should I say, *safer?*" She cocked one eyebrow. "Now you don't have to talk about your fella."

"He's not my fella," Jody ground out.

Two young men elbowed past, spilling Andrea's drink. "*Fils de putain!* Watch where you're going, *Bioque!*" She cast a glare in the men's direction.

"Sorry, lady." They stumbled down the street.

"Jeez, Andrea." Jody hissed, then pulled on her friend's arm. "Did you see the size of that one guy? Don't start any trouble." Sometimes she wondered if Andrea had any working brain cells.

Andrea pushed her blonde curls away from her face. "I'll kick his *tcheue* he be messin' with me," she huffed. She looked at Jody and began to laugh. "And if I can't do it, then I have a friend who can, eh?"

"You think so?" Jody grinned, the tension leaving her body.

"Yeah, you kick his ass for me and I'll drag it down to the swamps. We'll make gator bait out of him."

Jody shook her head wondering what she was going to do with her friend. Andrea was forever opening her mouth and inserting her foot. The girl never thought before she spoke.

"Come on, I think it's time we went home."

"What time is it?" Andrea glanced at her watch. "Only three."

"And we both have to work tomorrow afternoon. And I think you've had one too many daiquiris."

"Okay, okay. Whatever you say, but I want to meet your fella tomorrow, though. It was too dark in the club the other night for a good look."

"He's not my fella."

"I'm just surprised you haven't scared him off. Take him on a few gory homicides and he'll be out of your hair if that's what you're wanting. That reminds me, how come you were the last on scene when I dispatched tonight?"

"Captain's orders."

Andrea stopped, grabbing Jody's arm. Her eyes widened. "You mean *babysitting* him for a month? That's what you'll be doing?" She chuckled. "I can't see you letting a perp go just 'cause the captain told you to."

It rankled. But orders were orders. She'd managed quite well last shift. She could do it for another twenty-one days.

Maybe.

"You going to sleep with him again?" Andrea asked, taking her by surprise.

A delicious tingle tickled her tummy. She valiantly tried to ignore it. "No. It'd be too complicated."

Andrea tossed her plastic cup into a trash can and looped her arm through Jody's. "If it was the best sex you'd ever had, then why not enjoy the opportunity again. You might even call it fate."

She shook her head. "No, it wouldn't work out."

"You sound like a woman who's afraid she might have met her match. You said yourself there'd been a connection."

"I'm not afraid, and the connection I felt was because I

hadn't had sex in a hell of a long time," Jody scoffed. The idea was ludicrous. "Logan Hart means zip." She snapped her fingers.

"Maybe, maybe not, but you are afraid of committing to anyone. I've seen it too many times in the past."

Jody pulled away, planting her hands on her hips and stared at Andrea. "And just what do you call Paul? We dated for a while."

Andrea puckered her lips and wrinkled her nose. "Pretty boy? Ugh! Yeah, right. You knew from the start that relationship wouldn't work." She sighed deeply. "I've seen the same thing happening over and over in your life. You date guys you know aren't going to last."

"Maybe I'm just not ready to settle down," she hedged, feeling suddenly uncomfortable with the turn their conversation had taken. Andrea might be her best friend, but she damn sure didn't want to discuss her sex life with her.

"You won't let anyone get close," Andrea spoke softly.

The crowd had thinned, the music a distant hum the farther they walked down Bourbon Street until it was only the two of them. Jody sat on the curb, pulling her knees up until she could rest her head on them.

"You're right. You and *Mamere* are the only ones I've let into my life. I know I can't change what happened that day, but someday my uncle will return." Her laugh was cold and hard. "Isn't that what they say? The criminal always returns to the scene of the crime? I can't stay focused if there are too many people in my life."

Andrea sat beside her. "Revenge." She shook her head. "It'll eat you up on the inside if you let it."

"It's not revenge, just self-preservation."

"Are you sure?"

"What if it is revenge? John Cavenaugh killed my father, and I have no idea what happened to my sister. Wouldn't you want revenge?"

Andrea didn't know John Cavenaugh like Jody did. And if

she ever did come face to face with him again, she knew he would try to kill her, and this time he wouldn't graze her temple. He'd have no choice. She was the only witness who could testify against him. The only thing that had kept him away so far was the fact he thought he'd already murdered her, but if he did come back, she would be ready this time.

"It's been twenty years. In all that time you haven't been able to discover his whereabouts or your sister's, and I know you've looked. Let it go, *chere.*"

"I can't."

A shudder rippled over her when she remembered the cruelty in her uncle's eyes. Something inside her hoped they never crossed paths again, but she had a feeling they would.

When she crawled into bed in the wee hours of the morning, she'd managed to accomplish what she'd set out to do— she didn't dream of Logan Hart when she finally fell asleep.

Chapter 5

Cavenaugh took a long drag from his cigarette, inhaling deeply before slowly exhaling. Gray smoke curled in front of his face. He softly blew it away before glancing around with disdain. The guard had called the walled, concrete area the yard. The only thing that might resemble being outside was the open overhead making the sky visible. Fucking fresh air. He hated the outdoors. The only reason he'd taken his time was so he could have a smoke.

They were keeping him segregated from the other prisoners. He snorted. What was he going to do, corrupt one of them? Why the fuck did the cops think they were here in the first place?

He curled his hand into a fist. *How the hell had he ended up in a stinking jail in Two Creeks, Texas?*

But then, he knew the answer. Fallon, the niece he let get away. She'd changed her name and infiltrated his setup. He'd never even suspected they were related.

Hell, he hadn't thought there were any loose ends that mattered. Twenty fuckin' years and his past comes back to haunt him. How ironic could things get?

He laughed without mirth. Who the hell would've ever thought she'd end up with the DEA and had been searching for him all these years? He snorted. Talk about holding a grudge.

He maliciously grinned. But she couldn't prove he'd killed her father, or her little sister. If she could, she'd have gloated by now. Besides, he'd had a crooked cop do a background check on him once and there were no murder charges, only drug charges. He ground out his cigarette with the heel of his boot.

"Pick it up." The deputy spoke from behind him.

Cavenaugh's eyes narrowed, but he bent and retrieved the butt, dropping it in the can beside the concrete table. "Sorry about that, boss. Do you think I'd have time for another one?" He glanced over his shoulder and smiled. The skinny cop didn't look impressed with his submissive demeanor.

"One more."

As soon as Cavenaugh turned back, his smile vanished. *Bastard!* He wondered what the deputy would think about a late night visit after he was free. He'd give him an attitude adjustment the cop wouldn't soon forget. Teach him a little respect. No one spoke to John Cavenaugh like he was shit on the bottom of their boot. He'd had enough of that when he was a kid. He refused to take it as an adult.

He inhaled, then blew the smoke away from his face, and assessed what they had on him.

They could only pin him with dealing drugs, and more recently, money laundering. That was enough in itself to put him away for a long time, but it wouldn't get him the death penalty. They'd never be able to tie him to the deaths of Jody or Phillip Dupree.

He was thoughtful for a moment.

A damn shame Jody had gotten in the way. He hadn't known the seven-year-old was home. He'd kind of liked her. Maybe because she'd reminded him of her mother.

Angelina had been a damn fine-looking woman. He remembered the first time he'd laid eyes on her. Made his dick hard just thinking about those pouty, full lips. She had the kind of mouth that could suck a man dry. And big blue eyes. Exotic . . . sensual.

He sighed. Yeah, Angelina Dupree had been a damn fine

looker until the cancer ate away at her. He shuddered, disgusted by any form of disfigurement.

She'd died, leaving his half brother to raise the two girls. They'd kept Phillip busy, too busy to notice the drugs hidden in his basement. Well, almost too busy.

Phillip had deserved to die. He'd foolishly flushed the drugs down the toilet when he'd discovered them. *Merde!* So much money down the can. What a fucking idiot.

Cavenaugh's supplier wouldn't have hesitated to flush him down the toilet just as quickly if he didn't come up with the money from selling the drugs that no longer existed. But he'd taken care of that problem when he left the state—he'd stayed a healthy distance away all these years and kept his ear to the ground because as well as he'd done in the drug trade, his supplier had done better. The state of Louisiana wasn't the only one who wanted a piece of him. He'd always been able to keep one step ahead of everyone . . . until now.

"Time's up." The officer spoke from behind him.

He ground out his cigarette and stood, carefully masking the fury he barely held at bay. He'd escape. They might extradite him to New Orleans, but he would escape. There wasn't a jail that could keep him locked up. Not with his connections.

"He's locked down again," Andy said, as he entered Wade's office.

Fallon breathed a little easier. Every time they let her uncle out of his cell she stayed on edge. She didn't trust the bastard as far as she could spit.

"If you don't need anything else I thought I'd check with Mr. Edwards about his missing bull."

"Go ahead," Wade told his deputy.

Andy left, closing the door behind him.

Fallon stood, going to the window. A few minutes later she watched Andy exit the building and get inside his car. "How much longer?"

Wade came up behind her, drawing her close. "Not long. If he fights extradition, it could be a while."

"Do you think he will?"

"No. Not on drug charges alone. Right now, that's all he's facing in Louisiana." He sighed, hugging her close. "I still don't understand why you don't call Jody now that you know she's alive. I think you need her as much as she'll need you."

She shook her head. "And say what? Hi, this is your sister and I'm coming home. Oh, and I'm bringing our uncle with me. You remember, the man who killed our father and left you for dead." She raised her head and looked at him. "I can't do that to her. She probably thinks *I'm* dead. Hell, I thought she was until a short time ago.

"Besides, until Cavenaugh is locked away in a Louisiana jail, I won't feel comfortable. If he discovers he left a possible witness before then, Jody's life will be in danger. I have a strong feeling she saw what happened, and if so, he could get the death penalty."

"I don't think you're giving her enough credit. She isn't seven years old anymore. She's a cop. She'll know how to protect herself."

She moved from the warmth of Wade's arms and walked to the other side of the room. "Maybe I'm scared."

"Scared?"

She heard the surprise in his voice. It surprised her a hell of a lot more than it did him. She'd always prided herself on being tough, being strong. Right now, she didn't feel either.

"I didn't think anything could frighten you."

She looked at him. "She's going to think I deserted her. I went to the store because I had a stupid crush on the boy who worked there. When I returned and saw Cavenaugh leaving I knew something was wrong." She drew in a deep breath, hugging her middle. "I thought Jody and my father were dead. There was so much blood, and I was so damn scared I'd be next." God, she'd been petrified.

"She'll understand."

Her laugh held no mirth. "Understand what? That I went to the police, but saw Cavenaugh laughing and talking to the same cop I'd spoken with, and I ran again. That I was too damn terrified to go in to the swamps to find our grandmother?" She'd hated the swamps for as long as she could remember. There was something unnatural about alligators. A shudder rippled down her spine.

"You were fourteen. Only a child."

She closed her eyes tight. "But I never went back." She clenched her fists. "When I was older, I should've gone back, but I figured our grandmother was dead by then. What would there be to go back to? Nothing but a lot of painful memories. But will Jody understand that?"

Wade strode across the room, and put his hands on her shoulders, looking her straight in the eye. "She will if she's even a fraction of the woman you are."

She prayed he was right. She wouldn't be able to accept anything less, not without it destroying her.

After all she'd been through, she hadn't thought anything would ever get to her, until Wade Tanner had shown her how to feel again.

Chapter 6

Jody leaned against the patrol car, hoping Logan wouldn't show. She also hoped he would. It was going to be damn hard keeping her distance.

How could she let him get under her skin so quickly? Easy, no matter what was happening between them now, the night they'd spent together had been the best night of sex she'd ever had. Last night's kiss had only made things worse. She was as tight as a pair of rusty handcuffs.

She straightened when he came out of the building and strode toward her. "You're late," she told him as she opened her door.

"Yes, I know."

No apology. She watched as he went to the passenger side: squared jaw, thin lips; hell, he barely blinked.

He was pissed.

Logan folded his arms across his chest as he waited for her to unlock his door. Not even a hint of a smile danced in his eyes.

He might not look happy, but he did look good. Damn good. When he was angry, his eyes were dark, smoldering . . . and sexy as hell. Almost the exact shade as when he was in the throes of passion. A flush of heat stole over her. She pushed the button that unlocked the passenger door. *You have to stop thinking about that night,* she warned herself.

Yeah, right. Easier said than done when everything about him reminded her.

"Are we going to drive around the city again—arriving on the scene when it's safe?" Logan asked as he climbed inside and slammed his door shut. "That's going to get old after a while. I thought you were a real cop. I must've been mistaken."

He might as well have dumped a pail of ice water over her head. Her ardor cooled considerably. Well, what had she expected? He wasn't getting the stories he wanted. She hadn't thought for a moment he'd been fooled by their late arrivals, either. "If you get killed the captain will have my hide."

"Darn, that would be a damn shame. I'd hate for you to get into trouble if I got wasted."

A comedian.

"I'm serious," he told her and fastened his seat belt. "As much as I enjoy being in your company, I also have a job to do. This is my last assignment. I want it to be the best. I don't want to write a tour brochure of the city. I'm in the running for assistant editor. This assignment could make or break me. I'd prefer the former."

She hesitated before starting the car, feeling like the catalyst that *would* break his career. Damn it, why had the captain ordered her to hang back? She respected Logan for wanting to do a good job.

He'd certainly put his all into his performance the other night—onstage and off. She cleared her throat, and her mind. Starting a relationship with him would only cause her problems.

Still, he had a job to do and if she didn't give him something her life would be hell for the rest of the month. The least she could do was answer a few of his questions. "Okay, what do want to know?"

His hesitation was brief. "What's it like being in law enforcement? How'd you get started?"

Wariness crept over her. This was exactly what she'd been

afraid of. People prying into her life. There were too many secrets that she didn't want brought out in the open. She glanced across the seat. "Your questions sound personal to me."

"That's what makes the stories I write better than average. I want gut feelings, not a blow by blow list of the day in the life of an officer."

She started the car and backed out of the parking space as she gathered her thoughts. She didn't want to share her feelings. It would be like giving him a part of herself.

"They were simple questions, Jody."

Maybe they were. Maybe she was making more out of them than she should. "I like being a cop," she hesitantly began.

"Why?" He pulled a pad of paper from his pocket and began to write.

"Great pay and short hours?"

"Seriously."

She drove to the traffic light and turned left. He wouldn't let up on his questioning until she at least told him something he could use in his article. One of the other officers should have to deal with getting the third degree. She liked her privacy.

She glanced across the seat before returning her gaze to the street. He patiently waited for her to say something. At least he looked a little less angry. His features were more relaxed. His eyes a warm, caramel-brown. She caved.

"I don't like knowing there are people out there who hurt other people. I want the bad guys behind bars."

He nodded and scribbled something in his little book. "How old are you?"

"Twenty-six." She frowned. "What does my age have to do with law enforcement?"

"Nothing."

He grinned and her heart thumped double-time. Cute *and* sexy . . . a lethal combination.

"I was curious."

Her frown slipped, almost turning the other way. Damn, now he was making her smile. She straightened in her seat, trying not to get too comfortable with him. If she wasn't careful she might start liking the man, and she couldn't let that happen. "Try to restrain your inquisitiveness."

"I'll try," he told her, but didn't look at all repentant. "Okay, what does it feel like when you put someone dangerous away?"

That was a safe enough question. She thought for a moment, and remembered her last bad call. A stabbing at one of the local bars. The victim had lived, but the perp had cut the guy pretty bad—sixteen stitches.

The perp had been proud of his knife wielding, bragging all the way to the precinct. At least she'd taken the maniac out of circulation for a while.

She drew in a deep breath. "When I take someone off the streets, I feel relief. The city will be a little safer because I did my job."

"Is that how you got the scar?"

She went from hot to icy cold. "What?"

"The scar above your right ear. I noticed it the other night when I brushed your hair away from your face. It's a bullet wound, right? Did you get it on the job?"

"No." Unthinking, she reached up and touched the scar that was barely discernable. A neon light up ahead flashed red. Blood. So much of it. *Mamere!*

"You okay?" He touched her arm.

The past slipped back into the small space of her mind that she'd allotted it. A place where she wouldn't have to look at what had happened. Somewhere it couldn't hurt her. "Yeah, I'm fine." She stepped on the brake to let some tourists jaywalk and pulled herself together.

It wasn't Logan's fault his curiosity had been aroused. He'd only asked a simple question. "I'm fine," she repeated, more to assure herself, than him. "The scar happened when I was a child, not while I've been an officer . . . an accident." She glanced at him before quickly looking away. "I'd rather not talk about it."

Static crackled over the radio. *"Ten: twenty-four of unknown nature."* The dispatcher gave the address. *"Any unit responding identify."*

Jody hesitated. A medical emergency. It was Saturday afternoon in the Big Easy. Someone had probably started celebrating early. A drunk fell or something.

"Are you going to ignore this one, too? I do know some of the streets, and we're only a couple of blocks away."

His words challenged her to deny she was holding back. She grabbed the mike and went en route. "It's only a medical call. I doubt it's anything serious," she explained.

She went the two blocks, and turned the corner, pulling close to the curb, then called on scene before getting out of the car. "Do us both a favor and stay behind me. Remember, I'm the one with the gun."

Not that she really thought she'd have to use it. But then again, this wasn't the best part of town. She pushed open a gate that hung by only one hinge. It squeaked in protest. She had to sidestep a broken beer bottle as she carefully made her way over the cracked concrete sidewalk.

How could people live like this?

She ignored the shiver of revulsion that ran down her spine as they made their way through the overgrown yard that was more weeds than grass, and up the rickety steps.

She had to give Logan credit; he stayed behind her. She rapped her knuckles on the door. "Police." Nothing. She opened the screen and tested the knob. Unlocked. Slowly she turned it while at the same time pushing the door open.

Even though it was only four in the afternoon, the interior was dim. She pulled her flashlight from the loop at her waist and shined it inside the room. There was almost as much trash inside as out.

"Police," she called again. Was that a whimper? "Stay here," she told Logan, wondering if she'd brought him into something she would later regret.

She took a cautious step inside. The smell of gas burned

her nostrils. She stepped back out, drew in a deep breath, and went back inside, heading for what she hoped was the direction of the kitchen.

She'd guessed right.

Lying beside the open oven door was a man. She quickly turned off the gas and started to put her light away so she could get him outside, but strong arms moved her to the side and began dragging the man out of the kitchen.

Jody didn't say anything; she could use Logan's help.

There was another whimper. Her blood ran cold. She shined her light around the room, stopping in the corner. A small, trembling dog, and her three puppies, huddled on a pile of filthy rags. She scooped up a puppy, and shone the light so Logan wouldn't trip. They got the guy into the yard as the ambulance arrived.

The man began to cough and sputter. She set the sleepy but otherwise unharmed puppy on the ground, and narrowed her eyes on the man. She should've known. "Damn, Eugene, next time you try killing yourself, put the dogs outside. Hell, you might have killed one of them." She stomped back inside to get the rest of the animals.

Logan didn't say anything as he followed her to the kitchen, but she noticed how gently he carried the mother dog as they made their way back through the house.

They put them down once they were outside, and in the fresh air. The mother dog looked like a Scottish terrier mix. The first puppy they'd brought out immediately bounced over and tried to rouse the other two so they could play. She smiled. They were kind of cute.

She went back to Eugene and squatted next to him. Her nose wrinkled. She refused to even guess at the odor coming from his body. "Why were you trying to kill yourself *this* time?" she asked. The ambulance crew had oxygen on him and he was more alert.

He moved the mask. "The bitch left me."

"Charlotte?"

He nodded.

"And you think she's going to feel sorry for you? Once you're dead, it isn't going to matter. She'll find her another fella before they drop the first shovel of dirt on your casket." Maybe she should tell him if he showered, and shaved his scraggly black beard, Charlotte might hang around.

Instead, she looked at the paramedic. "Is he going to be okay?"

The paramedic removed the blood pressure cuff from Eugene's arm. "Yeah, his vitals are all fine. He doesn't need to go to the hospital. Probably wasn't in there more than a couple of minutes."

"Good, then I'm taking him to jail."

Eugene sat straighter as she stood. "Why you gonna take me in?"

"Endangering animals. It would've been a damn shame if that bitch and her puppies had died. And it's against the law to kill yourself."

"But I'm not dead."

The paramedics helped him to his feet, and she placed him in handcuffs.

"Then maybe I'll arrest you 'cause you *are* still alive." She read him his rights as she led him toward the car. Once she had him ensconced in the backseat, she called animal control to pick up the dogs. At least they would have a chance at getting a decent home.

And Logan had kept his word and stayed back. Except when he'd dragged Eugene out of the house. She couldn't really hold that against him.

But after they'd booked Eugene in, and were back on the streets, she couldn't help wondering what he was writing in that little black notebook.

Or what other stuff he'd already written.

"It's not all shoot-outs every time we go on a call," she warned. "Eugene tries to kill himself as often as he moves . . .

which is about every month or so. Hell, he was probably the one who called 9-1-1."

He snapped his notebook shut. "I realize that, but it's a lot more than the Eugenes of the city. You're holding back. I can't write a decent story if we arrive after the action." He ran his thumb along the inside of his seat belt and glanced out the window. "Do you really want me writing my story about cops who drive around the city sightseeing or eating beignets? Is that the kind of picture you want me to paint?"

"No, of course not." But she didn't want to go against the captain's orders, either. For once, she was really trying to play by the rules. She'd already discovered what happened when she colored outside the lines the night she ended up with Logan.

"Then show me what it takes to be a cop in this city. Unless, of course, this *is* your normal routine."

"Screw you, Hart." She kept her eyes on the road. Didn't he realize it was just as hard on her? She was a cop. Babysitting wasn't her cup of tea, either. It wasn't like the captain had given her a choice in the matter.

She'd like to show him what it was like behind the scenes. She could take him places that would turn his stomach. He'd get his story, all right. Probably more than he would ever want. He just might not live to write it.

She could show him stuff no tourist would ever see. Hell, most people who came here on vacation thought this was the party capital of the world, but they had crimes like every other town. Sometimes there was strange stuff that went down in the dark of night; she shuddered. Or in broad daylight.

She squared her shoulders. She wouldn't show him the seedier side. He was still a civilian. Her job was to protect and she wouldn't let her pride get in the way—unless he pushed her too damn far. Then she might just show him more than he'd bargained for.

Chapter 7

Logan killed the engine, then got out of his car, slipping the keys into his pocket. His footsteps were heavy as he trudged toward the newspaper office.

Not a damn thing had happened while patrolling the streets of New Orleans. Not one decent thing to report.

They'd arrived on a stabbing call after the scene was under control. The same happened when another call came in that a fight had broken out at a local bar. Then an elderly woman said the man next door had peeped into her bedroom window while she was undressing for bed, and she'd known for years he lusted after her body. Jody had suggested she pull her blinds down or undress in the bathroom.

Eugene's attempted suicide was the only excitement Logan had seen. Things were going to have to change or this last assignment would make for a pretty boring story. Besides the fact Hank had scored big when he'd covered the Icycles concert at the stadium.

How could the man get so lucky to be right there when the lead singer ripped his clothes off and flung himself into the crowd? Apparently, the kids had a little sense because it was like parting the Red Sea. The singer bruised more than his ego, and Hank's article had made a big splash in the entertainment section.

Logan pushed against one of the double doors that led into

the newspaper building. Some of his ire faded. It was busy this morning. More than a dozen cubicles were filled with people intent on getting the latest news to the public. A couple of clerks pushed their carts through the aisles dropping off or returning work.

He would've loved working in a newsroom before computers. He closed his eyes for a moment and could almost hear the tapping of keys on an old Remington. He inhaled and the scent of ink filled his nostrils.

When he opened his eyes, quietly efficient computers had replaced the antique typewriters in his mind's eye, but it didn't matter what year, or even what century it was, the excitement remained the same as eager reporters sought out the truth. Every time he walked into the building, his skin began to tingle.

He strolled to the other side and glanced inside the editor's office. Bradley wasn't at his desk. No big deal. Logan didn't have anything on the day in the life of a police officer anyway, and he didn't really think his boss would want to hear about Eugene. Hell, they'd had to fumigate the squad car after Jody booked the guy. Not only did his memory linger, so did his body odor. He'd catch Bradley later.

There was something else he wanted to check out first. He always liked to know whom he was working with, especially if he sensed another story, which he did, and maybe this would be the one that got him the job of assistant editor.

He turned, and almost ran over his competition. His gaze swept over Hank. The man was so thin he was almost on the point of anorexia. At carnival he wouldn't need a costume. He *looked* like one of the walking dead. The gloating expression on Hank's face said it wasn't an accidental meeting.

"Did you catch my story?" Hank opened the conversation, his beady gaze flitting around the room.

Not for the first time did Logan wonder if the man was on speed. He twitched, for Christ's sake. Logan didn't trust anyone who twitched as much as Hank.

"Yeah, great piece," Logan told him. The man deflated before his eyes. Apparently, Hank had expected him to be pissed—at the very least, irate.

"I especially liked how you misspelled the group's name and the name of the lead singer. It's *Icycles* with a *y* and the lead singer is *Rian,* with an *i.*"

Of course, Logan wouldn't have known that if Kevin hadn't mentioned it. His younger brother used to listen to the band before they became so popular they let their collective ego overshadow what got them to the top of the charts in the first place.

Hank grabbed one of the papers off the counter and began scanning his article, groaning when he found his mistakes. He sat heavily in the nearest chair.

Logan felt a deep sense of satisfaction as he strolled toward the room adjacent to the main newsroom where the news clip files were kept. He didn't like or trust Hank. Not one damn bit.

Large file cabinets contained all the articles prior to nineteen eighty-eight when they'd switched to computer. He knew Jody was twenty-six years old so he started his search then, at the beginning.

Everything was indexed by year and subject so it wasn't hard to locate the right drawer. His hands shook when he pulled open the file cabinet. Maybe because he knew his instincts were good. Jody was hiding something behind those sexy, deep blue eyes. He didn't think for a moment that if she knew he was researching her background, she'd likely hang him by his balls.

It didn't take him long to locate her birth announcement. Jody Lynn Dupree, born to Phillip and Angelina Dupree. It also listed an older sister as being on the little welcome wagon.

Logan paused, thinking about two Dupree women loose on the town wreaking havoc in men's lives. He smiled as he opened his notepad and jotted the names of her parents, her sister, and Jody's date of birth in case he might need the information later.

She'd just had a birthday. Maybe he'd buy her a present. *Like that would get him anywhere.* He probably didn't stand a chance. But he wasn't ready to give up. The memory of her lying in his arms, her naked body pressed intimately against his was too new, too fresh in his mind.

When he finished writing down the information, he shut his notebook and slipped it back inside his jacket pocket. Nothing else was in the folder for that year or the next few years. The rest would be on the computer files.

Glancing at his watch, he saw it was almost time for Jody's shift to begin. He closed the file cabinet. Tomorrow would be soon enough to begin another search. Something inside him knew there was a story here. Why else would she have a scar from a bullet? He left the room and walked toward the front door.

She'd been pretty evasive when he questioned her about what had happened. Instead of forgetting about it like she'd suggested, he'd been more curious to know the details. Of course, it might just have been a stray bullet—an accident of sorts, like she'd said. It could be nothing at all.

But he didn't think so.

"Caught your show the other night," Celia said as he passed her cubicle.

Logan came to a jarring stop. Heat spread up his face, but he tried to act nonchalant as he faced her.

The repercussions were starting. He'd been afraid of this, but he'd hoped the women from the office had stayed home, or at the very least, would be too shy to remark on his performance. Women had certainly changed over the years. Not that he was complaining that much. He kind of liked the woman of today.

Except for right now.

"Your husband let you go to a strip show?" he asked, trying to turn the tables. From the slow appraisal Celia gave him, he knew his ploy hadn't worked.

She chuckled. "You have something to learn about women—especially older, married ones." She leaned forward on her elbows. "John doesn't care where I get my appetite, as long as I come home to eat."

Slowly, her gaze roamed over him. He shifted his feet. Celia was at least twenty years his senior, even if she didn't look it. Hell, he'd seen men half her age give her a second look, then go back for a third.

"And I must say," she drawled, "I had quite an appetite by the time I crawled in bed that night."

Margaret chuckled from the next cubicle. He glared in her direction. She quickly covered it with a cough, and went back to typing.

He hadn't been this embarrassed since he and Rosalie were caught skinny-dipping in Mr. Crawford's pond after the senior prom—by half the senior class! He should've known Rosalie couldn't keep her mouth shut. She was the biggest gossip in school.

"I was there to do a job," he ground out.

Celia arched one finely penciled eyebrow. "And you did it very well."

With a frown marring his features, he turned and strode from the offices amid the snickering of women. They reminded him of a bunch of cackling chickens. He was glad they were enjoying themselves at his expense.

As he pushed on the door leading outside, he couldn't stop the smile tugging at the corners of his mouth. So maybe it was kind of funny now that he thought about it. Someday he might even be able to laugh, but he had a feeling that day wouldn't come around for some time.

He pulled his keys from his pocket before sliding into the front seat. It would take a while to live down his one night of stardom, he thought as he drove toward the police station.

His little brother had probably already called their mother. He groaned thinking about the repercussions from that quarter. He was sure by tomorrow she'd be calling to ask about his show business stint and trying the whole time not to laugh. How in the world had he ended up with a mother like his? He grinned. Just lucky he guessed.

He slowed at the corner and flipped his blinker on before turning right.

His mother had an unusual sense of humor. Raising four rambunctious boys and one daughter, who was just as rowdy as the boys, would either make a person crazy—or fill them with laughter. His mom had chosen to laugh.

Nope, he hadn't heard the last about his night as a stripper.

He parked his car and turned off the engine. He was down the street, but he had a clear view of Jody as she stood on the steps talking to the blonde who'd been with her the other night. Even though her friend was cute, in a flamboyant kind of way, it was Jody's dark beauty that captured and held Logan's gaze.

He couldn't see her eyes, but they were the kind he could get lost in: deep, sultry blue. And when she made love with him, they'd become even darker, almost black.

Leaning forward, he rested his arms on the top of the steering wheel. She seemed less rigid than when she was with him. He noticed she laughed easily at something her friend said.

Would she ever feel that comfortable around him?

As soon as the thought crossed his mind, he wondered why he should care. Just as quickly the answer came to him. There was something about Jody. Something different from the other women he'd known. He couldn't quite put his finger on it, but he knew he wanted to know more about her.

The two women went inside the building, but it was a moment more before he moved. He kept picturing the look on Jody's face when he was making love to her. The way she made little panting noises. And the way she arched her back when she came.

He wanted her again. He wanted to put that same look on her face one more time. As he exited his car he knew instinctively that once more would not be nearly enough to get her out of his system.

Chapter 8

Jody covertly looked across the expanse of vinyl seat to where Logan was partially slumped like he pondered the great mysteries of life. She glanced at the illuminated green numbers on the clock mounted in the dash. Nearly ten. She was off duty at eleven, another boring shift almost over.

Her only excitement had been the occasional glance at Logan that she stole. He sent her pulse racing, even though she knew he was ticked because they were always arriving at calls after the danger had passed, and the scene secure.

Right now the other two units in the area were working a possible homicide. No wonder he wasn't talking. But she was obeying orders—again, and keeping Logan safe.

Hell, she couldn't blame him for his irritation. This was her third shift of hanging back and already she felt like a caged animal looking for a break in the wire.

She was damned tired of showing up at the scene late, and watching Paul smirk. Apparently, he'd finally figured out she couldn't, or wouldn't, put a hex on him. Sheesh, he certainly wasn't the brightest bulb in the strand. Again, she wondered why she'd even dated the man.

Okay, so maybe he reminded her of a Californian—the blond surfer type. Nice tan—straight from a tanning booth, decent muscles—from a gym, killer smile—as in you'd better wear sunglasses or you'd go blind.

Everything about Paul had driven her crazy after a week of dating him. Hell, he acted like it was a major catastrophe if one hair on his head got mussed. As much hair spray as he used, she doubted one ever would.

And now this. Paul's attitude made arriving after the danger had passed that much harder to take. If he flashed her that knowing smile one more time, he might find himself sitting in the dentist's office. She completely understood Logan's ire.

"Listen, I'm sorry you're not getting the story you wanted," she finally conceded, breaking the silence.

He straightened in his seat. "At this rate, the only way I'll write a decent article is if I stumble over a dead body. Seen any lying around?"

"I don't like it any more than you." She pulled into the parking area at the side of a small, all-night coffee shop. "Want a cup? I'll buy."

"Since you're buying, sure."

It was the least she could do. He'd kept his word and stayed out of the way . . . and he hadn't touched her. She wasn't quite certain if she was relieved . . . or disappointed. Hell, he hadn't even mentioned their night together. Maybe it wasn't as memorable for him?

Was this what her life was coming to? Wondering if she was good in bed or not? Now, that was pathetic.

They went inside and ordered. Once they had their coffee, they took it to a small table near the storefront window that looked out onto the narrow street.

The silence stretched uncomfortably. Finally, she couldn't take it anymore. "How long have you lived here?" she asked, admitting to a mild curiosity.

"Almost a year. I'm from Texas originally."

For the first time tonight she began to relax. She should've guessed he was from Texas. He reminded her of a country song she'd once heard about a cowboy from Texas who didn't back down from an angry bull, or a hot-tempered woman.

She didn't know about the bull, but he certainly hadn't let her intimidate him.

"What?" He looked at her over the rim of his cup.

The shell she'd built around herself began to crack. She smiled. "That would explain your slow, southern drawl." She leaned back against the red-cushioned seat. "Your accent is a little different than someone from New Orleans—slower, the words more drawn out."

He blushed! She'd never seen a man's face redden. It made Logan more human. She sighed. More likable. This wasn't good. *Stick to the coffee,* she told herself.

"And you?" He nodded toward her before blowing on his coffee and taking a drink."

Her hesitation was brief. She wouldn't let herself get in too deep. They'd carry on a simple conversation . . . nothing more. "Born and raised here." Logan didn't need to know more than that, and she wasn't in the mood to step inside a confessional.

"In New Orleans?" he prodded.

She rearranged her plastic spoon on the paper napkin. "I've lived here most of my life, or nearby." For a brief moment she could almost envision a beige clapboard house. The screen door open so the afternoon breeze could pass through.

"Jody, come play," her sister called from the front porch.

"Any family?" Logan queried.

His question jerked her back to reality and the warmth she'd felt only seconds ago dissipated, leaving a cold emptiness in its wake. "This the third degree again?"

He didn't meet her eyes. "Idle curiosity. Worried I might discover something about you?"

"Of course not." She waved her arm. "There's nothing to tell. I have no family besides a grandmother."

She glanced out the picture window just as a hulk of a man crowbarred the gate across the street. It popped open like a can of soda. She sat forward, no longer listening to Logan, no longer concerned with his prying.

Damn, what the hell was she supposed to do now? Ignore

the fact someone was breaking into the courtyard across the street?

Not likely.

"What?" Logan turned in his seat and glanced out the window.

The perp had already slipped into the courtyard, though. Nothing looked amiss. Just another quiet night. "Stay here," she ordered. "Someone just broke into the home across the street. As she stood, she brought her radio out of the holder, and keyed the mike.

"Six two R in progress." She followed with the address.

"I don't have a unit clear," Andrea's voice came over the radio. "As soon as I do, I'll send them your way."

"I'm going to check it out." She glanced at Logan. "My rider will be at the coffee shop across the street." She replaced her radio in the leather holder. "Stay here," she ordered once more, just in case he'd started to get any ideas about following her.

The street outside the coffee shop was dark. Dampness hung in the air from the recent rains, making the street slick. Thankful for rubber soles, she silently crossed to the other side.

She undid the strap across her gun and lifted it from the holster as she neared the gate. The cold, hard steel weighted her hand. Sometimes she wondered why she'd become an officer. She hated guns. She hated what they could do. But as much as she disliked them, she knew sometimes it took violence to end violence.

No sound came from the courtyard. Slowly she eased the gate open and looked inside. About six feet of narrow space, then the passage opened into a dimly lit patio. She knew if she stepped inside, and met the perp as he was leaving, it could get messy.

Jody closed her eyes for a moment. She'd met death once before. She'd held its hand and walked down the tunnel. Hell, she'd even seen the light. Could she cheat it once more?

Sure, why not.

She drew in a deep breath and stepped inside, letting the wooden door close silently behind her. She reached the end without confrontation.

Something clicked behind her. She spun on her heel, gun raised, heart pounding.

Logan!

She closed her eyes and took a deep breath to calm her racing pulse. *Merde!*

"I told you to wait at the coffee shop," she hissed.

"I thought you might need some help. Besides, I have a story to write."

"You can't write it if you're dead."

He grinned and for a second she forgot where she was. *Concentrate!* "Stay behind me or I swear I'll be the one who shoots you."

"You got it."

The captain would kill her—right after he skinned her alive if he knew she'd let a civilian go with her on a robbery in progress. There wasn't a lot she could do about it now, but later . . .

She edged to the corner and scanned the courtyard. A sweet, tropical scent filled the night air. Up-lights on several trees cast a blend of dim light and shadows. In the corner was a café table and two matching black iron chairs. She didn't see anything out of the ordinary.

Hugging the wall, Jody made her way to a back door. It was slightly ajar, the wood splintered. It had been jimmied open. She'd expected as much. She glanced at Logan. She'd kill him later. Her attention returned to the crime in progress.

Adrenaline sped through her veins.

Her heart pounded.

This was her rush . . . her high in life. This was why she was a cop. She slipped inside, Logan right behind her.

A thump sounded from upstairs, followed by a muffled scream.

She raced down the hall and up the narrow staircase. Light spilled from an open door at the end of the hall.

"No, please, don't. Please don't hurt me," a female pleaded.

"Strip, bitch," a deep male voice followed.

Jody gripped her gun tighter and hurried forward. She stopped at the door and took a second to gather her wits. Saying a silent prayer, she peeked around the corner, then jerked back. One man, one woman. The man had an ugly-looking 357. Almost as ugly as him.

He looked even bigger up close than he had from across the street. Jeez, why couldn't she get the skinny runt criminal? This man probably weighed close to three hundred. He looked like a cross between a gorilla and a bulldozer.

Screw it!

In one swift movement, she wheeled to the doorway. "Drop your weapon!" she bellowed.

Startled, the two people in the room turned toward her. The woman was tiny, not much older than Jody. And her whole body trembled.

"Move real slow," she warned the perp. "And drop the gun."

When he grinned, her blood ran cold. A maniacal gleam glittered in his eyes, telling her he didn't plan on going down easy.

"Make me," he told her. "Tell you what, drop *your* gun, or I blow her brains out. He aimed his gun at the woman who began to cry hysterically. Jody didn't doubt for one minute he would, too.

She pulled the trigger.

The explosion vibrated through the room.

The woman screamed and scurried under the bed.

The perp yelled and grabbed his forearm, then quickly switched his gun to his other hand.

"I don't make deals." She tightened her grip.

"Son of a bitch, you shot me," he yelled, looking at the blood running down his arm.

The man was an intellectual giant. "Stop whining. I only grazed you. Now, drop the gun." She kept her weapon trained on him. He growled. She knew exactly what was going through his head. "I intended to hit your arm. Next time I'll aim for your heart. And I don't miss."

He hesitated before dropping his gun. It clattered to the floor. She didn't relax her stance.

"Now turn around and put your hands above your head."

"How the hell am I supposed to do that?"

"Think about it like this; if you have your wounded arm above your head it'll slow the bleeding. You might not bleed to death before an ambulance gets here."

Apparently, he didn't see any other way around it. He turned and faced the window. She jerked her handcuffs from the leather pouch fastened to her belt as she moved forward. She spared a second to kick his gun out of reach.

"Lower your right arm and bring your hand behind your back, and don't think for one second I won't blow your head off."

She quickly handcuffed him and forced him to his knees. Once she was sure he couldn't cause any more harm, she turned around. Logan was right behind her. The expression on his face told her that he was ready to help if the guy gave her any trouble. "You promised to stay back."

"I did." He almost pulled off that look of innocence. "I was right behind you."

"That's not what I meant, and you know it." She went to the edge of the bed and knelt down, raising the red dust ruffle. "You can come out now."

The woman scooted from under the bed, warily eyeing Logan. "Who's he?"

"He's with me." She held out her hand, the woman took it, and they stood. "Are you okay? Did he hurt you?"

Her bottom lip trembled. "He was going to . . . going to . . ."

"Shh . . , it's okay now." The woman fell into Jody's arms, almost knocking her down from the momentum.

After a moment the woman stepped back, her face a rosy hue. "I'm sorry. I didn't mean to drench your uniform with my tears." Her voice was timid. "Can I get some clothes to put on?"

Jody nodded as she reached for her radio. She let Andrea know the would-be burglar was in custody, and requested an ambulance for him.

She couldn't stop the flutter of pride that swept through her. One down, and she didn't care how many were to go. One at a time, that's all she had to worry about.

Her eyes went to the perp. Let Paul or Joe make one re-mark about the fact she was babysitting Logan and she'd . . .

Her eyes focused on the perp's bloody arm. She blinked several times, and another room came into focus. She felt a burning pain above her right ear, and something warm began to trickle down the side of her face.

"You okay?" Logan put his arm on her shoulder.

She drew in a deep, shuddering breath and glanced around: same bed, same bedspread, same dresser. The room was as it had been a moment ago. What the hell had hap-pened? She looked at Logan. A worried frown marred his features. "Yeah, I'm fine. Just beat."

He seemed to accept her explanation.

The world continued to function around her.

Another unit arrived on the scene. Someone took the vic-tim's statement. Logan was taking his own notes. She tried to be annoyed, at the very least irate that he'd followed her on the call, but neither emotion rose to the surface.

She was more concerned with why her past was rearing its ugly head. She hadn't had a vision like this in a long time, not since she was a child.

An omen? She shook her head. No, it was only nerves. The aftereffect from the rush of adrenaline when she'd taken the perp out of commission. It was nothing more than that.

Chapter 9

Fallon glared at the man behind the bars. "You're going down, and I'll be there to witness every second of it."

Cavenaugh chuckled as he scooted farther back on the thin mattress that covered the springs on the lower bunk. It was only marginally softer than the concrete floor. "You think you have me exactly where you want, eh *chere*?"

"I don't think . . . I know."

Damn, she was almost as mean as he was. She hadn't thought twice about fighting him on equal ground. Fought like a goddamned man. It still rubbed him raw she'd beaten him—this round. She'd live to regret it. His niece wasn't the only one who believed in the part of the Bible that said an eye for an eye. That was the only verse he *did* believe in.

He looked at his bandage. His wound still throbbed where the cop had shot the gun from his hand. He'd have to remember to stay alert around these country yokels. Maybe they weren't as stupid as he first thought.

His gaze moved back to Fallon—the niece with more than one name. Brigitte Dupree, his niece . . . Fallon Hargis, DEA agent. She probably had a lot more aliases he didn't know about. And faces, he thought, remembering the blonde wig she'd worn as she gathered evidence against him. Damn, why hadn't he seen the resemblance to his half brother? But then, he knew. Over the years he'd become lax in his vigil. He wouldn't let that happen again.

"So, you're planning on going to New Orleans with your uncle, eh, *chere*?" His voice lowered. "There are a lot of ghosts in that town."

He watched closely, saw the color drain from her face. He knew she was thinking about her dead sister and father. So, she did have a soul. He'd begun to wonder if she was alive on the inside. That was good. People who cared made mistakes.

"I'll nail you for murder if it's the last thing I do," she said between clenched teeth.

"But how you be doing that, *chere,* when you got no evidence?" He spoke softly, quietly, but he knew she heard and understood his words.

"Go to hell." She turned on her heel and strode out of his line of vision.

He chuckled. "I think that's where we'll probably both end up, but with me it's different. I'm not scared of going."

His smile faded. New Orleans, on the other hand, was a different matter. He had no desire to return. Had, in fact, avoided it since the unfortunate incident with Jody and his half brother. The place gave him the creeps. All that voodoo shit, the swamps. A shudder of revulsion rushed over him. He'd always hated the swamps. There was stuff there even he couldn't explain away.

No worry, though. He already had a plan. No one would get the best of John Cavenaugh. He was already setting the wheels in motion. One phone call a day, that's all he was allowed, but that's all it took. By the time he was in New Orleans everything would be ready.

Fallon shut the door that separated the good guys from the bad guys, and took a deep cleansing breath.

"You okay?" Wade asked as he came up beside her.

"Yeah, fuckin' fantastic."

He drew her into his arms and her fear and anger began slipping away. Why the hell had she let Cavenaugh get to her? She laid her cheek against Wade's chest, absorbing his strength. Without a doubt, she knew as long as Wade Tanner was in her life, she could manage to face anyone, or anything.

"I can see it's breaking your heart not to leave right away. I'll do whatever you want."

"Just keep doing what you're doing."

"It won't be long now," he reassured her.

Her heart skipped a beat. Soon she would have her little sister back again. She tamped down her excitement.

"Kids caught making out at the sheriff's office," a scratchy voice spoke behind them.

Fallon looked at Wade; he was smiling.

"Ben, I haven't been a kid for more years than I'd like to count, but thanks for the compliment."

She stepped out of Wade's arms and looked at the elderly gentleman who wore a slightly rumpled suit. He held a notebook and a pencil, and there was an extra pencil stuck behind his right ear.

"You and me both," Ben commiserated. "I'd feel a hell of a lot older if Dr. Canton wasn't still kicking. He'd make anyone look young."

"I won't tell him you said that," Wade told him.

"Don't matter to me one way or the other. I've been meaning to check out the new doctor they hired over in Nocona." He frowned. "But that's not the reason I'm here. How come every time I take a vacation, and mind you, I haven't taken one in two years, and shut the blasted newspaper office down for a week, the biggest news story of my career breaks wide open?"

She should've guessed. This was the editor. No wonder there hadn't been any reporters dogging the station.

Ben sighed. "Well, let's go to your office and I'll get what information you have. Can't believe Wichita Falls didn't send a reporter over to cover the story. I had to hear it from Mrs. Johnson."

"It didn't go over the scanner and besides, they had that big meth lab bust at the same time. Our news wasn't as big."

"Our news wasn't as big. . . ." he huffed. "Wait until they read about what they missed when I put the paper out next Thursday. That'll make them sit up and take notice."

Fallon smiled. This town was starting to grow on her.

Chapter 10

Logan glanced down at the open box. A smile tugged at his lips. The puppy inside was chewing on the red rubber ball he'd bought her. The pink bow around her neck was slightly askew. She was kind of odd-looking with her reddish-blonde hair sticking out in all directions. But her looks only endeared her to him more.

"Okay, remember the plan?" The puppy continued to chew. "Don't make a sound. Remember, you're a present." He rapped on the door.

He'd cajoled the captain's secretary until she'd finally given in and told him where Jody lived. When he put a little effort into it, he could be pretty charming. Ha! And his little brother thought he had the market cornered on wooing the women. Not the case this time. He could woo with the best of them.

His grin was a little cocky as he waited for her to answer his knock. He felt damn good. His first stripper article would run in tomorrow's paper, and he'd dropped off a rough draft about the perp breaking and entering. He might just get the job of assistant editor after all. He didn't want to admit it, but he'd begun to worry. Bradley had looked interested, anyway, and Hank hadn't come up with anything earth shattering.

The sound of locks sliding across metal reeled his thoughts back to the present.

Jody opened the door. His gaze swept over her. She looked damned cute in short-shorts, a white T-shirt with faded lettering, and fluffy green slippers that had lost their fluff a long time ago.

Something stirred deep inside him just looking at her. He returned his gaze to her face where her mouth had turned down into a very unbecoming frown. He wondered if she knew she could get wrinkles doing that. Not that he thought this would be a good time to mention it.

Other than not seeming too happy to see him, she was still damned cute. Logan's grin widened.

"It's my day off," she said, promptly shutting the door.

His grin slid off his face. Now that wasn't very polite. He looked at the pup. "She didn't really mean to shut the door. That's just her way. She really likes us a lot. Just wait and you'll see." He knocked again.

"Go away," came the muffled reply from the other side.

He knocked again, but with a little more determination this time.

The door opened again.

"What are you doing here?" She brushed her hair behind her ears. "I'm not working today. Our relationship only extends so far as my job."

He turned and picked up the box.

She never missed a beat as she continued talking. "I don't want any kind of relationship with you. . . ." Her eyes grew round. "What's that?" She warily eyed the box.

He lowered it until she could see inside. "Your birthday present."

"It's not my birthday."

He noticed she spoke with less conviction. "It *was* your birthday, though. This is a belated present." He grinned. "I named her Betty."

"Betty? You don't name a puppy Betty. That's a terrible name."

"Can we come in? I think she's thirsty. I forgot to water her, and I sure could use a cup of coffee."

She hesitated.

He sent his best forlorn look in her direction. The one that always worked on his mother.

"Okay." She sighed. "But in ten minutes you're leaving and taking the mutt with you. Agreed?"

"Anything you say."

She turned and strode back into the house leaving him to follow. He looked at the pup. "See, I told you it'd work. Don't ever doubt me again."

The pup stopped chewing on her toy long enough to wag her tail ninety miles an hour.

"And don't worry, you probably won't have to keep that name for long." He stepped into the house and shut the door behind him. "I think she really likes you," he whispered.

The foyer was modest with only a hat rack and umbrella stand. She had a stereo on somewhere, a soothing sound. New Age? The notes seemed to linger in the air along with the musky scent of incense.

He followed her, entranced with the seductive sway of her hips. Damn, she had a real nice rhythm, but then, he already knew that.

She entered a moderate-sized kitchen. The black and white tiled floor gleamed, as did the counters and appliances. He dropped into one of the cushioned chairs. Almost too clean. Life was meant to be a little messy.

Jody opened and closed cabinets as she set about making a pot of coffee. Logan placed the box on the floor and lifted the pup out, and set Betty on the floor along with her toy.

She quickly pounced on the rubber ball and began chewing. A few seconds passed before she realized she was in a new environment. She continued to chew, but looked around at the same time. Her eye caught the movement of Jody's slippers scooting about the kitchen.

The pup dropped the ball. It rolled away from her, but she didn't seem to care.

Transfixed on this new object of interest, Betty moved her gaze back and forth as Jody walked from sink to coffeepot, and back for a filter. The pup squatted on her front paws, butt in the air, tail wagging.

When Jody stopped to pour water into the coffeemaker, Betty pounced. Jody squealed as a bundle of fur was added to her not-so-furry slippers. The pup growled low in her throat, warning the slipper-predator not to mess with her. Logan thought it sounded rather menacing. She'd make a great watchdog if she ever got bigger than her current weight of approximately three pounds.

"Let go of my shoe, you mutt." Jody glared down at the pup, but Logan didn't think she looked that upset. "I could've been so startled that I might have dropped the coffeepot on your head."

Betty barked, then scampered to the stove and squatted in front of it. She had a very serious expression on her face for a moment, then raced back to Jody's shoe.

One eyebrow quirked upward as Jody turned her gaze toward Logan. "She peed on my floor."

He really tried to keep a straight face . . . but unfortunately for him, his serious demeanor didn't last long. He finally stifled his laughter when he saw Jody still wasn't amused. "Hey, it's only a floor. It'll mop up."

She picked up the puppy and for a moment he sort of worried what she was about to do, but she only went to a narrow utility closet and brought out a mop. "Good, then you can be the one to mop it up," she told him as she came back and handed him the mop. "And please dispose of the pad when you finish." One eyebrow quirked upward as she stared at him.

Her stern expression crumpled when Betty slurped her tongue up Jody's cheek.

Jody eyed the pup in her arms. "It's too late to ask forgiveness now. You should've thought about winning my affection before you ruined my clean floor."

Betty barked. A tiny little noise meant to melt the coldest heart.

It worked.

Jody snuggled her face into the puppy's downy soft fur. The puppy went ballistic as if she sensed she'd found the owner she wanted.

"Why did you bring her over, Logan?" she moaned. "I don't want—or need—a puppy."

Her words might have been intended to sound harsh, but he detected a slight softening. She leaned out of reach of Betty's tongue and frowned at the pup.

"Isn't this one of the puppies Eugene had in his house?"

He was hoping she wouldn't remember. He wasn't sure he wanted her to think he'd been worried about a dog and her pups. What if she thought he was some sappy jerk?

He came out of his chair and got busy cleaning the tiny puddle. "Well, yeah. I was sort of going by the shelter the other day and thought I'd stop in to check on them." He didn't meet her eyes. "This one looked so cute I couldn't leave her." He dropped the soiled pad in the trash and replaced the mop before washing his hands.

"And what exactly am I supposed to do with her?"

He walked over to stand in front of Jody. She was so damned beautiful, and as hard as she tried to be tough, she looked so damned alone. He turned his gaze on Betty. Absently he brushed a hand across the top of the pup's head. "Love her. Just love her. That's all you have to do," he spoke softly.

"Why did you bring her to me?"

"I thought you looked like you needed someone to love, and someone who would love you."

"I have Andrea, and my grandmother."

There was still something lurking deep in her eyes. At one time or another she'd suffered pain. She reminded him of a Vietnam vet he'd once interviewed. Reflected in the man's green eyes, he saw the trauma he'd suffered, things no human should have to see. The only thing different between the vet and Jody was the color of her eyes.

Somewhere along the line, she'd suffered, too. And it had something to do with her sister. Why else would she not mention her? He'd discover what lay hidden inside Jody eventually, but he sensed now was not the right time.

"I thought you needed unconditional love," he told her.

Her eyes narrowed. "Unconditional love?"

"Yeah, you know, the kind of love that never leaves no matter what happens, or what you do."

She scoffed. "There's no such thing."

He took the pup from her and placed it on the floor. She immediately found her ball and began to chew. "Yes there is. My parents are a great example. They have unconditional love for each other."

She still didn't look as if she understood. Damn, she was so beautiful, so sweet. He couldn't stand the thought of anyone hurting her. Before she could make another comment, he gently tugged her into his arms and lightly kissed her.

He didn't mean for the kiss to deepen, but it seemed like forever since he'd tasted her sweet lips. She had a tendency to make him forget everything around him. Then again, she wasn't pushing him away, either.

Maybe the pup had been a dirty trick. He didn't doubt that she saw through his plotting. That he'd thought to get to her through the big eyes of the pup. Still, he had a hard time feeling guilty—his plan had worked.

When she pressed her body closer, he lost himself in the heat emanating from her body, the feel of her arms around his neck. How had he survived this long?

When he ended the kiss, it was still a moment more before

he could catch his breath. She leaned against his chest, a perfect fit.

"You cheated," she said, finally breaking the silence. "It wasn't fair bringing the pup here."

"I know. But you have to admit Betty is pretty·darn cute."

"Ugh! Her name is not Betty."

"Then what is it?"

"I don't know yet, but it certainly won't be Betty."

"Okay. Want to make love while you think about it?"

Chapter 11

Jody drew in a sharp breath. It was a good thing she had her head against his chest so he couldn't see her expression. More than anything, she wanted to make love with Logan. She wanted to feel him buried inside her, stroking her.

But look where that kind of thinking had gotten her the last time. Stuck with him for a month! Something soft and warm swirled inside her. It had been a night she hadn't been able to forget.

Why the hell didn't she throw caution to the wind? But could she afford to let him into her life, even for a short time? He had a way of making her forget her uncle was still out there. She couldn't afford to forget . . . not completely.

"We were good together that night." He lightly caressed her back.

Logan didn't have to say what night he referred to. "Sometimes it isn't smart to let your guard down." And if she wasn't careful, that's exactly what she would do.

With her head resting on his chest, she could hear his heartbeat. The steady rhythm was soothing to her ears. Damn, she didn't want him to leave—to walk out of her life. At least, not right at this moment.

"Who scared you so much that you're afraid to let anyone get close?" He kissed the top of her head.

She tensed. "Scared? No, more like angry. Sometimes you

need to remember the bad things that happen in life. It makes you stronger."

"Or it destroys you."

"I won't let it."

Mamere said people like Jody cared too deeply. It was their nature. She was never so right as when she'd uttered those words.

"Take a chance," he whispered close to her ear. "You might even find you don't really like me."

A smile curved her lips and suddenly the pressure was no longer inside her. How had she ever managed to get tangled up with this man? She sighed. He was tempting, and right now, he tempted her. His body heat was nice as it wrapped around her. Even with the closeness she shared with her grandmother and Andrea, her loneliness was unbearable at times.

He waited for her to decide. She knew if she said no, nothing would change in their relationship. He would still ride out so he could get his articles. And he would still look at her in a way that sent a thrill through her. Nothing she did would make the chemistry any less.

After she'd told him there wouldn't be an encore performance of the night they'd made love, Logan had backed off and never mentioned it again—until now. There was no getting around the facts; she wanted him as much as he wanted her. It wasn't likely her uncle would show up on her doorstep today. He might never return.

She reached up and ran a hand down his cheek. It was still smooth from his shave that morning. For almost twenty years she'd kept vigil in case her uncle returned, that he would finish the job he'd started. Maybe it was time she stopped watching . . . and waiting.

"Yes," she said. "I want to make love."

Before she could change her mind, Logan scooped her up in his arms. One of her shoes came off and Betty pounced.

"Which way is the bedroom?"

It was as if a weight had suddenly been lifted from her shoulders. Jody couldn't help herself, she laughed.

He frowned. "I've been suffering since the morning when I woke up, expecting to make mad, passionate love to you again, only to find you'd slipped out like a thief during the night. I had nothing but a first name. No way to locate you.

"Then when I do discover where you are, you act like I'm the last man you ever expected, or wanted, to see in this lifetime.

"And now that I have you in my arms . . . you laugh. I'm deeply wounded."

How could one man turn her life around so much? "Down the hall and through the first door on your left."

"Good, I was afraid you were going to tell me it was upstairs." He headed in the direction she'd given.

Logan's humor was infectious. She found the restraints she'd placed on herself slipping away. Still, she hesitated.

The humor died in his eyes. "It's okay to let go."

He seemed to know her thoughts so well. Strange, but with Logan she did feel like it was okay to let go—at least for a little while.

She drew in a shaky breath and tried to move past the awkward moment. "You mean you wouldn't have carried me up a flight of stairs? This is the South, and all southern men are supposed to carry women up the stairs. Didn't you ever watch *Gone With the Wind?*"

"As much as I want you, I think I'd carry you just about anywhere." His slow grin melted her heart. "And my mother's seen the movie a dozen or so times. So yeah, I've seen bits and pieces."

When he stepped inside her bedroom, his eyes widened. She knew exactly what her room looked like: hot reds, dark, vibrant greens, and touches of gold. Out of her whole house, this had been her one indulgence. It was a sensual room made for making love, but no man had ever crossed the threshold. She'd never invited a man into her home—until now.

This was her special room, where she let all her barriers fade away and got in touch with her inner self. She liked the colors, the way they made her feel. She drew strength from the color combinations, and the muted music that played in the background from the speakers she had hidden in each corner. This room was her solace when she desperately needed to be alone to think.

She'd let Logan invade her space. She wouldn't think about what it might mean. Not right now, anyway.

He set her on her feet, his attention no longer focused on the room as he began tugging her T-shirt over her head. She knew her bra was in direct contrast to the old, faded shirt. It was feminine: pale blue trimmed in lace. The bra pushed her breasts up, barely covering her nipples.

He drew in a deep, ragged breath. "That should be illegal," he croaked.

"Glad you like it. Want me to keep it on?" she innocently asked.

"Nope."

He unclasped the front hook, and pushed it off her shoulders. Her breasts spilled into his hands. She arched her back when he began to knead them, rubbing his thumbs across the tight nubs.

"I love the way you feel." He leaned forward and took her in his mouth, flicking his tongue across her nipple before sucking on the tender flesh. "And taste."

She moaned, grabbing his shoulders so she wouldn't lose her balance. Her legs had begun to tremble and she suddenly felt unable to bear her own weight.

"No . . . stop," she barely managed the strength to utter her plea. It took him a moment before he realized she gently pushed on his shoulders.

Reluctantly he released her tender flesh and stepped away. Disbelief crossed his face. "Now?" he sputtered.

She took a moment to catch her breath. If her body didn't feel like it was on fire, she might have laughed. Instead, she just smiled wickedly.

"I don't want you to stop . . ."

"Good." He reached for her again.

She quickly backed away. "Last time you called most of the shots."

When he grinned, her heart collided with her breastbone.

"From the sounds you made I didn't think you minded that much." He reached out and ran the tips of his fingers across her abdomen.

She sucked in a breath and took another step back when all she really wanted to do was close her eyes and hope he never stopped touching her. "You're cheating." Her words trembled.

"I didn't realize there were rules." He raised his eyebrows.

She moved behind him, more because it would put her out of his reach, than anything else. "There are no rules, per se." She ran her fingers lightly over his back, moving down to the hem of his red Polo and tugging it free from his jeans. Her hands tingled with her need to touch him. She slid her hands beneath the material, gliding over the sinewy muscles of his back. She closed her eyes, memorizing the texture of his skin.

He drew in a deep breath. "Okay, you have my attention."

"Making love should be savored, not rushed. It should be experienced. Love games between two consenting adults." Not that she was that experienced. But she'd read a lot. Books Andrea had given her about the human anatomy and all the erogenous zones. She'd just never found a man she wanted to experiment with—until now.

She pushed his shirt upward. He took the hint, pulling it over his head. When she brushed her breasts against his back, he moaned.

"But then, who said I was in a hurry?" He turned, his chest hairs grazing her nipples.

She bit her bottom lip, suddenly feeling out of control. He pulled her toward a plush, red velvet chair and sat down, tugging her onto his lap so that she straddled him, her legs on either side of his.

"I have all the time in the world." He lightly squeezed her breasts. "God, I love the way your nipples pucker and harden every time my fingers brush over them."

His words thrilled her, sending deep, pulsing sensations down her body, settling in the vee of her legs. She enjoyed his hands on her as much as she enjoyed touching him.

She traced his nipple, and felt it harden beneath her touch as she swirled her finger over it. She moved to his other nipple and repeated the movement.

His reaction was immediate. Logan swelled beneath her. His hard length pushed against her through the material of their clothes. She relaxed her body. He grunted, but she didn't think it was from pain. For a moment, she savored the feel of him against her.

He slid his hands down her hips to the waistband of her shorts, and popped the metal button from the hole, tugging the zipper downward. She started to stand, but he grasped her closer to him.

"Not yet."

When he began to move her hips back and forth, she sucked in a breath. The friction started a fire inside her. Suddenly she didn't care what happened next. The only thing that mattered was this moment in time. Any inhibitions she might have harbored vanished. Whatever he asked her to do next, she would do without hesitation. She'd lost all control of her body.

He slid his hands inside her shorts and massaged her bottom, squeezing each time she slid forward. A sweet ache began to build deep inside her as she rubbed against the rough texture of the material.

The music paused as the CD player changed to another disc. A few seconds passed and the room came alive with deep, pulsating sounds. She closed her eyes, letting the lingering smell of incense, the throbbing music, and the movement of Logan's body capture each one of her senses until they all exploded inside her at once. Her body shook as the orgasm swept over her and she crumpled to his chest, her face nestled in his neck. She lay against him, unable to move.

"I don't think there will ever come a day when I get tired of watching you come."

His words sent a tremble of excitement over her, but she could only guess at his pain because he held back his own release. Forcing life into her sated limbs, she pushed out of the chair and stood.

"You make me feel very wanton, Logan Hart." She began to move to the sensuous rhythm of the music, moving her hands over her breasts, touching and squeezing before sliding her palms down her hips and slowly pushing her shorts the rest of the way down and kicking out of them. She stood before him in a lacy blue thong that hid very little of the dark triangle between her legs.

He gripped the arms of the chair, his eyes glazed with barely restrained passion.

"No man has ever made me feel wanton." Her words were husky. She tugged on the elastic and his gaze became transfixed on her movements; sliding the thong down, then bringing it back up at the last minute. She became a tease, in a deliciously sinful sort of way. Power filled her. She enjoyed knowing she controlled the situation and that her movements would heighten his sexual desire.

She shoved the thong all the way down and kicked it off, noting his knuckles blanched as his fingers dug into the arms of the chair.

"Maybe you should've been the stripper." He abruptly stood and kicked off his pants, his white Jockeys followed.

"Damn . . . forgot . . ." He scrambled for his pants. "I need a condom."

Before he could reach his jeans, she scooped them up. "Let me." He sat back down in the chair as she brought out the foil packet and tore across the opening with her teeth. Kneeling between his legs, she started to roll it on, but stopped for a moment to admire his hard length. Without taking the time to think about it, she flicked her tongue across the tip. He jerked his hips forward.

"You can experiment next time, but darlin', right now I'm about to embarrass myself." He grabbed the condom from her hand and slipped it on before reaching under her arms and drawing her forward.

It was nice to know she had the same effect on him that he had on her. When he slipped inside her, thoughts of who did what to whom quickly vanished.

"This feels so . . . damn . . . good." He moaned. "You don't know how I've ached to bury myself inside you again."

He raised his hips and she went a little deeper. She matched each of his thrusts, raising her hips slightly, then plunging downward, squeezing with her inner muscles, enjoying the way he filled her body.

Their ragged breathing blended with the beat of the music and the deep tones of the room. Haunting notes, vibrant colors crashing together in a symphony of unrestrained passion.

He cried out, closing his eyes tightly. Her release came seconds later. She squeezed her legs against his thighs as her juices flowed.

She closed her eyes, savoring the sensations running through her . . . but something happened. A subtle change in the way she felt. Almost like a black cloud hovered over her.

A shiver ran down her spine breaking the spell of contentment. She closed her eyes tight, not wanting to see what wasn't there. But she heard a scream . . . saw blood . . . and she looked death in the face. But this time she wasn't looking at her past. This was the future. Her future.

For a second she felt icy cold. She felt dead.

Chapter 12

Jody could deny it until she was blue in the face, but Logan knew something had happened. Her face had drained of color. When he'd questioned her, she shook her head, and refused to tell him. Had he hurt her? No, he didn't think so. The look on her face hadn't been one of pain.

Hell, he wasn't sure what it had been. Her eyes had glazed over, filled with passion. He was entranced watching her. The way she'd panted, biting her bottom lip, her breasts straining toward him.

But then something happened.

The sex? Damn it, he knew the sex had been great, and he thought she'd enjoyed it, too. Hell, he knew when a woman was in the throes of passion, and Jody had been in the zone. Still . . .

He pulled into a parking space in front of the newspaper office and climbed out of his car, jamming his keys into his pocket before taking the steps two at a time. Maybe today he would find something that would give him a little more insight into who Jody was.

He pushed on the glass door and went inside. What the hell else could go wrong today?

Damn, he'd felt so great when he delivered the puppy early this morning, and so crappy now. He'd almost sewn up the job of assistant editor. So why didn't he feel like he owned the world?

He strode across the building, but stopped when he heard his name called out. Bradley stood just inside his office, his shoulders squared. His boss wasn't frowning, but he wasn't smiling, either. He motioned for Logan to come over.

Damn. He eyed his computer before reluctantly turning away. He wondered what Bradley wanted as he walked toward the other man.

"That was a nice piece you wrote on the perp breaking and entering," he said after he took his chair behind his desk. He motioned for Logan to take a seat. "When we run the cop articles sales will be good."

"Thanks." His eyes narrowed. There was more to this than met the eye. "What's up?"

His boss smiled. "That's what I like about you—good instincts."

Logan waited for the other shoe to drop, and he was sure it would land with a clunk any second now.

Bradley leaned back in his chair and steepled his fingers. "The only two people who have a chance at the assistant editor position are you and Hank Johnson." He glanced at his hands, then back at Logan.

Logan's insides knotted.

"Hank is older, more experienced." He leaned forward, elbows on his desk, and looked Logan straight in the eye. "But even though you're younger there's a hunger inside you. It reminds me of when I was a reporter. A damn good one, too." He sighed. "Sometimes I miss those days."

Some of the knots loosened. Okay, he wasn't losing the job, at least, not at this moment.

Bradley didn't meet his gaze as he rotated a pencil between his thumb and forefinger. "They pulled a body out of Lake Ponchetrain about an hour ago," he began, like he hated saying what he had to say. "Hank was there and got the full story. It was the mayor's cousin."

He gripped the arms of his chair. Damn! When Jody ended her shift, he'd gone straight home to write about the arrest so he could drop it on Bradley's desk before going over to Jody's this morning—just to let Bradley get an idea of how he planned to write his series on the life of a cop.

"It doesn't mean he has the job," Bradley continued. "I'll give you until the articles are finished before I make up my mind, but if you want the job, you'll have to give me something substantial. I hope you won't disappoint me."

Logan recognized the dismissal and stood. "I'll get you a story."

He wheeled around and strode out the door. Damn it, he wanted that job. He'd always been caught in the middle. He was the middle child in a family of five, fighting for his place in his family and then later in society.

In high school he'd found it—editing the school's monthly newspaper, and again in college. Since then, Logan knew what he wanted to do with his life. The job of assistant editor would give him the experience he needed. He'd be learning directly from the best. Bradley hadn't lied when he said he'd been a damn good reporter.

This job meant a hell of a lot to him. Hell, it was more than a job. This was his dream. It seemed like he'd worked toward this one goal all his life.

He pulled out the chair in front of his desk and dropped into it. Maybe staring at old newspaper clippings would clear his mind and help him figure out what he needed to do. He couldn't let this opportunity slip between his fingers. At the rate he was going, that might just be the outcome.

Being there when Jody took down the perp had been a fluke. If she had her say, that would be the only call he ever made that involved weapons. He ran a hand through his hair. He felt like he was grasping at straws. Maybe if he knew more about Jody, he'd be able to come up with the right argument to convince her he needed some kick-ass articles.

He put her name in, but the only thing that came up was a brief article where she'd graduated from the police academy. He tried her mother's name. He found her—in the obits.

> *Angelina Dupree, loving wife and mother of two, passed away quietly in her sleep on December eighth. . . .*

What had it felt like to the little girls to lose their mother so young? Even worse, around the holidays. He scanned further. Donations to Hospice. Cancer maybe? Something terminal. A bad deal. He shook his head, took a deep breath and continued, looking under her father's name.

MAN FOUND MURDERED

The name Dupree jumped out at him. He sat forward, skimming the article.

> *The body of Phillip Dupree was found murdered in his home. A single gunshot wound at close range took the life of this widowed father of two. Neighbors stated they weren't home at the estimated time of death. A small pool of blood near the body of the dead man brought gloomy predictions to the fate of the two girls, a seven-year-old and her fourteen-year-old sister. At the time the paper went to press, the whereabouts of the children were still unknown, although we were informed the eldest daughter had been at the police station shortly after the murders would've taken place, that report has been unsubstantiated. No arrests have been made.*

Bradley had written the article, before he became editor. Excitement rushed through him.

He looked up Jody's older sister. Nothing. She might as well have vanished off the face of the earth.

Logan sat back in his chair. He stared at the screen but his thoughts weren't focused on the words in front of him as he put everything together.

Jody's father had been murdered. That must be how Jody got the scar above her right ear. She probably got caught in the crossfire. He grimaced. Had she seen her father murdered? No wonder she didn't want to talk about it.

But what had happened to her sister? Jody hadn't mentioned her the other night at the coffee shop, only a grandmother and her friend Andrea.

She was hiding something. He pushed out of his chair, the beginning of an article began to form in his mind.

Missing child discovered working in the same police department that couldn't locate her twenty years ago.

The captain might not like it that one of the missing Dupree children worked for his department. Especially if she could clear up a murder. Why hadn't she?

Again, the puzzle wasn't complete. Where was Jody's sister? Had she been the one who committed the murders? Fourteen-year-old? Possible. Or had she been a victim, too?

He froze.

Damn, why had it taken him so long to see what was right in front of him? Jody probably knew who killed her father, and possibly her sister.

But why hadn't she told anyone? Temporary amnesia? He'd read about that sort of thing happening more than once.

Adrenaline rushed through him. This story would get him the job of assistant editor. He could see the headlines now. TWENTY-YEAR-OLD MURDER SOLVED.

He pushed out of his chair and strode to Bradley's door, rapping on the glass before entering. He didn't even wait for his boss to say come in. Bradley looked up, but Logan didn't give him time to speak.

"You remember writing about a murder? Around twenty years ago? Phillip Dupree?"

Bradley dropped his pen on his desk and leaned back in his chair, a thoughtful expression on his face. "No, not off-hand . . ."

"They never found his daughters," the words tumbled out of him. "A seven- and fourteen-year-old."

He nodded. "Okay, now I remember. I think everyone eventually assumed the killer murdered them, too, then dumped their bodies in the swamp." He grimaced. "Ugly business."

"What if I told you I knew the whereabouts of one daughter?"

Bradley picked up his pencil and began to tap-tap it on his desk. After a moment, he looked at Logan. "Are you sure?"

"Almost one hundred percent."

"Does she know what happened? I mean, who killed her father? What about the other sister? Why hasn't she come forward?"

"I haven't questioned her about it yet."

Bradley's eyes glittered with interest. "Damn, a twenty-year-old mystery solved. Everyone likes a mystery. Especially if one of the girls survived. Readers love a happy ending even more." He reined his thoughts in. "Get me this story and I can almost guarantee you the job of assistant editor."

"It's practically written now." Excitement spiraled through him. His instincts had been right on target. He'd known Jody had a story locked inside her.

He left Bradley's office and went to his car. He had a few questions he needed answered. Not just about Jody's past or if she had seen who murdered her father.

What had happened after they made love? One minute she'd been right there with him, then she mentally drifted away. He'd never forget the look of panic on her face. There was some kind of connection between her present and her past. He started the car and drove straight to Jody's house. He'd take it slow and easy, but he'd find out what was going on.

Damn, he loved every second of being a reporter.

Chapter 13

Logan twice in one day. She wasn't sure she was comfortable with that or the way he stared at her—like he'd taken a clock apart, laying out all the mechanisms, then tried to discover what made it tick. Since opening the door, she'd sensed a difference in him. Almost as if he knew something about her he hadn't previously known. But that was impossible. He hadn't been gone that long.

"So, have you decided on a name for the pup?"

Idle conversation? He *did* know something. No, she wouldn't let herself become paranoid. He'd asked a simple question—nothing more. This was why she hated serious relationships. There were too many complications. Maybe she should've stuck with Paul. He'd only been concerned with himself. Just the thought of dating him again left a sour taste in her mouth.

"I think you'll probably have to buy a new pair of slippers." He glanced downward. "One of yours has been confiscated."

She looked over the side of the table. The pup raised her eyes to Jody and dropped the house shoe. Apparently, she decided it was now time to play with the humans because she began barking and wagging her tail.

Her suspicions of only a moment ago vanished. It was

crazy to question Logan's every move. Why couldn't she just accept the fact he might be interested in her?

Her attention focused on the puppy and she forced herself to relax. Odd how she could become attached to an animal so quickly when she had a tendency to keep people at arm's length. She rubbed the pup behind the ear and received a lick for her reward. And to think Eugene could've killed her. It was bad enough she'd had a pile of filthy rags for a bed.

"Ragamuffin, that's what I'll call her," she spoke quietly.

"Ragamuffin?"

She nodded. "Yeah, when we first saw her, she was on a pile of rags, and she looks kind of funny with her hair sticking out in all directions."

He nodded. "Rags for short."

She frowned. "No, that's a boy's name. Muffin for short."

He cringed. "Muffin? As in poppy seed, or blueberry? Don't you think that's a little . . . well . . . sissified?"

"No, I don't." She raised one eyebrow, daring him to make another snide remark. Muffin was a perfectly acceptable name. And it suited her.

"Muffin it is, then." His gaze locked with hers.

There was a subtle change in the air. Nothing she could quite put her finger on, but she suspected it was because of what happened after they made love this morning. He hadn't questioned her then, but let the matter drop. Would the reporter in him let her off the hook quite so easily, though?

"About this morning . . ." he began.

"Have you eaten lunch?" She jumped up from her chair and went to the refrigerator. "I have ham if you'd like a sandwich," she said as she looked inside." *Don't pry,* she silently prayed. Why couldn't their relationship stay exactly the same as it was now? How long would he hang around if she told him about her visions?

He'd asked what happened after they'd made love and

she'd told him nothing. She hadn't thought he believed her. Why did he have to be such a . . . a reporter?

"A sandwich sounds good." He stood, joining her at the counter. He grabbed a tomato and knife.

She sighed with relief, and set the plate of ham down. She spread mayo on bread and added a slice of the ham. And she began to relax. Maybe he sensed she didn't want to talk about what happened after they made love. A good thing, because she couldn't really explain it herself.

She'd had premonitions and visions in the past, but nothing like this. No, that wasn't quite true. She'd had something similar when she was a child. The day her father had been murdered. *Mamere* had told her that her mother had had premonitions and visions. The gift, she'd called it. It was one present she'd gladly give back.

She reached for a slice of tomato and placed one on each sandwich and topped it with the other slice of bread. While she carried the plates to the table, Logan washed his hands.

"So, are you going to tell me what happened after we made love, or are you going to make me guess?" he asked, drying his hands on a towel.

She stumbled, but caught herself. Why wouldn't he let the matter fade into oblivion?

Trying to remain calm, she set the plates on the table and went to the refrigerator. She opened the door and leaned forward, letting the cool air swirl around her. It felt good on her suddenly hot skin. "I don't know what you're talking about," she hedged.

"I think you do."

She removed two sodas and carried them to the table. He tossed the towel to the cabinet and followed. Before she could sit, he took her hand in his. Odd how his hold on her felt tender, yet firm, like he knew something had happened, and he wasn't about to let her brush aside his questions.

"If I hurt you, I'm sorry."

He meant their lovemaking. Is that what he thought? That he might have hurt her? She looked away. "You didn't." He dropped her hand, and she sat in the chair across from him.

The opposite was true. She didn't want Logan to think she hadn't enjoyed making love. He'd made her feel things she'd never felt before.

"Then what happened?"

She began ripping the crust off her bread, piling it on the side of her plate. "I have visions," she finally admitted. "It's no big deal." She bit her lip. "It's been a long time since I've had one." She glanced up.

"You're serious?" he asked.

Her spirits dropped. She'd known he'd think she was delusional. "That's why I didn't want to tell you. I knew you wouldn't believe me, that you would think I'd lost my mind. I don't have them often, in fact, not for a long time. I'm not sure why I've started having them now. I'm not crazy." She should've known better than to say anything. Damn it, when would she learn?

"Did I say you were?"

"No, but you thought it." She dared him to deny it.

He took a drink from his soda and set it back down. "Before I moved to New Orleans, I covered a beat in Dallas. Man, was it in a rough area. Hell, everyone was afraid to go on that side of town. Not me." He ruefully smiled. "Okay, maybe a little. But there was this woman who lived in a two-room shack. She might have been forty or seventy. It was hard to tell. Her neighbors called her a witch."

She wondered just where his story was going. Did he think she was a witch? Why should she care? Easy question. Difficult answer. She didn't want him to think she'd lost her mind or that she was odd in some way.

"This woman had an ability to predict things," he continued. "I discovered most of what she said came true. I never laughed at her, and I wouldn't laugh at you, either."

Relief swept through her. She tried to tell herself it wouldn't have mattered if he'd thought she was looney. But it did. More than she cared to admit.

"What happened to your sister?" he asked after a moment of silence.

She could feel the color draining from her face. Did he know something about her? For a brief moment the possibility he might have information about her elder sister sent hope soaring inside her, but just as quickly she stifled it. How many times had she thought she might have found something only to discover another dead end? Too many to count. She warily eyed Logan. "What do you know about her?"

"Nothing. I know you have a sister, but you've never mentioned her. When you spoke of the people in your life you only referred to Andrea and your grandmother."

She didn't like someone delving into her business, but how could she have expected Logan to do anything less? He was a reporter, and he was interested in her. Of course he would try to find out about her past so it would help him understand what made her tick. She didn't like nosy people. She had too much pain in her past to talk about it.

"All I know is that you have a sister. Nothing else." He reached across the narrow table and took her hand.

She immediately pulled hers away. "My family is none of your business," she ground out, pushing away from the table and standing. Damn it, for a second she'd let herself hope. She should've known better.

She grabbed her plate and took it to the sink. Half her sandwich remained, but the thought of eating more turned her stomach.

A thick, uncomfortable silence hung over the room. She closed her eyes. From the very beginning she'd never felt awkward with Logan. They'd clicked within the first few seconds of meeting. But now it was like a wedge had been hammered between them. It wasn't a good feeling.

"How much do you know?"

"That your father was murdered. No one knew what happened to his daughters. You're the youngest, aren't you? The seven-year-old. What happened to your sister?"

"I don't know where she is," she told him. "She could be dead. I suspect she is. Your guess is as good as mine." Pain ripped through her. Each time she admitted what she feared most, it was like she laid truth to her own words. She didn't want the big sister she'd adored to be forever dead. As long as she thought of her as just missing then her sister could remain alive—if only in her mind.

"What happened that day?"

Hell, he already knew everything. What difference did it make now? "I had a . . . a vision or something. I was only seven. I remember it scared me. I'd had a few in the past, but nothing like this."

Her sister had never really paid much attention to them, only *Mamere*. Jody had loved listening to their grandmother's tales of the supernatural, legends of the Louisiana swamps, spells and hexes. And about what she called Jody's *gift*.

She turned from the sink and met Logan's gaze. "You want to know what happened? A vision that came true."

"What did you see?" He leaned against the back of his chair and waited patiently for her to continue.

Jody reached down and scooped Muffin into her arms, smoothing the pup's scraggly hair. Even though sunshine streamed into the room, she felt cold. "Why should I tell you? So you can splash it across the front page of the newspaper?"

"Is that what you think?"

"No." She shook her head. "That isn't what I think." She'd been right about Logan from the start. There was some strange connection between them. More than the sex.

And maybe she was tired of holding it all inside. She took a deep breath and began telling him what happened that day. "My sister wanted to go to the store. I begged her not to leave. I knew something felt wrong. There were pictures—inside my head. I had a sick feeling in the pit of my stomach, a tightening in my chest." She hated explaining, but she wanted Logan to understand. She shifted her feet. "Like when you had to take a test in school, and you hadn't studied."

When he nodded, she continued.

"I told her we should go see *Mamere* instead. But she'd never felt comfortable around the old woman. She said *Mamere* spooked her, and besides, I had a cold that day. She told me I should stay in bed."

For a moment she could see her sister's face, her long, glossy black hair. That was the only resemblance they'd shared. Jody looked more like their tiny mother, her sister looked like their father, and she was so damn sassy and full of vinegar. Jody had been the wistful one, always daydreaming . . . until her daydreams were stolen from her.

"And then," Logan pulled her thoughts back to the present.

"My sister left, and I fell asleep. I don't know how long I slept, but I woke to arguing. Daddy was so angry. Uncle John had hidden something in the house, but Daddy didn't want it there so he flushed it down the toilet." She focused on the puppy she held and forced the past out of her mind. If she didn't think about the words, then it didn't hurt so much to say them. "They began to fight. I could hear furniture crashing to the floor. I was scared so I crawled out of bed and went into the other room to see what was happening."

Strange, but she could see everything play out like a movie running inside her head. She saw herself walking out of her bedroom and down the hall. Everything was in sharp detail, even down to her white nightgown with little blue flowers. Her feet were bare and she held a stuffed bunny tight to her chest. Suddenly, it wasn't her anymore, but someone else. She felt the little girl's fear—not her fear.

"I went to the doorway of the kitchen," she spoke in monotone, watching what the child would do next. She wanted to warn her away, but she knew she couldn't. The story had to unfold the same way each time. "They wrestled over a gun. There was an explosion." She reached up and touched her scar. She could feel the little girl's shock, her pain. Jody saw the blood. The little girl took a step back. Her father cried out his anger. The girl crumpled to the floor. Another explosion followed. Her father's body fell close to her. For a moment, their gazes met. She knew the exact instant his soul left.

For a second, she felt the darkness . . . the warmth that kept her from being scared. A bright light surrounded her, but it didn't hurt her eyes. She reached for her father's hand . . .

She drew in a sharp breath. "When I came to, I was at *Mamere*'s cabin, deep in the swamps. I asked about my sister and father. My grandmother told me that he was dead. That my sister didn't exist anymore, and it was best to leave the past alone so everyone would be safe."

"Your *uncle* shot you, and killed your father?"

"My father's half brother." She shivered. "I guess Uncle John was afraid he'd be implicated in the murder of his brother. He probably thought he'd killed me, too. I don't know where he went."

"And your sister?"

"*Mamere* told me she couldn't find her. My theory is that she'd returned as he was leaving. Maybe he killed her, then dumped the body in the swamp, and maybe he was coming back to dispose of me and my father, but the police came. I don't know. I was only seven at the time. I had a fever after the bullet grazed my temple. *Mamere* took care of me, nursed me back to health."

A cold chill ran over her. She vaguely remembered the nightmares when her fever soared.

Running through the streets of New Orleans, sleeping in cardboard boxes, afraid her uncle would find her and finish the job he'd started. Sometimes she almost felt as if she were in someone else's body as she ran far, far away.

"I tried searching for her when I was older . . . just in case she'd escaped. Too many years had passed. Any trail she might have left had grown cold."

"Wouldn't she have gone to your grandmother?"

She shook her head. "Not if it meant going into the swamps. Just the thought of that place terrified her, said the swamps were creepy. She always got lost, could never find her way around them."

"And your uncle?"

She swallowed past the bitter taste in her mouth. "I think he'd hidden drugs in our house. I'm pretty sure that's what my father flushed down the toilet. If that were the case, he would've had to answer to someone. I tried to discover his whereabouts, but ran up against a brick wall. Nothing. I figure he left the state, maybe the country."

He stood. For a moment she wondered if he were going to leave. Why would he want to get mixed up with a woman who had visions? Whose uncle was probably involved in a drug ring. He'd be a fool to hang around.

A sense of loss swept over her. She didn't want Logan to leave. With all her heart she knew he wasn't supposed to go.

But he walked toward her, not away. She raised her chin, met his gaze. He had the look of a man who wasn't going anywhere. Relief washed over her. She hadn't realized just how much he'd come to mean to her in the short time she'd known him.

He took Muffin from her and set the puppy on the floor before taking her in his arms. She didn't feel like she was in this alone anymore. Maybe she was burying her head in the sand, but Andrea was right. It had been almost twenty damn years since her father was murdered. Maybe it was time she let go of the past.

"I'm sorry for what happened. No child should have to go through so much trauma." He kissed her lightly on top of her head.

She moved so that her face was raised toward him. He took her invitation and lowered his mouth. His kiss was at first gentle and soft, but it soon turned into something much deeper. Her heart soared. Logan had taken the lonely ache out of her life.

The kiss ended and she rested her head against his chest. The steady rhythm of his heartbeat a comforting sound.

Logan lightly caressed her back. "Let me help you. I want to write your story for the newspaper."

Her heart crashed to her feet. She stepped out of the comfort of his arms. Logan faded away and in his place she saw dark red blood. . . .

"Jody?"

Tension threaded through his words, but it came from a distance.

Chapter 14

Fear swept through Logan. "Jody? Jody!" What the hell was happening?

Her eyes drifted closed. Almost in slow motion, her legs buckled, and she started falling to the floor. He scooped her into his arms and carried her toward the bedroom, his heart pounding against the wall of his chest.

As if sensing there was something wrong with her newfound mistress, the pup began to whine.

"I feel the same way, girl," he muttered. How long would she stay like this? What if . . . He clutched her closer to him. No, he wouldn't think about what-ifs.

He laid her gently on the bed, brushing her hair away from her face. She looked too damned pale. Maybe he should wet a cloth and place it on her forehead.

Somewhere in the back of his mind he could remember his mother doing that when he'd been ill. Would it be enough to snap her back to reality? Hell, right now he'd try anything— even if he were grasping at straws.

When he turned, his gaze landed on an address book lying on the nightstand beside the phone. Hope sprang inside him. The friend she'd mentioned would know what to do. What the hell was her name, though? He grabbed the book, his hands shaking as he thumbed through the pages.

There weren't many names to choose from. His address

book had more on one page than she had in her entire book. That bothered him. He didn't dwell on what it meant.

As soon as he saw the name Andrea, he remembered. She was listed under the P's. Andrea Potier. He reached for the phone and quickly punched in her number.

It rang once.

Twice.

He said a quick prayer.

"Yeah?" A surly female answered.

"Andrea?"

"You have the wrong number. I'm not the woman you met last night." Her voice became distant.

"Wait, don't hang up," his words rushed out. "It's about Jody."

"What's wrong?" Her alarm was apparent.

"I . . . I think she had a vision or something. I can't get her to talk. I carried her to the bed . . . she just lays there." Speaking the words made the situation more real. His gut twisted. Once, he'd read an article about some psychic going into a trance for hours, and when she came out of it, she never acted right again.

"Is this her stripper?"

"Reporter," he corrected.

"Whatever. Where is she?"

"Her house."

"I'll be there in ten minutes." The phone clunked when she hung up.

He pushed the END button, hesitated for only a moment, then called his apartment.

"This better be good," his brother grumbled as if he'd been in a sound sleep prior to the insistent ringing of the phone.

"I need you."

"Where?" Any traces of sleep were immediately erased from Kevin's voice.

Logan gave the address and hung up. He didn't know if his brother could do a damn thing, but he wanted him here. He never doubted Kevin would drop everything and rush over. He was family, and in his, they didn't question when they were needed. They just came.

He set the address book back on the nightstand. Jody hadn't moved since he laid her on the bed. He watched for a few seconds. Did her chest rise and fall? He couldn't tell. Fear maliciously weaved its way through him. He moved toward her, wanting to shake life into her body.

Then he saw it. A slight movement. Her chest rose and fell. He reached out and grabbed the back of the chair to steady himself. The same chair they'd made love in that morning. It seemed like a lifetime since then.

He pulled the chair close to the bed and sat down . . . and stared. An air of frailty surrounded her. There were no traces of the tough cop she'd been when she took down the perp.

Who was this woman? And why did he care so much what happened to her?

She had a dark, sultry kind of beauty he didn't see very often, but it was more than just her looks. He liked the way she wasn't afraid of making love, and even though he'd feared for her safety, he admired the way she handled herself as a cop. She was a damn good one.

But behind her dark blue eyes there lurked a deep sadness. He knew he could never make the pain she'd suffered as a child go away. Hell, he couldn't even imagine what she'd gone through.

His childhood had been so much different. His father had taught all his children a solid code of ethics, and his mother had added generous portions of laughter and hugs. Had anyone hugged Jody?

He looked at her still form. Could he ease some of her pain? What if he wasn't given the chance? What if she didn't return to him?

As he sat there time was no longer relevant. The ringing of the doorbell finally sunk into his muddled brain. He hurried to the door and opened it.

Andrea looked like ten miles of bad road. Obviously, she hadn't bothered to comb her hair. Blonde curls were going in all different directions. And he had a feeling she'd thrown on the same clothes she'd worn the night before, except maybe the pink tennis shoes.

She wore tight black jeans with gold sequins down the sides, and an equally snug, ruffled leopard-print top that veed almost to her navel nearly spilling out her breasts. Over her outlandish outfit she'd thrown a black bomber jacket.

But her face was free of makeup. Her skin shone with a healthy glow, and an innocence that didn't quite match the rest of her.

She suddenly frowned, sweeping him with a disgruntled gaze. "Don't just stand there like a damned fool, take me to her."

"Sorry," he mumbled. "She's in the bedroom."

He stepped back when she pushed past. She might be tall, at least five-eight, but she still had to raise her head to look at him. He didn't think that set well with her. Even so, she was taking charge of the situation whether he wanted her to or not.

"What happened?"

He hurried after her, words stumbling out of his mouth. "We were in the kitchen. Her eyes got this glazed look and she started to fall. I carried her to bed." He nearly ran over her when she skidded to a halt.

"What the hell is that?" She frowned at Muffin who was lying beside the bed on a small, gold fur throw. The pup growled.

"Muffin. Jody's puppy," he explained.

"She doesn't have a puppy."

"She does now."

"Well, get the runt out of here."

He scooped Muffin into his arms, along with the green slipper she'd dragged into the bedroom. He carefully kept his eyes off Jody. He couldn't stand seeing her like this. Every time his glance fell on her it was like someone ripped his heart out.

"Is there fresh coffee?"

"Maybe a couple of hours old."

"Make a fresh pot. Six scoops. No one ever makes their coffee strong enough."

Doing anything was better than standing around with his hands shoved in his pockets. He felt so damned helpless.

The doorbell rang again. Andrea raised her eyebrows.

"My brother. I called him."

"Whatever." She turned back to Jody, effectively dismissing him. "Shut the door on your way out."

He started to leave, but hesitated at the last minute. "Will she be okay?" he asked without turning. He desperately needed someone to tell him she'd be all right.

Her voice softened. "Yeah, I think she'll be just fine. I've never seen her have a vision as strong as this one must have been. She's starting to come around, though. I won't let nothin' or no one hurt my Jody."

Was she warning him? He didn't give a rat's ass as long as Andrea helped her, and she was right, Jody was starting to moan.

"Go on." Andrea motioned for him to leave. "Let me take care of her. She won't want a lot of people hovering over her."

Logan hesitated before he left to let Kevin inside. Maybe it was better that Andrea took care of her right now.

He opened the door and stared at his disheveled little brother. "What'd you do, sleep in your clothes?" Did no one get up at a decent hour anymore? It was past noon.

Kevin frowned, leaning a shoulder against the door frame to prop himself up. "When my brother begs me to come over, and sounds like he's on the verge of sure death, then I grab whatever clothes I have nearby, and throw them on." His frown deepened. "Excuse me for not taking time to decide the exact apparel to wear, or to shave." His frown deepened. "You don't look like you're dying, either."

"Sorry, I guess I'm a little strung out. I didn't mean to sound critical. Come on in and I'll explain while I make a pot of coffee."

"Good. And make it strong. You could read the newspaper through that muddy water you call coffee. At least six scoops. Who lives here, anyway?" Kevin glanced around as he sauntered inside.

Logan turned and headed in the direction of the kitchen. "Jody Dupree."

"The cop you're riding out with?"

"Yeah."

"You didn't kill her, did you? If so, I'm not helping you dispose of the body until after I've had at least one cup of coffee."

"Funny," he spoke dryly. "Here, take Muffin." He shoved the pup into his brother's arms and went about making coffee, trying to remember the motions Jody had gone through when she made the coffee and finding where she kept everything.

Kevin eyed the pup. "Hey, isn't this one of the pups you brought home with you? That momma dog isn't going to like you taking one of her babies. And what kind of name is Muffin? Sounds kind of sissy-ish if you ask me."

"I didn't name her. Jody did." He filled the glass pot with water and poured it into the coffeemaker. "And she's old enough to be weaned."

His hands shook slightly when he scooped coffee from the canister. He took a deep breath, then continued putting the pot of coffee together. She'd be okay, he told himself. He was certain Andrea knew what she was doing.

"Maybe," Kevin continued, forcing Logan to think about something besides Jody. "They just don't look very big."

He lightly grabbed the pup's snout and shook, growling at her. Muffin latched on to Kevin's finger and growled back. Kevin chuckled. "Feisty little thing."

Logan should've known Kevin would pick up on the fact Muffin was one of Blondie's babies. Jody would never let him live it down if she knew he'd adopted the mother and all her pups. He couldn't very well leave them in the overcrowded shelter, though. And besides, he'd already given one of the pups away—to Jody. It wouldn't be long before he found homes for the rest.

"You know, I'd just as soon Jody not find out I brought the dogs home."

"Why? Afraid she might think you're a softie?"

He frowned at Kevin.

"Okay, but I don't really see what the big secret is." Kevin put the pup on the floor, rolling the red ball toward her. Muffin pounced. "So, you going to tell me what's going on or not? I doubt very seriously you called me over to talk about a dog and her pups. Where is Jody, anyway? And why are you here on your day off? I thought you had to write an article or something?"

Logan began opening cabinets looking for the cups, and tried to think of a way to explain what happened without giving away too many of Jody's secrets. He doubted she'd appreciate him discussing her, but before he could think up a good lie, Andrea walked in.

She looked from Logan to Kevin. "Logan is here because he's been sleeping with Jody since the night he played stripper. Jody has visions. He showed up today, she tranced out on him. He got scared and called me." She looked back at Logan. "Is that coffee ready yet?"

Logan's jaw dropped open, then snapped closed. Kevin, on the other hand, was looking at Andrea like he hadn't seen a woman in a very long time. He glanced between the two. Andrea had more than caught his little brother's interest.

"What?" Andrea asked.

He brought three cups out of the cabinet. "I don't think I would've stated it quite so bluntly," he grumbled.

She planted her hands on her hips. "Isn't that what happened?"

"Well, yes."

She shrugged. "Then why dance around the truth?" She strolled forward and took one of the cups.

Fine, but there were more important issues to worry about. Mainly, the woman in the next room. "How's Jody?"

"She's awake, but her head is pounding worse than the morning after a Saturday night drunk. I gave her a couple of pills to help with the pain. She'll be fine. This must've been a bad one, though. I've never seen her out of it like this. They're usually very short. What was she talking about before she spaced out?"

"Her uncle."

Andrea paused with her hand on the handle of the coffeepot, her expression turned serious. "She told you about him?" Her gaze dropped from his as she poured coffee into her cup.

"About him. About her sister. About what happened," he told her.

"She doesn't talk about her past to anyone." She added sugar and slowly stirred. When her gaze met his, it held an unmistakable warning.

"I won't hurt her."

"Sometimes the best intentions can get twisted."

"Hey, can anyone join in on this conversation?" Kevin ambled over and picked up one of the cups Logan had set on the cabinet, then went to the coffeemaker.

"Nope, it's private." Andrea looked Kevin over. "I guess you're the brother."

"The best of the Hart clan." Kevin clearly let his gaze trail over Andrea. "Isn't it a little early for Mardi Gras, sweet thing?"

Andrea bristled, narrowing her eyes. "You're not from around here, are you? And I'm not anyone's *sweet thing*."

"Good." Kevin grinned. "Then you're available."

She cast a look in Kevin's direction that should've had him running for cover, but Kevin's grin only widened.

If Logan wasn't so worried about Jody, he might have enjoyed the sparring. He had a feeling his cocky little brother had met his match. But at the moment, he wasn't sure he trusted Andrea's diagnosis. Maybe he should take Jody to the ER just to be on the safe side. He vaguely watched Andrea and Kevin as he gathered his thoughts.

Kevin smiled. His lopsided grin had made women of all ages swoon at his feet since he was in junior high. Logan didn't think Andrea looked that impressed.

"Nope," Kevin said and poured himself a cup of coffee. "I'm from the Lone Star State—Texas."

She turned, taking her cup to the table and sat down. "I'll try not to hold it against you." She didn't bother looking at him when she spoke.

Kevin's ego was clearly bruised. "What do you have against Texas?" He sucked in air when he sloshed hot coffee over the side of his cup and onto his hand. He quickly grabbed a paper napkin, and headed toward the table, blotting the minor burn.

Logan might as well not be in the room as Kevin pulled out a chair across from Andrea and they got into a heated debate about the merits of living in the great state of Texas versus being raised in Louisiana.

Andrea seemed unconcerned her friend was lying in bed in the next room, yet Logan knew she cared a great deal for Jody. That had been evident from the moment she'd walked inside the house.

Maybe it was okay for her to sit at the table and pretend everything was all right, but he couldn't. The least he could do was check on Jody. Make sure she was okay. Even sit with her. He turned, and his heart skidded to a halt.

Jody stood in the doorway. He swiftly appraised her. She looked fine. In fact, she looked damned good, kind of rumpled with heavy-lidded eyes—bedroom eyes. If Kevin and Andrea weren't in the same room, he'd scoop her up in his arms and carry her right back to bed. If for no other reason than to just lie next to her.

Instead, he set his cup down and went to her. Their gazes locked. She quickly looked away. He paused. Why did she seem nervous? Worried? Maybe because he'd seen her go into a trance-like state.

"Feeling better?"

She hesitated, then nodded.

"Good. You scared the hell out of me." He took her in his arms and held her. Her body was stiff and unyielding. After-effect? He wanted to chase all her demons away. And he didn't want to ever let her go.

A few minutes passed before he realized the room had gone quiet. He kissed her on top of her head before moving away. "Want some coffee?"

She nodded, warily eyeing Kevin.

"That's my brother. I called him for moral support."

Kevin stood, pulling out a chair for her. "Wow." He cast his gaze toward his brother. "You never told me she looked like . . . like . . . this." He waved his arm toward Jody.

"What am I?" Andrea crossed her arms. "Chopped liver?"

"Nope." Kevin grinned. "You're dessert. The icing on the cake. You're temptation."

She cocked an eyebrow. "And you're full of shit."

Jody paused before sitting in the chair he'd pulled out. Logan came up beside her and set her cup on the table. "Don't worry. He's actually harmless. He usually keeps his raging hormones under control."

Kevin blushed as he sat down again.

Andrea snickered and earned a scowl from Kevin.

Logan sensed the undercurrent in the room. Andrea and Kevin were oblivious to the sudden chill in the air.

Even after he was seated, Logan found he couldn't take his gaze off Jody. On the outside she looked fine, except for the slight tremble he noticed when she raised her cup. She hid her tension well.

What had she seen that would upset her this much?

"Hey, I'm glad you're okay," Kevin told her.

Jody lowered her cup to the table. "It was nothing." She looked at Logan, effectively letting him know she didn't want to discuss the matter.

"But what—" Andrea began, only to be cut off by a quick look from Jody. "Yeah, I guess those things happen sometimes." She stood. "Glad you're feeling better. I think I'm going to wander around town and see what's happening on Jackson Square."

Kevin jumped to his feet. "Want some company?"

She quirked one eyebrow. "I'm not a tourist guide, Texan."

He straightened, and grinned. "Yeah, but darlin', you still have to convince me your state is better than mine."

Her stern expression slipped just slightly. "It is better." She turned and strolled toward the doorway, but stopped at the edge of the kitchen and glanced over her shoulder. "You coming or not?"

That was all the encouragement Kevin needed. He hurried after Andrea. A few moments later Logan heard the front door shut.

He turned back to Jody. She held her cup with both hands, like it had suddenly become her lifeline. She looked so damn vulnerable, unlike the strong woman he'd grown used to being around. Swift, murderous anger raged through him. When he thought of all she went through as a child, he wanted to kill her uncle. Were her visions tied to her past? He had to know what happened.

He took her hand in his. "What did you see?"

She pulled hers free. "I can't let you write my story."

He stilled. "What do you mean?"

"You might as well sign my death certificate if you write this story. I have to face my uncle on my terms, my time.

Someday he'll return. I have sources on the street. They'll let me know if he slithers back into town."

"And if he doesn't? Are you going to hide from him for the rest of your life?"

She laughed without mirth and turned away from him. "I damn well don't want him knocking on my door. When I meet him I want to pick the time and place. No surprises, and that's exactly what it would be if he discovers I'm alive."

He came up behind her and placed his hands on her shoulders, trying to pass some of his strength to her.

She pulled away. "Please, go away. Just go."

"You still haven't told me what you saw," he pressed for an answer. What the hell had upset her so much? He reached a hand toward her, but drew back at the last minute.

"I have to sort through the images . . . to understand what they mean. Please, I'll call you later."

He didn't like leaving her alone. It must've been some vision from the way she was acting. He drew in a deep breath and did the hardest thing he'd ever done in his life. He walked away.

Chapter 15

Cavenaugh narrowed his eyes on the man sitting across from him, Frank Burgoddi, supposedly one of the best lawyers money could buy, if you could afford him.

Cavenaugh could.

"They're going to extradite you to New Orleans for earlier drug charges," Frank stated matter-of-factly. "Fighting it will be a losing battle and it could take a few weeks or a few months. I've gone over all the papers and I doubt you'd stand a chance." He tapped his bony, pale fingers on top of a pile of papers. "It's up to you."

He hated losers. When he was free, he might have to show Burgoddi just how much. "I thought you were the best?"

Burgoddi shrugged. The movement caused barely a ripple in the brown linen suit that looked so damned out of place in this fuckin' Texas jail.

"I can get you a better deal than any lawyer in the state."

"What am I looking at?" He didn't give a fuck about deals. He wanted to know about all the goddamn fine print lawyers liked to hide until the very end.

"I can probably get your sentence reduced to ten years. I've only had time to scan your file. Louisiana's evidence is old, but you were linked with a cop. Bribing officials and drug trafficking are serious charges, but I'll go through everything closely. There're bound to be flaws in a case that's been dormant this many years."

Cavenaugh clenched his fists. Ten years. Ten fucking years. It might sound short to this prick, but it would ruin him. All his contacts would be worthless by then.

He studied the lawyer. What if he wasn't telling him everything? Cavenaugh knew he'd become an easy mark. Burgoddi could take his money and not do a damn thing.

His lip curled in distaste. He didn't like this Frank Burgoddi. "I don't want any jail time in New Orleans. No more than a week. Bribe some officials. Do whatever it takes to get the charges dropped."

Frank came to his feet. "That would be unethical."

Cavenaugh snickered. "You think defending me isn't?"

Burgoddi cleared his throat. "A couple of deputy marshals will be here in a few days to transport you to New Orleans." He stood, grasping his briefcase by the handle, his knuckles white. "If you would like another attorney, I understand perfectly."

He was running scared. "You want me to fire you?"

"Well, that is . . . uh . . . up to you of course. . . ."

"Get the hell out of my sight," Cavenaugh snarled.

Burgoddi stumbled to the door and pounded on it. The skinny deputy opened the cell and let the lawyer out.

"I want to make a phone call." Cavenaugh would be damned if they sent him to prison.

He stood and the skinny cop led him to a small room where the prisoner phone was kept. He quickly punched in a number. It was answered on the third ring.

"Ray . . . Cavenaugh, I'm tired of fuckin' with lawyers. I want you to find me a cop on the take." He wasn't about to leave anything to chance.

Chapter 16

Andrea glanced at Kevin from the corner of her eye. How in the hell had she let herself get maneuvered into bringing this long-legged Texan with her?

Okay, so maybe he wasn't hard on the eyes. She kind of liked the way his hair scraped the collar of his shirt. And he had the prettiest green eyes she'd ever seen on a man, with long sooty lashes.

And a body that could resurrect a dead woman.

But it still didn't mean she wanted him tagging along. Not her type at all. Too full of himself.

"You like me, admit it," he stated out of the blue in a soft southern drawl that made her nipples ache.

She came to a screeching halt on the sidewalk, crossing her arms in front of her. "And you're full of crap, cowboy. I let you tag back to my apartment, I even listened to your insults . . ."

He chuckled. "It isn't my fault your apartment looks like warehouse storage for the Salvation Army."

She spun on her heel and began striding toward Jackson Square, throwing over her shoulder, "I even listened to your *insults* when you downgraded my apartment," she continued through gritted teeth as if he hadn't so rudely interrupted her.

"Heck, you make even me look like a neat freak," he said as he caught up in two long strides.

"That's doubtful," she mumbled. Andrea didn't like smart-asses. Kevin was a smart-ass.

"But that's okay, I don't care that you're a slob."

He slung his arm across her shoulders. She tried to shake it off but it was too heavy. She had to admit that she sort of liked the weight of his arm. It had a snuggly warm feel. She could so get used to having him around.

Sheesh! Like that would ever happen. Kevin wasn't the type to hang around. He was a charmer for sure. She'd met plenty of his type. Just about the time she began to like having the cowboy around he'd be off to greener pastures. Piling on the fertilizer to some other poor female. Nope, his type was too easy to fall for and she didn't need a broken heart.

She tried to slip beneath his arm, but he only managed to pull her closer to his side.

"Come on. I'll buy you a daiquiri. Maybe it'll loosen you up a little."

The last thing she wanted to do was sit across from him and have a drink. Or did he have an ulterior motive for suggesting alcohol? A quickie? Did she look desperate?

"If you think buying me a drink will loosen me up enough so I'll crawl between the sheets with you, then you'd just better think again!"

"Nope, just being sociable. But I have to warn you, women beg me to make love to them. You've never experienced great sex until you've gone to bed with me."

She stopped and stared at him. Her eyes narrowed. He teased her. His eyes twinkled—and he was trying too hard to look serious. She should've worn boots for all the bullshit this cowboy dished out.

"I still don't want to have a drink with you, no matter how you try to sway me. And until I've had sex with you, then you can't prove anything by me, and I don't want to have sex with a cowboy." Hell, he'd probably wear spurs to bed. She might try a lot of stuff, but she wasn't into pain.

"Yes, you do. You're just being stubborn."

She didn't answer right away. He was tempting. She sighed. Maybe she would have a drink with him. At least her afternoon wouldn't be boring with him around.

But make him wait, make him wonder. The man was too full of himself. She frowned up at him. He didn't look like he was holding his breath as he waited.

She thrust her jaw forward. "You're paying."

"I'll get the first. You can buy the second."

She straightened to her full height of five feet eight inches and still didn't come close to his six feet four-inch frame. Damn, he almost made her feel . . . feminine. "Maybe I won't have a second drink."

"Are you always this stubborn?"

"No."

"Good."

"Sometimes I'm even more obstinate." They walked under the canopy of the outside café.

"Thanks for the warning," he said as he led the way to an empty table and pulled out her chair; but he was smiling with that cocky I-know-you're-attracted-to-me smile.

She ignored the little flip-flop her stomach did. "And I thought chivalry was dead." She looked pointedly at the chair.

"That's just simple politeness, ma'am," he affected a more pronounced drawl, and pulled down on the brim of an imaginary hat.

Definitely full of it. She bit the insides of her cheeks. It didn't work. Laughter bubbled out of her. He was cute, a born flirt, and she was so afraid she might get in over her head with this one. Damn, and she'd promised not to get attached to another man.

Friends. They could be friends.

Yeah, right.

He sat across from her, and nodded to the waitress that they were ready to order. When she left to get their drinks, Kevin turned to her.

"So, tell me about Jody and her visions."

Was that why he'd wanted to be with her? Just so he could wheedle information? She straightened in her seat. "That's a question you should be asking Jody, not me."

"I'm just looking out for my big brother. Seems to me like he might be getting in over his head." He shrugged. "I'm not sure I like this hocus-pocus stuff."

She bristled. What did he think? That everyone in New Orleans dabbled in voodoo? "But then your *big* brother should be able to take care of himself."

He studied her for a moment before taking a deep breath and expelling it. "You're right."

She quirked an eyebrow and wondered if he was trying a new tactic to get information. "About your brother being able to take care of himself?"

"No, that you can be very obstinate." He opened his hands in supplication. "I just don't want to see Logan get hurt."

"And I don't want to see Jody get hurt."

"It seems we're at a standoff."

Smart man. "It would seem that way."

He leaned toward her, elbows on the table. "So, you want to go back to Logan's apartment? We can have sex while we think about our problem."

Dead silence.

Damn it! This was serious stuff. Why the hell had he asked if she wanted to make love? "Were you kicked in the head by a bull when you were little?" She really tried for a frown but it reversed itself on her.

He grinned and her stomach fluttered with a thousand butterflies. Who taught him to smile like that?

"Okay, so sex is out of the question. Have another drink with me instead."

She hadn't exactly ruled out sex, but maybe it was a good thing they kept their relationship platonic. "Okay, cowboy, but you're buying." She certainly didn't want him to think she might be eager to go to bed with him—even if she was.

Their drinks came. She took a long gulp of her frozen daiquiri and got cold throat. You'd think the fire Kevin had lit inside her would melt anything. She stole a glance over the rim of her plastic cup. Damn, he was sexy. She wondered if he might still want to consider sex?

No, no, no! Not a good plan.

"A penny for your thoughts."

Like she'd tell him that she could picture him naked and lying sprawled on her bed.

His mouth dropped open.

It took her a moment to realize she had been slowly moving her mouth up and down the straw with slow, sensuous movements. She cleared her throat and set her cup on the table. It hadn't been that long since she'd had sex!

"So, what do you do in Texas?" Anything to get her mind off making love.

His jaw snapped shut. "Breed cattle."

"Personally?"

He frowned. "I have bulls. Holstein."

She nodded. "Oh." She wouldn't mind if he mounted her. Damn, not thinking about sex wasn't going to be easy. She sighed. Not as long as Kevin Hart was around.

Chapter 17

By the next morning nothing had changed. Jody still felt out of sorts. The vision had been cloying, suffocating as it clung to her, like being thrown into an open grave and feeling each shovel of dirt being tossed on her lifeless body.

This second one had been stronger, taking her by surprise. The last time she'd had one this bad, her uncle murdered her father.

But this time it was a little different. Maybe because she was older. With this vision, she was able to see past the mists shrouding her eyes. Just a flash. No more than that, but enough that she knew there was blood. *Injury or death.* And something shiny . . . like a badge.

There were other images, but no matter how hard she strained to see, she couldn't make out what they were before her head started hurting, making it too hard to concentrate.

"So, what did you see?" Andrea stepped to Jody's patio.

Jody jumped. Muffin barked from her lofty position on Jody's lap.

"You startled me." She brought her hand to her chest. The pounding of her heart thumped against her palm. There was nothing quite like aging ten years in the span of a few seconds.

"I startled *you?*" Andrea raised an eyebrow. "That must've been some vision you had, *chere.* And you forgot to dead-bolt your door." She scooped Muffin out of Jody's lap and brought the pup to her face. "And why'd you keep the mutt?"

Muffin apparently didn't take offense. The pup stuck out her tongue and licked Andrea's nose.

"Ugh!" She wiped the back of her hand across her face. "I don't like slobbers," she said, but a chuckle followed her words.

Jody crossed her hands. "You were saying *what* about Muffin?"

"Okay, so maybe she's kind of cute . . . for a mutt."

Andrea didn't attach herself to animals, and only a handful of people, which was odd since she thrived on crowds.

But she did collect just about everything else she came into contact with. The girl seldom threw even a straight pin away.

Jody understood why. Andrea hadn't had much in material possessions growing up. Coming from a large family, everything had been passed from one child to the next and Andrea was the youngest. By the time shoes or a dress got to her they were well worn.

Jody's life had been different. Just her and *Mamere*. The old woman sometimes had a strange way of showing affection, but Jody had always known *Mamere* loved her. As far as material things—the less clutter in her life the better.

Andrea sat cross-legged on the stone tiles, putting the puppy in front of her. She continued to focus on Muffin when she began to talk. "So, *chere*, you want me to not ask so many questions, maybe? Seems like there's a lot of stuff happening in your life. First this Logan fella, and now you start having stronger visions. Say the word, and I won't mention it again, but if you want to talk—I'm here."

When she raised her head, Jody saw sincerity, compassion and most of all, the kind of friendship that so rarely comes into someone's life. The kind that crossed the boundaries of blood. The kind you nurture and cherish. Jody knew exactly how lucky she was to have Andrea.

She leaned back in her chair, bringing her feet up to the little blue, cushioned stool in front of her. "Logan's not the problem. I think I knew there was something different about him from the first."

A patch of sun broke through the thunderous clouds. Jody closed her eyes for a moment, savoring the warmth.

"I sensed his presence before I saw him. I knew he watched me from the other side of the curtain. It's as if our souls merged before anything else."

"And the visions?" Andrea absently rubbed Muffin behind one ear.

Jody didn't answer right away. Cold chills swept through her when the clouds shifted, blocking the sun that had warmed her only moments ago.

She'd once gone on a ride that took her high in the air. It had paused for a moment at the top of its precarious position. She could see everything at the park. All the other rides, the people. She remembered thinking how wondrous it felt to be so high above the world. Then the bottom dropped out from under her and she went whooshing down to earth.

The vision she'd had earlier was the same as the ride. It jerked her back to reality.

"Jody?"

She drew in a deep breath. "Right before I had the vision Logan told me he wanted to write a story about what I went through as a child."

Andrea froze. "He can't. What if it somehow gets into your uncle's hands? A story like that could go national. It could lead Cavenaugh right to you. Do you think that's what triggered this episode?"

"Probably. At least I think that might be the reason."

"Is your uncle coming back?"

"If Logan goes ahead with the story, then yes, there's a good possibility he'll return."

"Do you think he'll write it? I have to tell you from what

I've seen of him I really don't think he will. At least not without your permission."

She didn't think Logan would stoop so low. "No, I don't think he will, either."

"But you saw something. What?"

"Blood, and something shiny. I've been trying to concentrate on the vision and I think I finally have most of it. It might have been a badge."

Andrea slowly came to her feet. "Take a leave of absence. This isn't good, Jody. I don't like the idea of you seeing blood and a badge. Don't you have some vacation time coming?"

"I'm not running away to hide." Jody stood. "I said it *might* have been a badge. I didn't say I was positive. It could be nothing."

"A vision this strong?" Andrea planted her hands on her hips.

Andrea was right, and Jody didn't really believe it was nothing. She shouldn't have told Andrea so much. Now her friend would only worry. There was nothing either one of them could do. It wasn't a gift she had. It was a damn curse.

Life was complicated.

She drew in a deep breath. "Let's have a cup of tea and forget about my visions for a little while."

Worry creased Andrea's brow. "But you'll be careful, won't you? Like that time you told me to be careful. I could've fallen through that broken step. But steps are a lot different than bullets and knives."

"I'm always careful, and I didn't say anything about bullets or knives." There was another piece to the puzzle if she could just make out the rest of the vision.

She hooked her arm through Andrea's and they walked back into the house with Muffin prancing beside them.

"Tell me about Logan's brother," she changed the subject, deciding to worry about her problem later, when she was alone and could think more clearly.

Her words brought a smile to Andrea's face, as she knew

they would. There had been just a little spark of interest shining in Andrea's eyes when she'd *grudgingly* invited him to leave with her yesterday. Andrea had tried to play it cool, but Jody quickly recognized the signs. She only hoped Kevin didn't hurt her. Maybe she would have to kick his *tcheue* if he did! Her thoughts brought laughter bubbling out.

"What?" Andrea stopped and looked at Jody like she'd lost her mind.

Jody gave her a quick squeeze before going to the cabinet and bringing out a tin of peach flavored tea. "I just realized how much alike we are."

"Yeah, right," Andrea scoffed.

She glanced over her shoulder. "And what's that supposed to mean?"

Andrea waved her arm toward her. "We're nothing alike. I'm pale and lackluster. You're dark and sultry. You have visions. I can't see two feet in front of me without my contacts. You're a police officer. I'm a dispatcher. You're petite, I'm tall."

Is that how she compared their life—how they looked? It was time she straightened out her friend's way of thinking. She put the tin on the cabinet and marched over to Andrea.

"You're joking, right?"

Andrea shook her head, blonde curls bounced around her face.

Sheesh, why couldn't she see what everyone else saw? Maybe it was time she did. Grabbing her wrist, she tugged her along with her.

"Where are we going? I thought you wanted to have a cup of tea."

"Not until you realize something." She didn't stop until they stood in front of the full-length mirror in her bedroom. "Now, tell me again what you see."

Andrea visibly cringed. "A rhinestone and a diamond. Guess which one is which."

She stared into her friend's eyes. Good grief, she really believed what she was saying. She shook her head. "No, you're wrong," she spoke softly.

"But, look at us." She waved her hand toward the mirror. Jody stepped away. "Now look."

Andrea shook her head in despair. "No matter how I dress, I always come off looking cheap."

"Do you want to know what I see?" Before Andrea could open her mouth to argue, Jody continued. "I see a beautiful woman who only needs a bit of tweaking."

For a moment a glimmer of hope sprang in her eyes, but when she looked back into the mirror the spark fizzled away. "Now I know why you're my friend. I need you around to boost my ego. Nothing I buy looks good on me. I can't be fixed. Believe me, I've tried."

"Okay, that's it. Time for a shopping trip."

"Huh?"

She grabbed Andrea's hand and pulled her toward the front door.

"I thought we were going to have tea?"

"Nope, what you need is a complete change. You're going to become a whole new person."

Andrea looked at her like she'd lost her mind. "Do you know what you're doing?"

She didn't, but she wasn't about to tell Andrea. Even Jody knew that when she had her hair done, or bought a different nail polish . . . she felt rejuvenated. Maybe that's all Andrea needed—to see herself in a new light.

She grabbed her purse off the side table before they trooped out the door.

A half hour later they were sitting in Sheila's House of Beauty. Jody had once kept Sheila's daughter, Darese, from going to jail after a wild night on the town. The teenager had eventually straightened her life out. Sheila told Jody if she ever needed anything at all, she should call her.

This seemed like as good a time as any. Andrea's expression said she'd rather have stayed home and drank tea.

Sheila rotated Andrea's chair one way then the other as she studied Andrea's face and hair. "Too many curls. It makes her look like Shirley Temple in drag." She squinted her eyes and latched on to Andrea's chin with her thumb and forefinger. "The foundation is all wrong. Too pale. The blush too dark. That shade of red lipstick is much too bold." She shook her head and clicked her tongue.

"Jooo . . . dy?" Andrea's eyes rounded.

"She's the best." At least Jody hoped Sheila knew what she was doing.

Sheila straightened, her nose slightly in the air. "Of course I'm the best. Everyone who is anyone comes to my salon." She scraped her gaze over Andrea. "Except you, which is obvious. But that will change. I will create a new, stunning woman." Her hand fluttered close to her chest. "You will be a goddess."

Jody clamped her lips tight. To laugh would be incredibly rude. Sheila might be a little over the top, but she was right, the woman could create a work of art from a pound of mud.

Four hours later, Jody and a very different Andrea left the salon. Excitement filled her. She couldn't believe the change, but she wasn't about to tell Andrea . . . yet. The butterfly hadn't quite emerged.

"Why can't I look in the mirror?" Andrea pouted.

Jody inwardly smiled. The transformation had to be dramatic. She wanted her to see everything at once. Only then could she shock Andrea into realizing just how beautiful she really was. "Not yet," was all she said as she dragged her down the street and into the best dressmaker in all New Orleans.

Shay Mary Beth was an exclusive shop with pricey clothes, but she knew for a fact Andrea hoarded money. Jody had a feeling after she saw how she could look, that would quickly change. She pushed the door open, a little bell jingled above them as they stepped inside.

A woman in her mid-fifties glanced up. Her bored expression changed to one of warmth as her face lit in recognition. "Jodeeeee! Hello, *mon ami*. It has been so long." Mary Beth rushed forward, grabbed Jody's hands, and leaned forward to kiss her lightly on each cheek.

"I need a favor," Jody told her.

"*Oui*, I will help. I remember zee time you stopped that awful man from robbing my store." She slapped a hand to her chest. "It was terrible." She shook her head.

"Can you change the way my friend dresses?" She tugged Andrea from behind her.

"Eghhh!" Mary Beth stepped back, a look of horror on her face. "Oh, good Lord, drape a couple of dead swans around her neck and she could pass for a rock star!"

Mary Beth's French accent completely vanished, but then, Jody had never really thought she did a great imitation in the first place. She supposed the customers liked it, though.

Mary Beth's hand fluttered to her face. "I mean, zee clothes you wear are all wrong." She took a deep breath. "But we will fix."

"What's wrong with what I'm wearing?" Andrea glared at the shopkeeper.

Jody had been afraid this might happen. First the hairdresser, now Mary Beth. Andrea was starting to resent their comments about her appearance. She was actually surprised her friend had lasted this long without blowing her temper. She'd better run interference.

She patted Andrea's shoulder. "This is the last place, then we'll go to a really nice restaurant and eat lunch. Are you hungry?"

Her bottom lip trembled, but she nodded.

Apparently Mary Beth realized how she'd acted. "Don't worry, *cherie*, you are vereee beautiful. With the right clothes, you will be *magnifique*. And I will give you a ten, no, twenty percent discount because you will showcase my clothes. Just do not forget to tell them where you shop."

For the next two hours Andrea tried on clothes, from casual to elegant, but when she stepped out in a sleek black dress, the skirt softly swirling around her ankles, Jody knew this was the dress that would turn men's heads. The front was low cut to show off her sexy cleavage, and hugged all her delicious curves. It was unadorned, nothing like the frills, ruffles or flashy sequins that Andrea usually wore. Just simple perfection.

"Now can I look in the mirror?" Andrea asked for the millionth time.

A slow smile curved Jody's lips.

Andrea raised her eyebrows in question. "I can?"

Jody nodded and walked over to the full-length mirror she'd had Mary Beth cover with a shawl. Andrea faced the mirror, expectation twinkling in her eyes. Jody removed the covering.

Andrea's expression didn't change. She looked behind her, frowned, moved a little to the left, then the right. Then it dawned on her, that was her reflection in the mirror. There wasn't anyone standing behind her, or beside her. She was the gorgeous creature staring back.

"Oh." She looked at Jody, tears brimming in her eyes. "That's me."

"Oh, don't cry." Jody scrambled inside her purse for a tissue and handed it to Andrea so she could dab her eyes without mussing her makeup.

"*Oui,* that eez you."

Warmth swirled inside Jody. Andrea was truly beautiful, but she'd already known that, she just wanted Andrea to see.

"Thank you." Andrea hugged Jody.

"I just polished the diamond that was already there. See, you're not a rhinestone. You're the real deal." She held her by the shoulders and looked into her eyes. "You've always been beautiful. Before the makeup, before the new hairstyle, before the clothes. Your inner beauty has always been right there for everyone to see, and that's what truly counts."

"I don't have to give all this back, do I? I mean, I kind of like the outer beauty, too."

Jody laughed. "I'd strangle you if you did."

They left the store after Andrea changed into a casual outfit and paid for her purchases. Andrea talked nonstop as Jody drove to the restaurant they'd agreed upon.

Jody only caught every other word. She basked in the knowledge her friend felt as good on the inside as she looked on the outside.

But that was all changed now. She wouldn't let Andrea feel bad about the way she dressed.

"And Kevin is taking me out to eat tomorrow night." Andrea whirled around so fast in her seat Jody was afraid she'd gotten whiplash. "You'll have to help me get ready. Please, promise me you will. I want Kevin to see me in that black dress. In fact, I want you and Logan to join us."

"I wouldn't miss seeing Kevin's expression for anything." She pulled into a parking space in front of the restaurant and they got out, still talking about what Kevin's reaction would be.

An ominous clap of thunder reverberated across the sky, jarring Jody. She shivered, wondering if the thunder had been a psychic warning that her life was about to come crashing down around her.

Chapter 18

"Stop fidgeting," Jody told Andrea as she zipped her dress.

"I can't help it." She frowned at her reflection in the mirror. "What if Kevin laughs." She doubled her fists. "I swear, I'll flatten him."

Jody shook her head and began to chuckle.

"What?"

How could she explain? She plopped onto the bed. When she saw the confusion on Andrea's face, her laughter bubbled anew. "You can't, you'll break a nail if you flatten him."

"Oh, yeah." Andrea admired her perfectly filed, rose-colored, false fingernails. "That would really piss me off." She grinned.

Andrea might look like she never got her hands dirty the way she was dressed right now in the sexy black dress, her hair softly framing her face, and strappy black sandals, but on the inside she was the same old Andrea . . . with a tad more confidence. Jody had a feeling after tonight, her confidence would soar.

Andrea sat on the bed beside her. "Hey, did you read Logan's article in the paper?"

Jody wiggled her eyebrows. "About learning to bump and grind?"

"That's the one. Okay, so tell me, did the lessons pay off? How well *does* he bump and grind?"

"Very well." She chuckled.

"I haven't heard you laugh like that since you had that vision."

Her insides twisted.

"Damn, I'm sorry I brought it up." Andrea bit her bottom lip.

"It's okay."

"Have you figured out any more of it?"

She shook her head. How could she tell Andrea she was positive the shiny object was a badge? It would only scare her. Maybe she had the right idea—take a vacation—but until more of the vision was revealed, she'd only be running backwards.

"Just be careful. Okay?"

"I'm always careful on the job, you know that."

"And Logan? You still think he won't write your story?"

She'd put off talking to him. He'd called and left messages on her answering machine until she'd finally given in and answered. Because Andrea hadn't let her back out, she agreed to have dinner with him tonight as long as it was a foursome.

"You're not spacing out on me, are you?"

She looked up. "What?" She realized Andrea referred to her silence. "No, I'm fine."

"You don't look fine." Andrea's eyes narrowed. "He isn't going to write your story—right?"

Jody jumped off the bed, and went to stand in front of the window. "He hasn't said anything more, but we haven't really talked." The streetlight cast an eerie glow on the shadowed pavement outside. A cold chill ran up her spine. She turned away.

Andrea glanced down, plucking at the bedspread, then smoothed her hand over the red satin material. "Have you ever thought that your visions might have started up again . . . I mean . . . this strong, because you're letting yourself get close to someone?" Worry etched her face.

The thought had crossed her mind, she couldn't deny it.

She'd always been cautious about letting people into her life. She didn't want to take the chance of feeling the kind of pain when she lost someone she cared deeply about. She and her sister had been closer than most siblings. Sure, they'd had their fights, their arguments, but they'd shared a deep, lasting love. Maybe because their mother had died when they were both young. It had created a bond between them.

Then her family was ripped apart.

She drew in a deep, ragged breath. She wished her vision had been something as simple as not wanting to get close to someone else, but she didn't think that was the case. "I don't think so," she finally admitted.

Andrea hopped off the bed and went to Jody, hugging her tight. "But you've always been afraid to let people into your tight circle. Remember how you'd give me that awful scowl when I'd sit at your table in the break room?"

She frowned. "I didn't . . ."

Andrea arched one finely penciled eyebrow.

Suddenly the corners of Jody's mouth turned up. She shrugged. "Okay, so maybe I did try to scare you away. It didn't work."

"Nope. I'd already seen through your act when that stupid detective said all those nasty things about me. You took him down more than a peg or two. So when you acted like you didn't care, I wasn't buying it."

"Apparently not since you're here now." She was so glad Andrea hadn't given up. It was nice having a friend like her.

"I have a feeling you won't run Logan off, either. And the way you're dressed tonight, writing a story will be the furthest thing from his mind," Andrea predicted.

Her heart fluttered inside her chest at the thought of him hanging around for a while. Just as quickly, doubt crept in. Which interested him more—her, or the story? She sighed, not wanting to dwell on anything having to do with her past, or her present.

She squared her shoulders; enough about her relationships

or visions. This was Andrea's night to shine. She examined her with a discerning eye. "You've chewed your lipstick off, and they'll be here any minute."

"You think Kevin will like the different me?" She struck a saucy pose.

Jody chuckled. "I think he'll be tripping all over himself to do your bidding."

Andrea waltzed over to the mirror. "I like the idea of him tripping all over the place. That's one cowboy who has an ego problem."

"He is pretty cute, though."

"That he is."

It should prove to be an interesting night. She had to admit, she looked forward to seeing Logan.

"You're acting awfully nervous tonight," Kevin remarked.

Logan unknotted his tie once more. Nervous? Too mild a word. Terrified? Better, more accurate. Probably because it took fifteen calls before Jody picked up, then she offered a lame excuse about her ringer being turned low.

He'd imagined the worst, had been at the point of tossing his pen, forgetting that his next article about male strippers was due, and rushing off to her home just to make sure she hadn't slipped into another trance.

Then she'd picked up, her voice drizzling over him like warm honey. He'd been casual when he asked her out. She'd said only if they made it a foursome.

Didn't she trust being alone with him? Hell, he didn't trust himself alone with her—why should she?

"And you're acting spacey. Sure some of her trances aren't wearing off on you?" Kevin adjusted his jacket, glanced at his reflection and grinned.

"Did you ever think I might just be ignoring you?" Logan adjusted his tie, gave a satisfied grunt, and reached for his keys.

Kevin wore a thoughtful expression. "No, I'm much too interesting to be ignored." He chuckled.

"I have no idea why Jody wanted me to drag you along." He headed for the door.

"It's not Jody, it's Andrea. The woman is fascinated with me."

Logan just shook his head. Kevin was a born flirt. He pitied Andrea, fearing her heart would be broken. Not that Kevin ever intended to break anyone's heart. He just happened to love women.

Maybe he should've warned Jody about his brother's reputation. Behind him lay a trail of broken hearts. He could understand Jody wanting to fix her friend up with him, though. Poor Andrea probably didn't get asked out very often. Not with her brusqueness. But again, he sensed there was more to her than met the eye.

He put his hand on Kevin's arm. "Hey, try to go easy on Andrea, okay?"

"*Me* go easy on *her*?" Kevin's smile slipped. "You're serious."

He nodded.

"That woman could break concrete with her sharp tongue. She can freeze a man with one glance. She can . . ."

"Don't break her heart."

Kevin studied him. "I don't intend to," he solemnly replied, then smiled. "There's something about her that I like. She gives as good as she gets. Feisty." He sobered. "And the assistant editor job? How's it looking?"

"Hank scooped me on the drowning in the Ponchetrain." Bitterness rose inside him.

"The mayor's cousin? I read about that." He grimaced. "Will it matter that much when you measure it against your articles?"

"The way it looks right now? Yeah, it will." Unless he wrote Jody's story. But what if she was right? What if it did draw her uncle back to New Orleans and put her life in danger? Would he be willing to take that chance? Not for a job.

He couldn't. But damn, the thought of Hank as his boss rankled.

Just before they left, he checked on Blondie and her two pups. They were snuggled on the oversize plaid pillow Logan had picked up at a local pet store—and paid way too much for. He'd kept remembering her other bed. The pile of rags. She deserved more than that. And besides, it was only money.

"You don't mind that Andrea dresses . . . kind of odd?" Logan asked on the drive to Jody's.

"You think she dresses odd?"

Logan glanced across the seat. Was he serious? She'd looked fine in uniform, but off duty, then yes, she had strange taste in clothes.

"You don't?"

Kevin chuckled. "A little. Okay, maybe a lot, but other than the way she dresses, she's damned cute."

To each his own. Maybe Kevin and Andrea were more suited than he'd first thought.

"So tell me more about Jody and her visions."

"Let's just forget about them, okay?"

"Must be pretty important if you don't want to tell me."

"We're here," he brought the conversation to an abrupt halt as he parked in front of Jody's house. Jody didn't want to talk about it, and right now, neither did he. Just for tonight, he wanted to forget about everything except being with her.

Damn, he should've brought flowers or a box of candy or something. Maybe a bottle of wine. He glanced down the street as if a store would suddenly appear where he could run in and buy something. None did.

"Why didn't you remind me to pick up flowers?"

"We're buying them dinner."

He shook his head as he rang the bell. A few minutes passed before he heard locks sliding across metal. The door opened. He could only stare. Jody stole his breath.

She wore a golden dress that molded her body, with some kind of gauzy fabric that draped over it. Earrings dangled from her lobes and she'd pulled her hair back and twisted it on top of her head reminding him of an Egyptian princess.

Her gaze flitted to him, then away. "Andrea isn't quite ready. Please, come in."

He cleared his throat. Heat rushed up his face. "You look great." Great? Why hadn't he said something more eloquent? After all, he was a writer. Words were supposed to come easy.

"Thank you." She turned to his brother. "Hello, Kevin."

Kevin moved to stand beside him, and took Jody's hand, bowing and bestowing a light kiss. "My brother has superb taste. No star could shine brighter than you do right now."

Since when had Kevin started talking like that? *No star could shine brighter*? What kind of crap was that?

Jody chuckled. "Would you like a glass of wine?"

"Sure, okay." He followed behind her, but not before he glowered at Kevin. His bother raised his eyebrows as if to ask what Logan's problem was. Maybe he should watch little brother around Jody. Blood relation or not, he'd better keep his distance.

"Did a green-eyed monster bite you on the ass, bro?" Kevin spoke under his breath as Jody removed wineglasses from the cabinet.

"Yeah, right." Jealous? Him? The idea was laughable. He barely knew her. He . . . son of a bitch, he was jealous. Of his little brother. That bordered on crazy.

He shook his head, grinning wryly at Kevin. So maybe he was a little jealous. As he watched the way she glided around the room in a shimmer of silver and gold he knew he had every right to be jealous of anyone who looked twice at her, including his little brother. Jody was a temptress. Hell, even he hadn't been able to resist her charm.

When Jody brought out the corkscrew, he sauntered over. "Would you like me to open it?" She handed him the bottle. She was treating him differently. It was nothing he could really put his finger on. She smiled, she talked, she even lightly joked. It was like she'd erected an invisible wall between them. He wondered if he'd be able to storm her defenses.

He deftly opened the wine, pouring some in each of the four glasses. "What shall we drink to?" He handed a glass to Jody and one to Kevin.

It was almost as if a curtain lifted and he saw a return of the sassy Jody. A wicked gleam sparkled in her eyes. He wondered what she was up to. Something was going on. Maybe he wouldn't need armor and a white steed after all. Maybe her defenses wouldn't be that hard to storm.

"Let's drink to new friends," she spoke softly.

He liked the sound of that.

"And new beginnings," she continued.

"Shouldn't we wait for Andrea?" Kevin asked.

"By all means, don't start without me." Andrea stood framed by the doorway, a vision in a long black gown. She strolled across the room, each sway of her hips meant to raise a man's temperature by at least a degree—and from the look on Kevin's face, it did. She took the glass Jody held out for her.

This wasn't Andrea. It couldn't be the same woman who came barreling into Jody's home just the other morning. This woman was . . . was . . . stunning.

"What's the matter, boys? Cat got your tongue?" She wrapped slender fingers around the stem of her glass.

"What'd you . . . uh . . . do to yourself?" Kevin swallowed the wine in his glass and stretched the glass out for more.

She shrugged. "Just changed a few things."

"A few . . ." He shook his head. "You look . . . great!"

Okay, Logan rationalized, so maybe the Hart men lost their wits when a stunning woman came into the room. An affliction his little brother seemed to be stricken with at the moment.

Logan stepped forward and took Andrea's hand, bowing over it before placing a light kiss on her soft skin. "My brother seems to be incapable of coherent thought at the moment, Ms. Potier. Let me just say how ravishing you look tonight."

After only a second's hesitation, she briefly acknowledged his compliment with a slight nod of her head.

Jody watched silently, feeling like the proud mother of a debutante. The new hairstyle, different clothes, softer makeup had transformed Andrea. The rhinestone was indeed a precious gem.

"Is everyone ready? Our reservations are for eight o'clock." Logan set his glass on the counter by Jody's.

Kevin held his arm out for Andrea to take. Andrea looked at him like he'd lost his mind.

"What?" She planted her hands on her hips. "Just because I was raised in the swamps doesn't mean I can't walk in heels."

Jody quickly took Logan's arm.

"Oh." Andrea grimaced. "So okay, I haven't been out of the swamp that long." She took Kevin's arm and with a regal air, they went to the front door.

"A good thing for me," Kevin told her. "I have you all to myself."

Jody knew that Andrea would be talking about this night for a long time. Kevin treated her like a princess, and yes, he was falling all over himself to do her bidding. She so deserved this and much, much more. They tossed sarcastic remarks back and forth all the way to the restaurant.

Jody was grateful for their chatter. It meant she didn't have to talk.

Logan pulled up to the restaurant and got out, coming around to her side of the car and opening the door. She slid across the seat, then stood.

"You all right?" he asked.

"Yes, fine," she murmured. For a moment her gaze lingered on Logan. All she'd wanted was a night free from her everyday life. Hot, wild sex to release bottled up tension.

She'd only managed to give herself a whole new set of problems.

Logan handed the valet the car keys and they went inside.

Immediately upon entering, some of Jody's anxiety melted away. The foyer was done in creams and soft beiges. Deep, rich burgundy drapes hung majestically from the windows. Above their head a chandelier sparkled like an expensive diamond.

Delectable aromas swirled around her, enticing her taste buds, and making her mouth water, while in the background someone softly sang a soulful tune. Her feet sank into the plush carpet as the maître d' led them to their table.

"How can he keep his nose so high in the air and not trip over something?" Andrea whispered.

Jody covered her laughter with a cough. She only hoped he didn't hear what she'd said. If he had, he certainly didn't show it.

They were seated. A waiter arrived with menus, and after a few minutes, took their orders.

"Pretty swanky place," Andrea remarked.

"Yes, it's very nice," Jody added. She couldn't help feeling a little intimidated. She'd never been in a restaurant quite this impressive, and she had to admit she was feeling a little like Julia Roberts in *Pretty Woman,* except two of the forks beside her plate were the same size, then a small fork and two spoons. On the other side were two knives. Did they think she'd order everything on the menu?

"I came here with a friend once. I thought you might enjoy it, too," Logan told them.

His confession only made Jody more uncomfortable. Had it been with another woman? She mentally chastised herself. What would it matter? She didn't have exclusive rights to him. But it did.

"Would you like to work up an appetite?" Kevin asked Andrea.

She frowned, looking at the small dance floor where two

couples moved gracefully across the white tiles. "I'm not sure . . ."

"Not scared, are you?"

She jutted her chin forward. "Lead on." She stood, started to walk in front of him, but changed her mind at the last minute and held her hand out for him to take. He chuckled lightly, tucking her hand in his.

Jody reached for her fork but stopped herself just short of rearranging the already perfect silverware. *Quit being so nervous,* she told herself. But she couldn't help it. Logan was staring. She could feel his gaze slowly caressing her, lingering, and her body responded. Her nipples tightened, aching for more than just his slow perusal of her body. Wanting him to touch, to stroke with his hands.

"You're staring." She drew in a ragged breath.

"Can't help it. God, you're beautiful. Just be glad I haven't scooped you up and carried you out of here because all I can think about is making love to you."

Delicious tingles spread up her calves, over her thighs and settled in the vee between her legs. She clamped her legs together, but it only increased the pressure, making her ache even more. She had to change the subject; talk about anything else or she'd melt into a puddle at his feet.

"But isn't there something else you're thinking about?" When he didn't make a comment, she continued. "Like writing my story?" Damn, it sounded like she was picking a fight with him.

Apparently he wasn't too concerned with her argumentative tone. He took her hand, rubbing his thumb over her palm. He might as well be rubbing two sticks together. The friction he created easily lit her fire.

"Not tonight. I didn't bring you here as a bribe to get a story out of you. I asked you to go out with me because I wanted to be with you. I don't even want to think about the newspaper, my articles, or your life story. I want to concentrate on us."

Kevin and Andrea returned to the table before she had a chance to comment. What could she say? She'd already said the same thing to herself. But was this just a trick to get more information? She studied his face. She couldn't tell.

Kevin pulled Andrea's chair out for her, then went to Jody. "Can I steal you away for one dance? You'll break my heart if you don't say yes."

His words were lightly spoken, but when Jody looked up into his face she saw something else. His creased brow. Worry? Concern for Logan? She glanced at Andrea, saw her slight shrug.

"I'd love to dance with you." She stood, taking his hand, and they went to the dance floor.

They glided around the smooth tiles, his steps easy to follow. But Jody knew wanting to dance with her wasn't the reason he'd asked her out here.

He looked a lot like Logan when he was bothered about something. The same furrowed brow. The same slant to his mouth.

"What did you want to ask me?"

He looked momentarily startled. "You can read minds, too?" A look of awe crossed his face.

She smiled. "No, but I could read your expression. It's the same as Logan's when he wants to ask me something but doesn't exactly know how."

"Oh." He grinned ruefully, then sobered. "Logan hasn't said anything. I only know you have this power . . ."

"It's not a power, or even a gift," she said, cutting him off. "Sometimes I think it's more of a curse."

"But you saw something that scared Logan or he wouldn't have called me to come over to your house. Now, I'm not saying I believe all this stuff or anything, but I don't want my brother getting hurt."

The more she tried to decipher the vision, she was more certain it had to do with her and the police department.

"Hey, you okay?"

She drew in a deep breath. "I'm fine." But she didn't feel fine.

"What exactly did you see?"

She searched his face. It wasn't curiosity she saw, but concern for his brother. "Nothing specific."

She looked across the restaurant at him. He was laughing at something Andrea had said. Her lips started to curve . . . the floor beneath her feet rocked. She grabbed Kevin's shoulders to steady herself. The room blacked out. Blood . . . a badge . . . and Logan.

"You okay?"

In the space of a few seconds the curtain came up and the last of her vision was revealed. Her stomach twisted in knots. No, no, no. Why Logan? Why couldn't she be the only one involved?

"Jody?"

She dragged her attention back to Kevin. "I'm fine. New shoes." Her smile wavered. "I don't normally wear heels."

The dance ended. She looked into his face. "I won't let anything happen to Logan." This was one vision that would have a different ending.

His hesitation was brief, then he nodded.

As the evening progressed, Kevin and Andrea carried on most of the conversation with their teasing. Jody could only think about what she'd seen.

Blood, a badge and Logan.

Riding out with her when she patrolled the streets. That was the only thing it could be. She'd already told him he couldn't write her story. She stole a glance in his direction. What would this do to their relationship? Now she had to tell him he couldn't write his articles either. There was no way she would let him continue to ride with her. She had a feeling she already knew what it would do, and it wasn't a good feeling.

They dropped Andrea at her house, and she invited Kevin inside for a drink.

Then it was just the two of them. Logan parked the car and walked her to the door.

She invited him inside, hoping it wouldn't be for the last time. Damn, life could be a real bitch sometimes.

Chapter 19

"I need you," Logan said as soon as the door shut behind them.

"I need you, too." She lightly caressed his face. How did she tell him what she'd seen in her vision when all she wanted to do was lie in his arms and forget everything existed except the two of them? It was something she had to do, though, but it didn't mean she had to like it. She just couldn't let him risk his life . . . not on her beat.

She struggled for the words, but before she could say anything, he pulled her into his arms, his mouth lowering to hers and all she could think about was the heat from his touch. The desire coursing through her.

No! This wasn't right. She pulled away. His brow furrowed in confusion, cutting her to the quick.

"Would you like a drink, or . . . something?" She had to look away. Damn it, she didn't want to hurt him or his career, but she couldn't see any way around it. Not that she thought alcohol would help, but she damn sure needed a drink.

Regretfully, he stepped away. "A drink would be nice. Maybe some of that wine we had earlier."

She exhaled a sigh of relief. "Great, I'll pour us a glass. Why don't we go to the patio? It's . . . uh . . . such a pretty evening." She needed a moment to compose herself after his kiss. He certainly didn't make this any easier on her.

"I'll help."

"I'll meet you out there."

He hesitated before nodding. "Okay." As he walked to the French doors, he looked around. "Where's Muffin?"

"Worried? Don't, she's in the washroom probably snuggled on the pillows I fixed for her—down filled by the way, along with a ticking clock and a pretty blue blanket. Satisfied?"

He grinned a lopsided grin before stepping to the patio. Her heart did double time. Why did he have to be so darn sexy? She poured them each a glass, his of wine, hers filled with what she hoped was courage. She covertly looked around, took a long drink, then refilled her glass. Oh, yeah, the words would come much easier if she slurred them. She put some music on before joining him.

Logan had his back to her. She glanced around the private patio. This probably wasn't the best place to discuss what she needed to say. The trees and plants made it an even more intimate setting along with the water splashing over the rocks from a fountain in the corner.

Small up-lights enclosed the area in a soft glow of muted white. He'd lit the fat candle that sat beneath a hurricane globe on top of the black, café-style table. The light breeze whispering through the leaves filled the area with the scent of vanilla.

"I thought it would be relaxing to listen to some music. Do you like Enya?"

"It's nice. Not country and western, but I don't mind an occasional change."

She smiled and handed him a glass of wine. "She makes me think of green hills and heather." She motioned for him to have a seat as she kicked off her shoes and curled up on the cushioned love seat, needing to put a little distance between them. When his eyes moved to her legs, she realized her dress had ridden up. She quickly tugged it back in place. She wanted his attention—but not that kind.

Now was the time. She opened her mouth, but something happened between her brain and the words she wanted to say. "Tell me about yourself," she said, then could've kicked herself. She'd never had any trouble talking before tonight. She knew what her problem was, and he sat in a chair not six feet away. Damn it, she really liked Logan.

"There's not a lot to tell," he said. "I was born and raised in central Texas."

"What's it like there?"

He took a drink of wine and set his glass on the table, running his thumb back and forth over the rim.

"Texas is so big it's a country all by itself. We have an ocean on one end and prairie on the other. Tall pines to the east and oil fields in the west—and in between we've got a little bit of everything." He raised his thumb to his mouth and licked the wine off.

Sweat beaded her brow. Did he realize the torture he was putting her through? All she could think about was the other ways he could use his tongue. She wasn't sure if it was the amount of wine she was drinking that made her feel tipsy or watching him from across the room.

"Is it a little warm to you?"

He shook his head. "Actually, I wondered if you might be getting cool."

Her nipples were getting hard, but not from the temperature.

He looked around. "Even closed off there's a slight breeze."

She had to think of something else besides sex or she'd be ripping off his clothes and having her way with him. But she wasn't ready to talk about what needed to be said. Just another half hour in his company, then she'd tell him. She wanted to listen to his soft, southern drawl a little longer.

"Tell me more about Texas, and your family."

He took a drink, then slowly licked his lips before answering. She leaned forward on the love seat, barely catching herself before she tumbled off.

"You okay?" He started to his feet, but she motioned him to sit.

"Fine, just fine," she lied.

"My family all live there. My parents have been married for forty-one years. They were childhood sweethearts." He smiled, thinking about them. "I guess they still are. I've never heard them get into a serious argument."

"Brothers or sisters? Besides Kevin."

"Two older brothers, Gabe and Lane. Then me, Kevin, and the baby, Haley. Except she's not that much of a baby anymore. Twenty-seven years old and full of piss and vinegar. I pity the man who tangles with her."

"How does Haley manage with four older brothers?"

"Let me put it this way, we try not to make her mad. The first time a boy asked her out, I politely told him she was much too young to go on a date. The next day I was treated to itch powder in my underwear. I decided right then and there she could take care of herself."

He chuckled and she realized just how much she liked the deep, reverberating sound.

"And what does it look like in central Texas?" She drank the last of the wine in her glass.

"We have a lot of cedar trees, and gently rolling hills. My parents have a ranch, not real big, only about a hundred and seventy-five acres, but it's like stepping back in time. There's a wild ruggedness to the region." He leaned back in his chair, a wistful expression on his face.

"You miss it, don't you?"

He shrugged. "It's not much of a drive if I want to go back for a visit."

She came to her feet, and sauntered barefoot to where he sat. "Want some more?" One more glass, she reasoned. Then she would tell him.

It took Logan a moment to realize she was talking about

wine. Like an idiot, he glanced at his empty glass. More wine? He didn't think so. He was already drunk from looking at her.

"Actually, what I want is to make love to you."

She drew in a deep breath. "I've been wanting to tell you something. . . . Please, don't look at me like that. I can't think straight when you stare at me that way."

"What way? Like I want to strip your clothes off and kiss every inch of your sweet skin? Is that how I'm looking at you?"

Before she could answer, he stood, pulling her into his arms, and lowered his mouth to hers. She tasted like the wine they'd been drinking . . . sweet, intoxicating. And so damn hot she almost burned him.

Please don't let her pull away, he silently begged.

But instead of resisting, she rubbed her body against his, a soft sigh escaping her lips as she wrapped her arms around his neck. He worked his hands to the back of her dress, tugging the zipper down. She moved her arms down to her sides and stepped back; he was afraid she *was* pulling away.

"Maybe you're right. What I have to tell you can wait until later."

She shrugged out of her dress. It glided to the floor, leaving her covered by the gauzy material that was more like a semi-transparent poncho, and sexy as hell. He drew in a deep breath as she stood there, quite unconcerned that she wore nothing under the dress except a black thong, and black thigh-highs held up by sexy little garters with a tiny gold rose on each one. What she had to tell him couldn't be more important than what they were doing right now.

"You're staring." She smiled, but she didn't look that upset to him.

"Damn right."

"How about that wine?"

He wasn't sure what she was up to, but he didn't mind a

bit going along with her. He nodded, still unable to take his gaze off her.

She was like a nymph as she took his glass and glided into the kitchen. He walked to the doorway and leaned against the frame, watching as she floated to the refrigerator and retrieved the wine, then back to the cabinet where she'd set the glasses. Her breasts pushed against the gauzy material, the nipples tight little nubs straining to be set free.

He shifted his pants away from his rock hard dick, but the release of pressure didn't stop his growing need for fulfillment.

"Would you like some cheese? Fruit?" She raised her eyebrows in question.

"That's not what I'm hungry for." He pushed away from the doorway and sauntered toward her, his gaze touching on every delectable inch of her body. "What I want to do is suck on your breasts. I want to scrape my teeth across your nipples. I want to taste all of you on my lips."

She drew in a sharp breath, her chest rising, her naked breasts pushing against the gauzy, silvery material.

He took the two glasses of wine from her hands and set them back on the cabinet. When he faced her again, only a few inches separated them. He tested the weight of her breasts in his hands. She gasped, closing her eyes.

"Do you like that?"

"Umm."

"I thought you would. You're a sensuous woman and you have to fill what's inside you to be complete." He rubbed his thumbs back and forth across her swollen nipples. "That's why you surround yourself with earth, wind, water and fire. They arouse the mind, but it won't ever be enough unless you fuel the body as well."

He tugged on her nipples. She gasped, grabbing his shoulders. Her eyes closed and she arched toward him.

"But stimulating the *mind* doesn't . . . umm, that feels . . .

nice . . . it . . . uh . . . doesn't create complications like our relationship could."

"But what's life without complications? If you don't jump off a cliff occasionally, how can you experience the adrenaline rush of the fall?"

"It's not the jump I'm afraid of, but the sudden stop at the bottom."

"I'll catch you," he murmured. Before she could argue more, he lowered his mouth, pulling at her bottom lip with his teeth while continuing the assault on her hard nipples. God, he loved touching her, tasting her. Feeling the way she responded to his touch. Knowing that he was in complete control of her body.

His tongue delved inside her mouth. Her tongue stroked his, stoking the fire building inside him. If he didn't pull back soon, he wouldn't be able to continue the game, and he wanted to take her higher than she could ever imagine. He wanted her to remember this night for the rest of her life.

A soft moan escaped her parted lips when he pulled away, tugging the gauzy material over her head as he did until she stood in front of him wearing only the black lacy thong, hose and garters. Her eyes were heavy-lidded, passion filled as she waited for him to continue the game.

"Has anyone ever told you just how damn sexy you are?" His words were raw, full of pent-up emotions.

Jody's body ached with her need to feel him buried inside her. "Maybe they know it wouldn't do them any good, *cher.*" She reached for her glass of wine, her mouth suddenly dry. "I don't go out with just anyone."

He grinned. "Then I feel privileged."

She swallowed some of the deep purple wine in her glass. "So, what are you going to do now that you know?"

"I think maybe I am a little hungry."

Jody's hand trembled as she set her glass on the cabinet. She'd drank way too much alcohol tonight. Her head was a little fuzzy, and she felt warm and tingly all over, but his implication was clear, and she was more than ready for a night of hot sex and let tomorrow be damned.

Disappointment filled her when he went to the refrigerator instead of taking her in his arms.

Her frown deepened when he brought out the chocolate pudding she'd made that morning, her chocolate syrup and a container of whipped cream. Was he going on a chocolate binge? Now? He carried it to the table and set it down, then looked at her with a leering grin.

Guilty heat spread over her, but in its wake a sudden desire to experiment. To do some of the things Andrea talked about. Jody was never sure if she exaggerated, or if people actually did that kind of stuff. Maybe it was time she found out for herself rather than relying on secondhand information.

She waltzed over to stand near the table. "Having a low blood sugar attack, are we?" She cocked an eyebrow.

A devilish grin lifted the corners of his mouth. "Didn't I tell you I have a sweet tooth? I just can't get enough of the stuff." He curved his finger and beckoned her closer.

She laughed lightly and obeyed. What else was a girl supposed to do when two of her favorite things were right there in front of her—a sexy man and chocolate?

He angled her in front of him, then before she knew it, he'd placed a cup towel over her eyes and knotted it at the back of her head. Andrea hadn't mentioned blindfolds in any of her tales. She reached her hands toward the covering. "Not fair . . ."

He stole the rest of her words when he lifted her up. Oh, God, she was going to fall. She blindly grabbed his arms to catch her balance.

"Easy now," he said as he set her on the table.

She sucked in her breath when the cheeks of her butt touched the table. "That's cold."

"It'll get warm soon enough." He chuckled. "I want you to relax. Tell me what you feel."

"Cold." She shivered. It sounded like he was rubbing his hands together.

He began to massage her shoulders. "Getting warmer?"

Heat spread over her shoulders and down her arms. She nodded. Umm, nice. Every bone in her body began to melt. She didn't realize just how tense she'd been the last couple of days. And Logan certainly had a way with his hands. She sighed with regret when he moved away.

She listened. A cabinet squeaked. Was that the microwave door opening, then closing? Yes, he'd turned the timer on. She wasn't concerned because she *did* trust him. Odd how she would so quickly after meeting him when she'd always been so guarded in the past. Giving of herself didn't come easily, but then, maybe it was as *Mamere* had always told her—with some people there was a special connection.

Footsteps, and he was beside her once more. She inhaled. Spicy aftershave . . . and chocolate? Okay . . .

He lightly brushed wet fingers across her lips. Automatically, she licked. Warm chocolate—of course. "Are you trying to make me fat?" She could almost hear his smile.

"I don't think you'll have much problem working off the calories."

The night was sounding better and better. She liked the idea of someone besides herself being in charge. It seemed everyone turned to her for answers: people needing help when she patrolled the streets, Andrea wanting advice about something. And then there was her grandmother. *Mamere,* well, she was . . . an entity of her own. Jody still hadn't figured her out.

But she did know tonight she wanted Logan in charge. She didn't want to think . . . only feel.

"I'm going to lay you back," he told her.

"It's strange not being able to see." She grabbed his arms. "Like I'm falling into empty space."

"Just remember what I told you, I'll always be there to catch you."

A cold shiver washed over her and she knew it wasn't just from lying back on the table. "Always is a long time."

"Don't think. Just feel." He ran his hand down the front on her body, stopping short of her thong. She gritted her teeth.

"Damn, you look sweet lying on the table with hardly any clothes on." He sucked in a deep breath. "I'm going to take your panties off."

The fact that he wasn't asking her permission, and knowing he was going to remove them no matter what she said, sent a rush of heat spiraling downward. When he tucked his fingers barely inside the waistband and began slowly tugging them off, she arched her hips, but his fingers didn't come close to her most sensitive area. She bit her lip as he slid them over her legs, grazing the insides of her thighs.

"I'm going to leave the hose on. You make a very sexy picture wearing black hose and lacy garters, your legs dangling over the side of the table as if you're waiting for a lover to spread your thighs and taste you."

Sweet torture! Anticipation of what she knew he was going to do was killing her. She wanted him to make love to her, but the thrill of the game was like a burst of fire flowing through her veins, and she found herself wanting the foreplay to last longer.

The whisper of material, a zipper sliding across metal teeth, and she knew he was removing his clothes. Mental images filled her mind of his broad chest, slim hips and strong thighs. An aching need to feel him buried deep inside her left her wanting more than words.

Without realizing it, she began inching her thighs open. He groaned. Awareness stilled her movement. What was she doing? No, don't think about anything, just let nature take its course, she told herself.

He smeared something cold on her nipples. She gasped at the initial shock.

"Tell me how that makes you feel. How else will I know if I'm giving you pleasure . . . or causing you pain?"

As she got used to the temperature, tingles began to spread outward from her nipples. "Erotic, exciting, wanton."

He began drizzling warm liquid over her body. Chocolate syrup?

"And now?"

"I smell chocolate." She smiled. "You warmed it in the microwave. It tickles, and I feel very decadent." When he drizzled the chocolate between her legs and the heated liquid slid down her clit, she arched her hips and moaned. Tantalizing spasms of pleasure washed over her.

"Like that?"

"Oh . . . yes."

He slipped his hands behind her head and removed the blindfold. She blinked several times, until her eyes adjusted to the light. She was covered with chocolate syrup, pudding and whipped cream.

He stood beside the table in all his naked glory, and it was definitely glorious.

Reckless abandon filled her. "And what do you plan on doing about this mess?" she asked in a husky voice.

"Don't worry. I plan on cleaning every inch of you." He lowered his head, drawing her nipple into his mouth. He sucked gently before moving to her other breast. Ripples of delight spread through her. She didn't want him to stop. Ah, God, it felt incredible, heat wave after heat wave spreading over her body.

He moved to stand between her legs, lowered his head and began to lick the chocolate off her. His tongue scraped back and forth across her clit. She grabbed her thighs as coherent thought fled, leaving behind only the pleasure his mouth gave her.

"Now," she pleaded.

He slipped on a condom just before he entered her. His hard length caused a friction inside her. Each thrust brought her closer and closer. She grasped his buttocks, pulling her feet up until she rested them on the edge of the table, and he drove deeper. Their heavy breathing filled the room.

He suddenly groaned, arching his back. Her inner muscles clasped him tightly as she was caught in the throes of her own orgasm, a tide of quivering pleasure that pulsated through her body, leaving her trembling and exhausted.

She fought to catch her breath. He rested his head on her abdomen, his arms on the table so she didn't bear his weight.

"What kind of spell have you cast over *me* Logan Hart?" she murmured, lightly brushing his hair away from his face.

"The same one you've cast over me."

After a few moments, he raised his head and grinned. "God, you're a mess."

She laughed. "You should see yourself if you think I look bad."

He straightened, tugging on her hand, pulling her toward the bathroom even though her body protested any movement whatsoever.

Showering seemed surreal. Jody knew the time was nearing when she had to tell Logan that he couldn't ride with her anymore, but when he glided the soapy sponge over her body and the spray of warm water washed away the last remnants of what they'd shared, the only thing she could think about was how right it was they were together.

He didn't seem to mind there were no words between them. Maybe he sensed her inner turmoil. It wouldn't be the first time he'd accurately guessed her thoughts.

But when they were seated on her sofa, Logan in his suit pants and partially buttoned shirt and her in a white terry cloth robe, she knew she could put it off no longer. He patted the cushion beside him. She stayed on the opposite end. She couldn't say what needed to be said if she was snuggled next to him.

She took a deep breath. "I don't want you riding out with me anymore."

His body tensed. "What are you talking about?"

"The vision I had." She looked at her hands. "I saw blood—your blood."

Silence.

She did look at him then. His face showed no emotion. "You don't believe me, do you?" Had everything he told her been a lie? Did he think she might be making this up?

He stood, walking to the window. "If I don't write the articles I can kiss the assistant editor position good-bye."

"I'm sorry."

He turned. "You're sorry? That's it? What if the vision is wrong?"

She shook her head. "I don't have them often, but what I see always happens."

"And what did you see?"

She cringed at his clipped words. "I saw blood. Your blood. A badge . . . and you."

He relaxed. "That's all?"

She jumped to her feet. "Isn't that enough?"

"Okay." He planted his hands on his hips. "If that's all you saw then you don't know for a fact where or when I'll get hurt."

"Not exactly . . ."

He shook his head. "Have you ever been able to warn someone and they don't get hurt?"

She'd felt a dark cloud hovering over Andrea once. She'd warned her. Andrea narrowly missed falling down a staircase because one of the steps was loose, but that was different.

"It doesn't matter." She shook her head. "I can warn you until I'm blue in the face but I can't stop a bullet, or . . . or . . ."

"Jump tall buildings?"

She glared at him. "That's not a damn bit funny."

"I know." He sobered. "But writing these articles is important to me." He paused. "If I don't ride out with you, I'll have the captain put me with someone else. It's your call."

From the look on his face she knew he wasn't about to

back down. Stubborn, irritating . . . man! Damn it, she'd rather be where she could at least take special precautions. Besides, it wasn't likely they would go on anything danger- ous. Surely she could protect him.

"I don't like it."

"But this is the way it has to be."

His tone told her she wouldn't be able to change his mind. There was one other story that he could write. That one would get him the job he wanted. But if he wrote it her life would be plastered on the front page.

She would be exposed. Dredging up the past wouldn't change anything. It wouldn't put back the pieces of her child- hood. It would only cause speculation and rumors.

And if her uncle were alive, it would bring him home. She had the training to meet him head on, but she already knew he didn't play by the rules. He wouldn't hesitate to put a bul- let in her back and slip out as quietly as he came in.

No, it was better to let old dogs sleep. As long as he didn't know she was alive, she'd have the element of surprise if he did return.

She looked at Logan. He waited patiently for her answer. She could keep him safe. "Okay, we'll continue on as be- fore."

He opened his mouth, but closed it without saying any- thing. He wasn't telling her something.

Andrea would say she was just being paranoid, and she'd probably be right.

Chapter 20

P-*u*-*s*-*s*-*y*
Andrea read the tiles when she glanced at the board on the coffee table. She warily eyed Kevin as he rested against the pile of pillows on the floor.

"That's not a word."

"If you can use cock, I can use pussy." His grin was smug. "I believe that's ten points."

She arched an eyebrow. "Cock is a word. You're from Texas. Cock . . . rooster? Duh."

"Pussy . . . meow . . . cat."

"You probably cheated while I refilled our wineglasses." She absently watched his face as she set the glasses on the table and sat on the sofa.

His mouth twitched. He glanced away.

"I knew it!" She jumped to her feet. "You picked the tiles you wanted while I refilled *your* glass." She narrowed her eyes. "That is so low. Even for you. I should've known you'd cheat."

He fell over on his side, laughing. "You're the one who chose the game."

She frowned as she sat on the sofa again, glancing at his words on the Scrabble board. "You're words are all sexual. Vigor, climax, lick." She quirked an eyebrow. "The only word you didn't use was . . ."

"I didn't have an F."

"Funny."

"That wasn't the word. Do they make you horny, though? We could make love to release the pressure building inside you."

She wanted to make love. Her whole body was starting to go into meltdown, but she wanted to do something different. She wanted to actually get to know him. Then they could have hot and wild sex.

"It's me, isn't it? You don't like Texans."

"That's crazy." She frowned.

"You don't like tall men?"

"No . . . it's . . ."

"Men with dark hair?"

"No, no, no! I just want my next relationship to have more substance. You're on vacation. You'll leave in a few days." There! That sounded pretty darn good. This time she wanted the kind of relationship where she could really get to know the man.

"Okay. I see what you're getting at. You don't want a wham, bam, thank you, ma'am." He nodded.

"Yes! Exactly right!"

"I'm from Texas. I have a ranch. I breed cattle. I think you're the sexiest woman alive."

He thought she was sexy. Of course she was sexy, and she was already tired of being proper. "Good enough!" With a wicked grin, she leaned forward. "But are you sure you can handle me, *cher*?" She slid her hand between his legs and rubbed her palm against him.

"Ah . . ."

He reached for her, but she quickly stood. "You're in the Big Easy, we do this my way, cowboy."

Kevin fell against the pillows. "You like torture, right?"

She laughed. "I like a lot of things. Give me five minutes and then bring the wine and glasses to the bedroom."

He rolled over so he'd have a better view as she sauntered

away. Man, she was the sexiest woman he'd ever been with. He could watch the sway of her hips all day long. He wondered if she realized what she did to him.

The clock on the wall slowly ticked the seconds.

She was killing him. This erection was killing him. What the hell was she doing in there? Mental images flashed across his brain. He groaned, rolling on his side.

Three minutes. Was that *all* the time that had passed?

He was going to die. Kevin Hart—cause of death: Hard-on. At least it kind of rhymed. Cripes! The blood supply had left his brain and swelled his dick. He had no oxygen. Nothing to feed his brain. He . . .

Jumped to his feet. Four . . . three . . . two . . . one! Five minutes. Grabbing the glasses and the wine he went to the door and tapped lightly.

"Come in."

"My idea exactly." He pushed the door open.

It was dark, except for the half dozen or so candles placed around the room. Hide and seek? He grinned. Might be kind of fun. Especially when he caught her.

"Come out, come out, wherever you are," he sang slightly off-key.

She laughed. "Don't give up your day job." She stepped out of the shadows holding a jewel-handled whip with velvet strips, but that wasn't what intrigued him.

She stood beside the closet holding the whip—and wearing a beaded and sequined, bright green lacy teddy, yellow hose held up by purple satin garters and she had on the sexiest pair of red stiletto heels he'd ever seen. His dick quivered. What made this teddy unique were the holes cut for her nipples and at the vee of her legs.

"You going to stand there staring all night or are you going to get out of those clothes and let me show you what a real woman can do?"

He set the glasses and bottle on the floor and kicked off his shoes while at the same time he was unfastening his pants. In record time, he was naked and walking toward her.

"On the bed, *cher*." She tested the handle of her whip against her open palm.

"I love it when you talk French." He climbed to the middle of the bed, more than happy to oblige.

"Turn over."

His brow wrinkled. He was pretty open-minded when it came to sex, but he would kind of like to know what she had in mind.

"Unless you're scared," she murmured.

He rolled to his stomach.

"Just relax. This is going to feel a little cold."

She drizzled something wet on him. He sucked in a deep breath. Cold his ass . . . She began to massage the oil on his back and over the cheeks of his butt. Cinnamon wafted to his nose as heat spread over his body.

"Is it getting warm?"

"Oh, yeah." His body was getting really hot, but in a good way.

She slapped her whip across his butt. Rather than hurt, it tickled . . . sensuously so.

"Turn over."

He didn't hesitate. She drizzled more oil on his front and massaged it into his skin. Tingles of heat spread over him in waves.

"My turn," he said, reaching for the bottle. She probably thought he looked like a starving kid who hadn't been weaned from the breast yet, but he couldn't drag his gaze from her delectable titties.

"Not this time." She moved it out of his reach.

He fell back on the bed in abject despair. She laughed. Lord, she had a rich, throaty voice that sent shivers of pleasure up and down his spine.

She stood, going to a small cabinet and opened the double

doors. His eyes widened. She had a shelf full of sex toys. He grinned. He loved a woman with a hobby. She sauntered back to him, her nipples hard and erect. The thatch of dark pubic hair hiding all her womanly secrets and making him hungry to explore every last one of them.

She slipped a condom on him. The inside of the rubber wasn't smooth. It was like tiny fingers touching all over his dick and when she stroked him, he almost lost it.

Before he could mention that fact, she slipped a rubber ring over him, then straddled him.

He easily slid into her moist heat. "Damn, that feels nice. Jeez, you're hot and . . ." He arched when she turned the vibrating ring on.

"I'm hot and what?" Laughter was in her voice.

She moved up and down his dick. He no longer cared if she laughed or not. One glance at her face and he saw she wasn't laughing anymore.

He met each of her thrusts, trembling as the heat of her body wrapped around his erection, stroking and massaging him. It was an effort, but he held back until she cried out. He gritted his teeth and grabbed her hips when his world rocked beneath him. This was better than a Ranger baseball game, better than the Fourth of July—hell, nothing he could ever experience in this lifetime could top making love with Andrea Potier.

He'd known making love with her would be great, but he never thought it could ever be like this. He rolled to his side, taking her with him, wrapping his arms around her and pulling her against him.

"Like I said before. You're fantastic. You're wonderful . . ."

"I'll give you two hours to stop talking like that or you'll have me blushing." She yawned and snuggled close.

"And funny. And . . ." He drew in a deep breath. "But next time it's my turn."

Chapter 21

Sitting in the captain's office, waiting for him to return gave Jody plenty of time to think about the night before. Had she really thought Logan would agree to stop riding out? Her plan backfired like a Ford with a bad muffler.

A shiver of longing swept over her body. She couldn't get the man out of her system. *Mamere* would tell her to stop fighting fate, some people were meant to be together.

And if he was injured while patrolling with her? Then how would she feel?

She looked at her watch. Speaking of which, he should be here within the next ten minutes. Unless he'd decided to take her advice after all. She could only hope.

She pulled her thoughts back to the present and straightened when the captain came back into his office.

"Sorry about being called away."

"No problem." She had a pretty strong feeling he was about to explain why she'd been summoned to his office in the first place. It didn't bode well for her. Damn it, why had Logan followed her the other night when the burglar broke into that woman's home?

She grimaced. It wasn't *all* his fault. Letting him tag along had been really stupid on her part. She shouldn't have proceeded on the call, but instead, waited for another unit to arrive on scene. She might as well accept the responsibility of what she'd let happen and get it over with. "About the other night, sir."

"The other night?" He raised his eyebrows in question.

Or maybe she didn't know what he'd called her in for. "Nothing," she hedged. "I just thought you might want to talk about something else, but I guess I was wrong." She discreetly took a deep breath, and exhaled. The noose loosened around her neck.

"I called you in here because I've been on the phone with the editor of the paper this morning. We talked for quite some time."

Okay, now she had a bad feeling.

"It seems Logan covered a pretty tough beat in Dallas. He's an experienced reporter. Oliver Bradley and I think he can handle himself enough that you shouldn't have to hold back." He paused. "Still, don't take any unnecessary risks."

"Captain, I don't think that's wise . . ."

"Apparently it hasn't troubled you too much in the past, Dupree. You did take him with you on the B and E call the other night."

Damn, she knew he'd find out. "But . . ."

"No buts, Dupree. Now, I have work to do and tell your rider if he doesn't stay out of the way, I'll pull him off the beat—articles or not. He's only there to observe."

She turned toward the door.

"You did a hell of a good job on the break-in by the way."

"Thank you." But her thoughts weren't on arresting the perp. Damn it, Logan had known last night that his editor was going to call the captain, and he hadn't said a word to her. He'd lied by omission.

She didn't notice anyone coming toward her until she slammed into a hard chest. The man caught her by the elbows to steady her.

"Easy now." Logan's slow southern drawl wrapped around her like sunshine on a cold day.

His words were soft, seductive, forcing her to remember

the intimacies they'd shared—whether he meant them to or not. She cleared her throat and her mind, and glared up at him. "Did you have anything to do with the fact I'm supposed to roll on calls now?"

"I mentioned something to Bradley the other day."

"Well, it worked and I don't like it. Stay back or I'll shoot you in the foot and put you out of commission. Got it?"

He chuckled. "Got it."

"Not funny, Hart. Are you ready?"

"Always." A lazy smile lifted the corners of his mouth.

She chose to ignore his implication and strode past him, but she couldn't ignore the fire he'd kindled inside her. Did he not realize how serious the situation could get? It made her wonder if he really did believe her visions; either that, or he was incredibly stupid. And right now, she wasn't quite sure which to believe!

He didn't speak again, for which she was profoundly grateful, until they were in the patrol car.

"Are you going to give me the silent treatment like you did the first time I rode with you?"

She turned the key and backed out of the parking space, turning left as they left the garage. "Maybe." She wasn't ready to let him off the hook.

"I do believe you saw me and blood . . . and a badge. I'll be careful . . . swear."

"But then you haven't given me any other choice, have you?"

"How about if we change the subject."

"Fine." There was nothing better she'd like to do.

"Nice weather?"

She frowned. Had Andrea coached him or what?

"It's muggy."

"Okay, did you know the editor, Oliver Bradley, covered the story when your father was murdered? When I mentioned . . ."

Her heart pounded. "You told him?" She slammed her

foot on the brake. Logan grabbed the dash. The driver of the car behind them blared his horn. He'd told her he wouldn't write her story. But no, he hadn't said anything. Just let the matter drop. Fool! She'd assumed because of their relationship and knowing how she felt, he wouldn't write her story.

It was almost the same as him not telling her about the change in how she patrolled the streets. She let off the brake and stepped on the gas, but she was so pissed she couldn't stop shaking.

Her story would be front page news!

"It's not what you think."

"Then explain just what the hell it is." She glanced out the window. A man hurried down the street. He wore a white suit. Her uncle had liked white suits.

"Watch it!"

She slammed on the brake again . . . just before she almost hit the car in front of her.

The man behind her yelled out his window as he whipped into the other lane and went around her, "If this is what my tax dollars are paying for, then I want a damned refund!"

She took the next right and made a beeline for the city park. She had to catch her breath before she killed someone. Her gaze briefly fell on Logan. Nice thought, but was he worth prison?

"Listen. My editor knows very little."

"Why did you tell him anything in the first place? Oh, never mind. I forgot; you're a reporter. Get the story and don't worry about the people you hurt."

"Is that what you think?"

She didn't want to, but he wasn't giving her much of a choice. In her fantasy Logan would tell her that he wouldn't write her story. He would know how much damage it would do. But like all fantasies—it wasn't real. It only existed in her mind.

She pulled into an empty parking space and put the car in

park. She needed fresh air to clear her head. After turning off the engine, she pulled the keys, and stepped out of the car. She heard his door open, then shut. He kept his distance. At least he had a little sense. If he touched her right now Jody was afraid she'd do something she might not regret for a good thirty minutes. From the corner of her eye she saw him lean against the hood.

This area had always given her peace. The old oaks rose majestically toward the clear blue sky. They almost touched the clouds, their branches outstretching like wise old men with beards of gray, tattered moss.

"I researched your background because I wanted to know more about you." His words were soft, but they broke past the quiet as he began to explain.

"Did you suspect there might be a story even then?" Her lip curled.

"Yes, I did. I sensed a deep sadness. I wanted to see if I could find out what had put it there. In the beginning I thought whatever it was might make a good story. But later, after I began to know you better, I knew a story wasn't as important. I thought I could make the sadness go away."

She hadn't expected him to tell her that he'd been thinking about getting a story since the very beginning. Not that it mattered. He'd told his editor. She hardened herself toward anything Logan might say.

"I knew your age, so I began there," he continued. I found your birth announcement in the archived newspapers, the death of your mother when you were four. Then nothing until your father was killed."

"And you immediately ran to your boss with the juicy tid-bit about the crazy Duprees," she snarled. When he wouldn't meet her eyes, she knew she had her answer. "Like I said, you're a reporter."

"No."

She cocked an eyebrow.

"I only told him I thought I had a lead on one of Phillip Dupree's missing daughters. Nothing else. I admit, I did get caught up in the moment, but it *is* what I do for a living."

"But you're going to tell him."

"Not if you don't want me to."

How could she be certain he told the truth? "You'd give up the job of assistant editor?"

He did put his arms around her then, drawing her against him, wrapping her in a cocoon of safety. She resisted for almost ten seconds before relaxing against him. She sighed deeply, letting all her problems disappear and languishing in the heat emanating from his body.

"You promise you won't write my story? Even if it costs you the job?" She had to hear him say it once more. Just to know she'd heard him right the first time. Or maybe so he would understand exactly what he was giving up.

He hesitated. She closed her eyes tightly.

"I won't write the story."

"I'm sorry."

"Don't be. It's just a job."

But it was the one he wanted. Guilt settled over her like a heavy blanket she couldn't push off. Not just because he wasn't writing about her, but because she still didn't quite trust him. After all, he hadn't told her she wouldn't be playing chauffeur while patrolling the streets. She didn't want to feel like that, but she couldn't seem to help it. Only time would give her the answers she needed. Time, she had lots of that.

Chapter 22

Cavenaugh adjusted his position on the leather seat. His butt had gone to sleep and his damn toes were starting to cramp. He probably wouldn't be able to fuckin' stand by the time they decided to stop for the night.

He glanced out the window, watching the scenery roll past. At least there were some damn trees here. He'd never gotten so sick of a town as quickly as he had Two Creeks—not that he'd seen much from his jail cell. He'd garnered a laugh from one of the cops when he'd remarked about the sparse landscape. The cop told him some crazy story about crossing an invisible line—the ninety-eighth parallel. Apparently, the land became flat, with few trees, once you crossed this imaginary line.

So maybe the cop hadn't been trying to pull something, he thought. The landscape had changed abruptly from flat and treeless to trees so thick you could barely walk between them. He shook his head. He must be losing his mind or be really bored to even give a crap.

After attempting to find another comfortable spot, he crossed his arms. One of the deputy U.S. marshals broke the silence. Cavenaugh tried to look as if he wasn't paying attention to their conversation, but he heard every word they said. And he made a mental note of everything about the two men.

Al Williams. Late thirties, he guessed. There were no wrinkles in Al's starched shirt. His badge had been polished so bright Cavenaugh could almost see his refection. He wore no jewelry, other than a plain gold band.

For the last couple of hours he'd listened to the on-again, off-again conversation. Al talked about his wife, who was running for secretary of the school board, and his two kids. Cavenaugh dismissed him.

But the other one . . . He narrowed his eyes on the dark-haired man. Early forties maybe. He wore a shit-eating grin most of the time, and he barely spared a glance in his direction.

Corruptible? Maybe.

He always enjoyed manipulating people. Funny what a supposedly upright citizen would do when he waved money under their nose.

He settled back against the seat. And these assholes—they might get him to New Orleans, but if everything went according to plan—they wouldn't have him long. His hands curled into fists. He hadn't spoken to Ray in two days. The son of a bitch better not bail on him.

He glanced over his shoulder. His gaze narrowed on the SUV behind them. His niece and her boyfriend were one car length back. She'd make sure he didn't try anything funny between here and a Louisiana jail. He had no doubt Fallon wouldn't hesitate to put a bullet between his eyes if he tried to escape. She was smart. If she hadn't been behind them, he would've made his move on the road. Too risky now. He smiled. But she'd let her guard down once they arrived in New Orleans. Then, if anyone got in his way . . . he'd kill them. If Ray didn't fuck up.

They stopped for a piss break an hour later. Al went in first to check the station out while Tom guarded him. Fallon and her boyfriend pulled in practically on top of the patrol car.

Bitch.

"Do they really think I'll be able to escape with all the

hardware?" he asked conversationally, raising his hands and dangling the handcuffs.

Tom turned in his seat. "Yeah, they are a little anal retentive."

"But you're different."

"When someone pays me as much as you are then I can afford to be more relaxed."

Cavenaugh's eyes narrowed. "Explain."

"I transported your friend Ray the first time he went down the river. We got to know one another pretty well over the two days we were together."

"I haven't been able to reach him."

"Don't worry, he's been busy. Found a cop on the take in New Orleans, Paul Leger, just in case we couldn't pull together an escape en route." He nodded toward the SUV behind them. "Good thing. That DEA agent and sheriff are right up your ass." He chuckled.

Cavenaugh didn't find his situation amusing. "Careful, my friend."

"Don't worry. Ray had a backup plan all along. Said he wouldn't leave anything to chance."

"And what about this cop? Can he be trusted?"

"Ray told me pretty boy wants out of law enforcement. Said he's going into politics. Maybe run for senator. He's looking for the big bucks."

Cavenaugh inwardly grinned. With the men he had waiting in the wings, a cop on the inside, he wouldn't be in jail for very long.

Their gazes locked in the rearview mirror. *No,* he thought, not long at all.

Chapter 23

Fallon watched as they led John Cavenaugh inside the jail. He turned and for just a second, they made eye contact. Hatred burned deep in his dark orbs, then he smiled. A cold chill ran down her spine.

"Don't let him get to you. Your revenge will come when he learns he'll face murder charges as well as drug trafficking." Wade hugged her close to him.

"But first I have to talk to Jody." Her glance fell on the police station. A different kind of fear swept over her. What if Jody couldn't care less if she were alive or dead? What would she think? That she'd abandoned her?

She glanced around. Time slipped away. There was a familiarity, a feeling of coming home. She closed her eyes as memories rushed back: running through the streets, stumbling into a cemetery, seeing a name carved in stone, taking it as her own.

"Fallon? You okay?" Wade asked.

She straightened, looking at Wade. "Yeah, fine."

He hugged her. "Are you ready to meet your sister?"

Heart racing, palms sweating, she calmly looked at Wade. "Let's go."

She walked up the steps as if she were going to an executioner. Once inside, she looked at the people passing back and forth. None of the women resembled what she thought her sister might look like as an adult.

Now or never. She approached a blonde. "Excuse me."

The woman turned. "Yeah?"

"I'm looking for Jody Dupree."

Her eyes narrowed. "And?"

She glanced at her name tag, Andrea Potier. Rude bitch. Fallon had no intention of telling her anything. She didn't want it getting back to Jody that someone claiming to be her sister had been asking questions. "A friend. Are you going to tell me how I can find her, or do I need to ask someone else?"

She shrugged. "Ask away, but it won't do you any good. Jody's shift won't start for another two hours and we make it a policy not to give out personal information."

"We'll come back." She turned and strode out of the police station. Once outside, her shoulders slumped. She wasn't sure if it was from relief that she had a little more time to prepare herself, or disappointment that she wouldn't be immediately reunited.

"Why don't we see about getting a room? You can rest, then freshen up before you meet Jody."

It took a moment for his words to sink in. Had she lost what few working brain cells she had? Nothing seemed to be functioning. Finally she nodded, glad Wade was taking charge.

He was right. She wanted to look her best when she met her baby sister. Tears formed in her eyes and that queasy feeling was rumbling around in her stomach again. She sniffed, quickly looking away. He must think her a sap. But whatever he thought, he wasn't saying anything, just silently giving her the support she needed. How had she been so lucky finding him? She chuckled inwardly. She didn't think holding him at gunpoint and ordering him to strip could actually be considered a normal first meeting. She only hoped the one with her sister would go a little smoother.

Chapter 24

Jody glanced around the parking garage as she walked toward her unit. Logan was late. A niggle of doubt crept into her thoughts. What if he was turning in a story this very minute?

Guilt washed over her. No, it wasn't that. She was almost positive. But the strange feeling she'd had all day persisted. She didn't like the odd sensation creeping around her. The tickle at the back of her neck. Something just wasn't right.

A shrill whistle called her attention. She turned. Logan. A smile of greeting formed. Lord, even from across the parking garage he looked pretty damn tempting. She raised her hand to wave. She had to admit, he was being cautious when they patrolled the city and so far nothing had happened. Maybe she'd been wrong. . . .

An explosion from inside the police department rocked her feet. She grabbed the side of the patrol car nearest her to steady herself. *What the hell was that?*

She looked over her shoulder, slightly dazed. Realization dawned. Andrea! She was inside the building. She could be hurt . . . bleeding . . . She swallowed past the lump in her throat. Oh, my God, please let her be all right.

She whirled toward the door just as it burst open. Two men came barreling out. She skidded to a stop. One was in street clothes, the other wore white coveralls emblazoned with one word: *Prisoner.*

Time seemed to hang in the air as everything moved in slow motion.

The lead man's gaze landed on her. Recognition widened his eyes. "Angelina?"

The air left her lungs. He'd called her by her mother's name. She took one step back, then another. "Uncle John," she whispered his name. *Go away!* Her mind screamed.

"Fuck! I killed you." He raised his gun.

"No!" Logan lunged toward her, pushing her behind a patrol car as another explosion reverberated through the air.

She slammed into the concrete. Her breath whooshed out. Pain stabbed her left side, her arm, her head.

"You ain't got time to kill the bitch," someone said. "Unless you want them to catch me and you both, and that ain't gonna happen."

Footsteps slapped the cement, moving away from them. The world spun around her, a black void seemed to be swallowing her. She touched her head. Pain shot through.

"There they are," someone yelled.

More people running.

A car started, peeled out.

Another followed.

Her uncle! No! She wanted him dead. She'd hoped he was. She squeezed her eyes shut. Oh, God, she'd looked into the face of death, and almost died once again. Her body began to tremble.

"You okay?" Logan asked.

"I've got to go after him." She started to sit up, but a wave of nausea forced her back down.

"You're not going anywhere. Where are you hurt?"

"My head, but I don't think anything is too bad. I just need to catch my breath."

Why had John Cavenaugh come back to New Orleans?

Why was he a prisoner? Why hadn't she been warned, but no, the captain wouldn't have known John Cavenaugh was her uncle.

He was alive. Damn! She clenched her fists. Somewhere deep in her mind she'd hoped he might be dead.

Now her uncle knew he hadn't killed her. That she was still alive. And that she knew he was the one who killed her father. She was vulnerable, and she didn't like how it made her feel.

"What the hell happened?" Logan's words rushed out; not waiting for her answer, he continued. "It sounded like someone tried to blow up the police station. I can't believe that son of a bitch took a shot at you." He barely paused to take a deep breath before he continued. "A breakout. Damn, I need to call my editor."

Apparently, he realized she wasn't talking.

"Jody? Are you sure he didn't hurt you?"

"I'm . . . I'm fine. You?"

"Actually, I think I've been shot."

For a second time, the breath was knocked out of her. She scrambled to her knees as she turned to face him, fighting past another wave of dizziness. "What do you mean, you think you've been shot?" Her voice cracked when she saw blood on the sleeve of his shirt.

He started to sit up, but wobbled. She grabbed his good arm, helping him keep his balance, then raised his sleeve. An ugly red furrow branded his arm. It was a graze, but it was still bleeding. "Come on. I have a first-aid kit in my car."

As they stood, she glanced around. Her vision blurred, then cleared. The place looked like a war zone as injured people streamed out of the building. Sirens and traffic blasters from ambulances and fire trucks screamed through the air as they approached the station. A short distance away, the captain directed people, but as soon as he saw them he hurried over.

"You two okay?" He looked at Logan's arm. "He shot at you?"

"Actually, I was the one he aimed at. Logan pushed me out of the way. What happened?" she asked as they hurried to her patrol car.

"The son of a bitch just came in from Texas this morning. He was being extradited on earlier drug charges. They were still processing him in."

"And the bomb?"

He paused. "Inside job. He managed to bribe someone. It's the only way it could've gone down so smoothly."

Her stomach turned. "Cop?" She got her first-aid kit out of her car and quickly began bandaging Logan's arm.

"I don't want to think so."

His handheld radio crackled.

"We lost them. They apparently had their escape route planned."

He keyed the radio. "Keep looking. I want that . . ." He clamped his lips together. "I want that prisoner." He let off the button. "Damn it, I'll have to find the paperwork in all this mess to get the statistics on him."

"His name is John Cavenaugh." She taped the bandage.

"What do you know about him?" The captain's eyes narrowed on her.

"That he's my uncle, that he murdered my father twenty years ago, and that he left me for dead when a bullet grazed me." She met Logan's gaze as she taped the bandage. She wished she could read his mind, know what he thought, but maybe it was better she couldn't read minds.

"And you don't think this was something worth telling me?" The captain's forehead wrinkled.

"Captain Franklin knew about it. I made him swear not to tell anyone else. When he retired, I asked him to keep his promise. You were new. I didn't know you." She glanced around at the people who looked as dazed as she felt. "I need to go inside where I can help. Andrea's in there." Her stomach twisted another notch, but before she could take a step, a familiar voice called to her.

"Jody!" Andrea ran up to them. "It was horrible. Is everyone okay?"

She did a quick visual. The sleeve of Andrea's uniform was torn and she had a small cut above her eye. Jody sighed with relief. "I'm fine. A bullet grazed Logan, though. The prisoner who escaped was my uncle."

"Your uncle? Did he see you?"

She nodded.

"You have to leave," Andrea spoke with determination. "Captain, she has to get somewhere safe."

"There's too much to do." Jody shook her head. "Look at all the hurt people." They were still trailing out of the building.

"Most of the injuries are minor cuts and scrapes. They just look bad because dust billowed in from the back." She shook her head. "You're a witness who could get him the death penalty. For Christ's sake, you saw him murder your father. He can't let you live . . . or Logan. He's a witness that your uncle tried to kill you again. Attempted murder."

"No, I won't sit back while someone else chases him. I've been waiting twenty years for this."

The captain told them, "Excuse me but the last time I looked I was still running the show. Dupree, you're too emotionally involved. If you get careless you could hurt not only yourself, but someone else. As of right now, you're on vacation."

She opened her mouth.

"Whether you like it or not," the captain growled. "You'll stay at one of the safe houses. You too, Logan."

"He won't hang around," Jody argued. "He'd leave the state . . . the country . . . as fast as possible."

Andrea raised an eyebrow. "Can you be sure?"

She looked at the bandage on Logan's arm. Another vision that came true. Damn it, she'd take a chance with her life, join the search, but she wouldn't take a chance with his—not again. Besides, it looked like the captain wasn't giving her a choice.

She drew in a deep breath. "Okay, but not in a safe house. There's only one place I know where we'll be out of harm's way. The swamps. He won't follow us there."

"I don't have time to worry about the two of you," the captain said. "Safe house or the swamps. The choice is yours, but right now you're on leave and I have a hell of a mess to clean up." His radio crackled again. He began talking as he moved away, expecting his orders to be followed without question.

She closed her eyes and nodded. "Okay." She looked at Logan. "Muffin. I can't leave her."

"I'll go by and get the puppy. I have your key."

"Kevin needs to know what's going on. We can stop by there before we leave."

"Too chancey." Andrea bit her bottom lip as if she were deciding something. "I'll take care of him, too. He can stay with me."

Through the soot, Andrea's cheeks turned a rosy hue when everyone looked at her.

"What?" Andrea bristled.

"Nothing." Even with everything going on, Jody was happy Andrea had found someone.

"Each minute you hang around, you're putting yourself and Logan in danger," Andrea warned. "Go."

She was right. Jody glanced around, as if expecting John Cavenaugh to appear. Her stomach churned. She handed Andrea the keys to her cruiser and dug her car keys out of her pocket. Then took a deep breath. "Remember that small cove we went to last summer?" When Andrea nodded, she continued. "I'll meet you there in two days. Four o'clock in the evening."

Tears welled in Andrea's eyes but she nodded. "Be safe, *chere.*"

Some of the tension left her body. She hugged Andrea close. "Always, *mon ami.*"

When Logan started to stand, Jody hurried to help, but he brushed away her arm. "I'm okay. Just sore . . . and really ticked off."

He looked around, as if John Cavenaugh might appear, then he could show him just how angry he was. She understood exactly how he felt. Now that the initial shock was wearing off she was angry. How many times had she imagined coming face to face with him? Well, she had, and he was still alive. She should've drawn her gun and shot the bastard.

Damn, why hadn't she paid attention to the vision? She glanced at Logan's arm. Blood. He was hurt. A badge. Not patrolling the streets, but the police station itself. She'd grown lax in her interpretation of her visions because she disliked having them.

"My car is over there." She hesitated. She couldn't ask Logan to sacrifice another story for her. "If you want to call your editor . . ."

"I will, later. At the moment, safety is more important than a newspaper story and right now you're in more danger than I am."

She'd been worried that Logan would write her story. Afraid her life would be splashed on the front page of a newspaper. That her uncle would discover she lived and take her by surprise. She shook her head. Fate had stepped in and played a cruel joke. She couldn't help wondering what else fate would dish out.

Chapter 25

Cavenaugh's gut twisted. He should've taken the time to kill Jody. He slammed his hand on the dash. He didn't like loose ends. Damn it, he had *two* nieces to worry about now.

"You're free. Forget the woman. What the hell did she do, anyway? You haven't been in town long enough to piss anyone off." The man behind the wheel snorted with laughter. "At least not until the explosion. That's liable to make a few cops mad."

"Ya think?" Cavenaugh glared at him. He didn't like Ray. The man was a real bastard—in and out of prison all his life. He'd used him for small stuff in the past. Since Jack and George were still in jail, Ray had come in handy. He had to admit, the son of a bitch had come through this time.

"I hooked us up with this man I know. He has a shanty we can use. It's close to the water, in the middle of nowhere. They won't find you."

A shiver of revulsion ran over him. "As long as it isn't close to the swamp. I hate the fuckin' swamp."

"Don't tell me you're afraid of little old gators." He chuckled.

Alligators, voodoo, swamp creatures . . . he'd hated it as a kid, and he hated it as an adult. There was something unnatural about the place. He always figured if he died, it would be in the swamp.

"Can't say as I like the place, either," Ray said, breaking into his thoughts. "As soon as everything quiets down, we'll leave. Too risky right now."

Yeah, they'd leave, but not before he tied up a few unraveled threads. He pictured the look of surprise on Jody's face, then anger. Shit, he didn't want two nieces hunting him. The hatred inside him slowly dissolved.

He'd known she'd look like her mother. Angelina had been an exotic beauty—before the cancer. Her hair had been as black as a velvety night, full lips and dark, mysterious eyes.

He could still remember the first time he'd kissed her. Damn, she'd been sweet. That had been the first, and last time, she'd let him get that close to her. As soon as she met Phillip, he ceased to exist. Another good reason for his half brother to die.

Maybe he wouldn't kill Jody after all. Closing his eyes, he pictured her naked, lying in the bed, waiting for him. She'd open her legs, inviting him to fuck her.

His dick grew hard. He rubbed his hand over the front of his pants and could almost feel himself entering her. A cruel smile curved his lips. No, maybe he wouldn't kill her. At least not right away.

Sweet Angelina.

Coming home might not be so bad after all.

Chapter 26

Jody plunged the pole into the muddy bottom and pushed. The pirogue glided silently through the murky waters of the swamp. She'd stopped looking over her shoulder an hour ago as they crisscrossed a maze of waterways, cutting through dense curtains of willows, and hardwood trees with clinging, tattered moss.

Anger had driven her from the time they left the police station. Anger at herself that she'd been so close to her uncle and froze. But once again, she couldn't turn back the hands of time. They'd catch her uncle: what goes around comes around. Uncle John wouldn't follow her here, but if he did, she inwardly smiled, he'd be on her turf. She just didn't think he had enough courage to venture into the swamps.

Not long after he killed her father, *Mamere* had found her crying beneath one of the willows, not far from the cabin. When her grandmother had asked what was wrong, Jody told her she was afraid Uncle John would come back. That's when her grandmother told her about the time he fell into the swamp and had almost gotten eaten by an alligator. He'd sworn not to return.

Jody had never forgotten the story. She glanced around. This place was her haven . . . her sanctuary. She always felt like a different person here. As if on the trip to *Mamere*'s cabin the protective armor she usually wore fell away, making her lighter and less worried about the world around her. This was a place of renewal of the body and the spirit. Maybe what people said about the swamps was true—it abounded in magic.

Her gaze fell on Logan. She didn't think he was having the same kind of experience. For the first time since running into her uncle, she smiled. His attempts to maneuver the pirogue had almost sent him overboard. She'd motioned for him to sit on the wooden bench, and had taken the pole from him before he capsized them and they both became gator bait.

Now, he gripped the seat until his knuckles turned white. With alligators, snakes, water crickets almost as big as fish, and spiders, to name a few of the swamp's inhabitants, he would probably disagree with her vision of safety.

But this was home to her. And here she found beauty in the snowy white feathers of the egret, turtles sunning on logs, raccoons scavenging for a morsel of food.

Then there were the tall, elegant water cypress, their roots, cypress knees, rising out of the water. The water lilies with big, colorful blooms . . . she even liked the duck weed. It wasn't a layer of green scum on the water like a lot of people thought, unless you'd lived around swamps, but actually a plant. Tiny, green pads with featherlike hairs on top. *Mamere* once told her little water fairies lived on the pads. Even though she'd stared at them for hours one day, she hadn't seen one. She grinned. It still didn't stop her from taking a second glance, even now.

Logan cleared his throat and nodded. "Alligator."

Jody glanced to the left. She cocked an eyebrow in his direction. "You want I should hit him over the head with my pole, drag him home, and maybe make you some gator soup, *cher*?"

"Funny. I hope you're having a good laugh," he grumbled.

She chuckled. "I'm sorry." She really tried to sound contrite.

"Now, why don't I believe you? Could it be the way your

eyes twinkle? Or the fact you look perfectly relaxed in your surroundings?"

His gaze slid over her, but rather than make her feel guilty that she'd made a joke at his expense, she had a strong desire to pull closer to land, find a comfortable spot, and make sweet love for the rest of the afternoon. Forget about what had happened. Wipe the explosion, and her uncle, from her mind—at least for a while.

She resisted the urge to swing into the nearest inlet and instead, concentrated on their conversation. "Can you blame me for feeling at home? This is where I grew up. Even though the bayous are forever changing, I know every twist and turn the swamp makes." She inhaled the woodsy, slightly musty smell. Some people might wrinkle their nose, but to her it was like sweet perfume.

They passed the reptile. It stared without blinking. Logan eyed it with more than a little trepidation.

"You really grew up here?"

She nodded. "In a two-room cabin." She remembered waking in the mornings to the aroma of *Mamere*'s scrambled eggs and fried bread. Sometimes her grandmother would help a neighbor, and they'd pay her with a thick slab of bacon. Her grandmother would cut and fry up slices to go with the morning meal. And in the evenings she'd bring out her papa's accordion, and the night would fill with music.

"This quiet didn't bother you?" He waved his arm over the water, apparently remembered what was lurking beneath the dark surface, and quickly drew his hand back to the bench. "I think the solitude would drive me nuts."

"Quiet?" She laughed. "But it's noisy today."

He glanced around as if he expected to see half-naked natives pounding on drums. "I don't hear anything."

"Because you're not listening." She nodded toward the land. "Look."

A family of raccoons scavenged for food, rustling through the brush. Close by, a young gator slid into the water like a small mudslide. Somewhere overhead a bird called to its mate. Quiet? She didn't think so.

"Besides, we weren't completely shut off from civilization," she continued. "People occasionally dropped by, people who considered *Mamere* the local *bruja* . . . witch," she clarified.

His forehead wrinkled in confusion.

"You know, potions to ward off evil, or to cure an illness." Okay, now he thought she'd lost her mind, or was teasing him again. Maybe she shouldn't have mentioned her grandmother and how she cured people. "It's the truth, I swear."

"And they fell for her hocus-pocus?"

She squared her shoulders. "How do you think medicine first came about? Most of the drugs in pharmacies are just a synthetic version of plants." She was thoughtful for a moment. "I know you've heard of the aloe vera plant. The clear gel you get when you break a leaf is used to heal wounds and burns. And basil can lower blood sugar and blood pressure among other things. Plants have wonderful healing powers, if you know how to use them."

"Sorry." He held up his hand. "I didn't mean to offend you."

Mamere was respected for her doctoring, and more than one woman had gotten married because she'd slipped a love potion into her man's drink. Jody secretly thought her grandmother had been the first to discover something similar to Viagra and that was her famous aphrodisiac, but *Mamere* hadn't revealed the formula to her. She said the knowledge was too dangerous in the hands of an unmarried female. She only gave out small portions to those wanting a love potion.

She eyed Logan, who still didn't look convinced. He wouldn't be the first person to disregard the things her grandmother concocted. She normally didn't let people's ideas of what they considered normal get to her, but Logan's opinion meant something to her. She wanted him to understand how she felt. "My grandmother took me in and raised me. I've seen her cure people who doctors gave up on. She knows what she's doing."

She guided the boat close to land and jumped out, grabbing the rope as she did and tying off. "Here, give me your hand. Sometimes sitting in one place will cut the circulation off to your legs and make you unsteady. I certainly don't want you to fall in the swamp."

"No more than I want to take a swim," he mumbled, looking down into the water like he expected an alligator to jump out and grab him by the throat.

Their fingers met, his hand encircled hers in warmth, and as he stepped from the boat, their gazes locked. She could feel the heat rising up her neck. Did he know she wanted him to make love to her? That she hadn't been able to think of much else since the last time?

From the heavy-lidded look he sent in her direction she rather thought he did.

"Welcome to my home, *cher*," she breathed, then turned and stepped through the trees, the crunch of his footsteps telling her that he followed.

Peace settled over her. Her uncle wouldn't follow her to the swamps. Just like when she was seven, and *Mamere* had carried her nearly lifeless body to the tiny cabin, it became a refuge from everything bad that had happened in her life.

The cabin sat nestled in a small grove of trees, hidden from anyone passing by. A fisherman's shack some would call it. Just a small wooden structure that didn't really keep out the chill on a cold winter's night. They'd stuffed old newspapers in the cracks between the boards, and *Mamere* had traded her doctoring for firewood. And they'd made do just fine.

She moved forward, feeling at peace until the sun glinted off her badge, transporting her back to the police station. Anger trembled through her. She closed her eyes, heard the shot Cavenaugh fired, felt her body slam into the concrete. Saw the furrow the bullet made across Logan's arm.

No! She wouldn't let her uncle invade her sanctuary. He wasn't welcome here.

She drew in a deep, calming breath and surveyed the scene in front of her.

Mamere liked to cook outside, but inside the circle of rocks the ash had been carried away by the wind. No one had made a fire for at least a couple of nights. There were other signs that told her the old woman wasn't there. No washing hanging on the lines. The front door closed to discourage small animals from coming inside.

It wasn't unusual for her to be gone. She often spent weeks hunting for the herbs and berries she used for her potions.

She breathed a sigh of relief, needing this time alone with Logan, needing the connection with him. There was no reason why they couldn't make love. He'd be the first here, just as he'd been the first in her home.

Full circle.

Her life had begun here; the day terror had tried to steal her soul. The swamps would once again become her shelter until her uncle could be recaptured.

She looked at Logan. She wanted to feel completely alive. Slowly, she began to unbutton her shirt, pushed it off her shoulders, and let it fall to the ground.

They didn't need words between them. His eyes said it all. They told her of his longing to take her in his arms, to pull her close, taste her lips. To reaffirm her brush with death had been only that.

Their clothes dropped to the ground until they stood in front of each other naked, only their need between them. She reached out, sliding the palm of her hand down his chest, feeling the sinewy texture of his skin.

Her gaze strayed to his bandaged arm. A few inches over and the bullet would've slammed into his chest. She couldn't breathe. Her throat began to close.

"Don't," he said, taking her hand in his, drawing her away

from the memory. "It's barely more than a scratch. I won't let your uncle harm you ever again."

He'd protected her. "But I'm the cop, the one who's supposed to protect." If not for him, she would be lying in a cold bin in the city morgue.

"It's okay to let someone take care of you. Your badge won't dissolve or anything. Remember, I said I would be there to catch you."

He grazed her nipple with his finger. She sucked in a breath as tingles spread over her breast, spiraling downward to settle in the vee of her legs. She wondered if it was a ploy to get her mind off her uncle? Probably. It was working. Already she ached to feel him buried inside her.

Thoughts of Cavenaugh faded as they explored each other's bodies. She loved the texture of his skin, the strength in his muscles. Where his tan started . . . and ended. She stepped closer, wanting to taste. She ran her tongue over and around his tight nipple. "Salty."

He drew in a sharp breath. "Do you realize we're out in the open, bare-assed naked?"

She glanced up, met his eyes, and smiled, finally starting to relax. "The freedom is exhilarating, but don't worry, it still doesn't top chocolate. I doubt anything ever will. I like that you have a sweet tooth." She stuck her tongue out and flicked across his nipple again.

He grabbed her shoulders, but it didn't stop her from moving downward, resting on her knees in front of him.

When she circled her tongue around his erect penis, he arched forward. She glanced up. His eyes were closed, a look of rapture on his face. He didn't look like he cared where he was anymore, not that anyone could see them.

They were protected by the trees, cloaked in a veil of limbs and leaves and Spanish moss. She closed her eyes. He groaned as she tasted the essence of him. She gently began to suck, drawing him deeper into her mouth, stroking him with her tongue.

His hands tangled in her hair. "Ahh, you . . . need to . . . ahhh . . . stop now," he gasped. "I want to be inside you when I come."

She pulled away, licking the taste of him off her lips. As she came to her feet, she couldn't help placing small kisses on his thigh, his hip, his abdomen—until she stood on tiptoe and kissed his lips.

He pulled her closer, their bodies melding, their souls joining. Every inch of her body was pressed intimately against his. And above them, sunlight streamed through the trees, covering them in a patchwork of light and shadows, casting warmth over them.

"You're so beautiful," he whispered after he ended the kiss. He stared into her face as if he would memorize each of her features.

"Make love to me. I need to feel whole again," she breathed.

"Inside the cabin?"

She shook her head and lay down on the ground. "Here, outside." She had to be one with nature. This is where her strength came from. Her renewal of not only her body, but her mind as well.

He didn't argue as he lay beside her. Maybe their connection was strong enough that he instinctively knew the reasons why she needed to be here.

Instead of immediately entering her, he began intensifying the heat inside her. Lying on his side, he explored her body as if for the first time. He touched her breast, rubbing her taut nipple, teasing it between his thumb and forefinger. The ache inside began to build as the tension inside her mounted.

She lightly scraped her fingernails through his chest hairs before moving her hand lower. A ripple washed over his abdomen.

He sucked in a deep breath. "That tickles."

"What about this?" She stroked her nails over his penis. His pupils dilated, darkened with smoldering passion.

"You tell me what it feels like." He tangled his fingers in the curls between her legs, rasping his finger down her clit, then back up.

"Ahh," she struggled to get even that out as sensations of heat spread over her body.

"Only ahh?" He tugged on the skin before moving lower and slipping his finger inside her. "You're wet . . . and hot . . . and ready for me to take you."

A moan escaped her lips. "Yes."

"Not yet. I'm not quite through exploring everything you have to offer."

She was mindless as delectable sensations began to spread over her body. Damn, what he was doing to her felt so good. She began to rock her hips back and forth against the movement his finger made. She could feel herself growing wetter, losing concept of time and place as she moved her body. She closed her eyes, not caring if Logan watched her. It actually brought her more pleasure.

A kaleidoscope of color swirled around her as she came. *Petite morte.* Little death. Her body arched toward the fire. Letting it burn her. Letting it scorch every inch.

Then slowly returning to earth. It took a few minutes for her breathing to return to normal.

"Only ahh?" he asked again.

The man was full of himself, but she inwardly smiled before shrugging. "It was okay." When he stroked between her legs, she grabbed his hand and laughed. "No, no, not yet. Let me catch my breath."

He raised on one elbow. "So, what do you propose we do in the meantime?"

"I'm sure something will come up." Actually, he already was, and had been the moment they stepped off the boat and their eyes met. It felt good knowing she could turn him on so easily.

She slowly began the motion he'd started with her, sliding his foreskin down, then back up. He gasped. He was wonderful . . . larger than any man she'd ever been with. Only a few seconds passed before she knew she had to have more. She pushed him onto his back and quickly slipped a condom on him before straddling him and lowering her body over his.

He filled her, their bodies fusing. When she looked into his eyes, she saw something besides passion and need. She trembled, knowing it was more than just their bodies joining.

A sudden wind whipped across them and a need as primitive as the beginning of life centuries ago swept over her.

She rose above him, lowered her body again. He grabbed her hips, met her thrusts. Their gazes locked. The connection was complete when the first waves of an orgasm hit them both at the same time. He cried out. Liquid heat washed over her, over him.

When she collapsed to his chest, something had changed in their relationship. In her heart, she knew there was no turning back. But like a fragile limb during a storm, she wondered if what they had would break, be torn away.

She closed her eyes, listening to the steady rhythm of his heart.

The vision came swiftly. She saw blood, and she sensed death. She cried out. Logan gathered her in his arms.

"He can't hurt you. Not as long as I'm around," he fiercely whispered.

His words came from a distance, but the sound of his voice was enough to bring her out of the nightmare. After only a moment, she raised her head and lightly touched his face. Maybe Logan *would* be able to protect her . . . but could she protect him?

Chapter 27

Andrea rang Kevin's doorbell, then without waiting, pounded on the door.

"Okay, okay, give me a sec," he said from the other side. Locks slid across metal and then he was opening the door. "Unless you're delivering pizza . . ."

She pushed past him. "You have to get out of here. Grab some clothes, you're moving in with me." She whirled around and faced him.

He wasn't wearing a shirt and the top button of his jeans was undone, displaying a sexy expanse of sinewy muscles. Kevin Hart exuded raw maleness. Her mouth went dry. He gave new meaning to the term no shoes, no shirt, no service. She had a feeling most women would gladly service him without question if they could see him like this.

Her gaze returned to his face. His cocky, one-sided grin sent tremors down her body. She stopped herself at the last moment from reaching down to rub the ache between her legs. Damn, all he had to do was look at her and she was wet, willing and more than ready for him to plunge inside her.

"I knew you wouldn't be able to resist having me around all the time. What was it? My sexy looks? My witty banter? My . . ."

"John Cavenaugh blew up the police station."

The color drained from his face. He started out the door,

apparently remembered he was only half dressed, turned around, and hurried to his bedroom. "Logan? Jody?" he tossed over his shoulder as he strode past.

Crap, she shouldn't have put it so bluntly. She hurried after him. How many times did she have to open her mouth and insert her foot before she learned to watch her words?

"Andrea? They are okay, aren't they?" His hands shook as he pulled a black T-shirt over his head.

"Yes, yes, they're both fine. Well, not exactly, Cavenaugh shot Logan . . ."

She grabbed Kevin when he swayed and helped him sit on the side of the bed. Damn it!

"Not shot actually, just grazed, but if it hadn't been for him, Jody would've taken a bullet." She collapsed to the bed as the reality of her words sank in. Jody would've died today if not for Logan. She swallowed past the lump of fear that formed in her throat.

"He's okay, then?"

She nodded. "They're both fine, but her uncle escaped."

"Her uncle?"

"It's a long story. I'll explain later. She and Logan went to her grandmother's in the swamps. It's the only safe place for her right now." She stood and began pulling clothes out of his closet and stuffing them into a suitcase. "But you might not be safe. If he discovers who took the bullet intended for his niece, he might show up on your doorstep. My apartment will be safer."

"But you're her best friend. Who's to say he won't go there?"

"I can't guarantee it, but at least there will be two of us. Besides, my apartment complex looks like the recruiting offices for all the police departments. There's an ocean of blue uniforms going on and off duty."

Not waiting for Kevin's help, she dragged the suitcase off the bed. It clunked to the floor when she saw the dog sitting in the doorway quietly watching her.

"What's that?"

Kevin grabbed the suitcase, looking over his shoulder. "Blondie." Two puppies peeked around the corner, then hid again. "And her pups. Logan rescued them from the shelter." His eyes brightened. "He gave Jody one. You want one, too?"

She arched an eyebrow. "No. It's bad enough I have Jody's mutt in my car. Get what they'll need. We can't leave them behind."

"Why can't we?"

What kind of game was he playing? "They can't very well fend for themselves."

He smiled a knowing grin.

"What?"

He grabbed the suitcase and Blondie before heading for the door. "I love a good game of poker. Maybe because I can spot a bluff a mile off," he threw over his shoulder, leaving her to grab the two pups and follow.

"What the hell do you mean by that? I don't care for animals. Is that such a crime?" She glanced down at them. They looked like Muffin except one had a black spot and the other, after she picked it up, she noticed, was a male.

Mangy dogs. What the hell was she supposed to do with a dog, her three puppies, *and* Kevin all in her tiny apartment for who knew how long? She shook her head. The most she could hope for was the cops would capture John Cavenaugh today. The thought of Kevin sleeping on the other half of her bed flashed across her mind. Okay, maybe tomorrow would be okay.

She carefully cradled the puppies close to her. Bluffing? She didn't even like cards . . . or dogs. Scrabble had been fun, though.

They'd been stuck in traffic over a half hour before Fallon blew her cool. They'd parked the SUV and decided to take their chances on foot. Another half hour passed before they were close enough to see what was happening.

"Damn!" The outside of the police building where they'd watched Cavenaugh being escorted inside was intact, but surrounded by patrol cars, fire trucks and ambulances all with lights flashing. It looked more like the start of Mardi Gras, except for the injured people sitting on the steps as a paramedic on the scene triaged.

She scanned the people, but it was hard to tell if one might be her sister. Why hadn't she stayed, waited until Jody arrived. Maybe she could've averted this . . .

"You couldn't have done anything to stop it," Wade said, correctly guessing her thoughts.

"I could have . . ."

". . . done nothing. Now let's see if we can find out exactly what happened." He took her hand, lightly squeezing. "Jody is okay."

She looked into his eyes as tears formed in hers. His were full of sincerity. She knew he meant what he said, but Wade couldn't be sure Jody was okay, that she hadn't been harmed in the blast. With the back of her hand, she scrubbed across her eyes. God, she was turning into such a wuss. Of course Jody was okay. Surely God wouldn't be that cruel.

They hurried up the steps and started inside but were stopped by a cop. In unison, they flashed their IDs and the officer stepped to the side.

The front had been spared except for the thick layer of dust that must've barreled its way from the back. They went directly to the man issuing orders. His once dark suit was now a light gray, and he didn't look one bit happy about the events that had taken place today.

"I need to see the captain." She squared her shoulders and didn't back down when he turned a fierce glare in her direction.

"I'm the captain and right now I'm just a little busy. If you hadn't noticed, someone tried to blow up my station," he ground out.

"It was John Cavenaugh, the prisoner extradited from

Texas." She knew without a doubt he was the cause of the explosion.

His eyes narrowed. "What do you know about it?"

"We followed the car that brought him here."

"The sheriff and the agent?"

She nodded. "John Cavenaugh is my uncle."

Captain Williams's lips thinned. "How many nieces does this man have?"

He knew about Jody. The room blurred.

Wade caught her arm to steady her. "I think we need to talk where we won't be interrupted."

His hesitation was brief. Maybe he saw something in her eyes that hinted there was a lot more to the story than he knew.

He nodded toward the other side of the building, away from the confusion going on around them. "We'll go to one of the vacant offices." They didn't say anything else until he walked down the hall and inside one of the rooms. He closed the door firmly behind them. After they were seated across from him he said, "Okay, I think you better tell me exactly what's going on."

"John Cavenaugh is my uncle."

"And?"

"About twenty years ago, he murdered my father. I'd gone to the store, and as I was returning, I saw him leaving our house." She gripped the arms of the chair. The room closed in on her, making it difficult to breathe. She shut her eyes, and for a moment, she could almost see her father's face. Smiling and laughing, that was her daddy. He'd taken over the role of mother and father when Angelina had passed away. He'd been a good man. Too good to die like he had.

Wade squeezed her hand, gently bringing her back to the present. She opened her eyes and looked at him. Another damn fine man had come into her life. She'd make sure this one was around for a long time.

She drew in a deep breath. "When I went inside, I saw my

father lying on the floor, a puddle of blood near his head. My sister was next to him."

"You didn't go to the police?" the captain asked.

She laughed without mirth. "Oh, yeah, that was the first place I went. They put me in a room. I got tired of waiting. I wanted someone to tell me it was all a bad dream, but when I went to the window and looked out, I saw my uncle laughing and talking to one of the officers. Then my uncle turned and walked away. I knew my life wasn't worth a wooden nickel. I ran away, took a name from a tombstone, left town and didn't return . . . until today."

"And your sister is Jody Dupree." Captain Williams stated.

She wanted to ask if Jody had been injured or maybe . . . maybe . . . The words choked up in her throat.

Please, God, don't take her away from me again. A single tear ran down her face. She hurriedly brushed it away. What was her life coming to? She never cried . . . never. Strength had always been her shield. But right now she didn't feel very strong.

Chapter 28

Logan eased from the bed they'd moved to after making love outside. Careful not to wake Jody, he stepped to the cabin's porch, stretching his hands high above his head and drawing in a deep breath. Jody was right—there was something to be said about the freedom of living in the middle of nowhere. . . .

"You be makin' good babies," the old woman spoke in a crackly voice after she rounded the corner. She wore a dark shirt, and a tattered, full skirt. A bright red bandanna covered most of her gray hair. When she grinned, he saw she was missing a front tooth.

"Jesus! You scared the hell out of me." Suddenly realizing what she'd said, and the fact he was still bare-assed naked, he quickly covered himself with his hands. "Who the hell are you?" He took a quick step back and rammed his butt into the cabin.

All the stories his two older brothers had scared him with when he was growing up were right in front of him, clomping up the steps. She'd spoken in an odd mixture of Cajun and broken English, with a slight French accent. He expected the hag to lay a curse on him at any moment.

Instead of answering, she stepped closer, her eyes narrowing on his blood-tinged bandage. He took another step back. She frowned.

"That be gettin' da rot if you don't take care. I make you better."

Yeah, right, like that was going to happen. He looked at her hands. They were clean, the fingernails trimmed. In fact, even though her clothes looked as old as her, they weren't dirty. He still wasn't going to let her touch him.

"*Mamere,*" Jody spoke softly from the doorway.

Her grandmother? For some reason he'd thought the old woman was dead. Apparently not—unless she'd been resurrected, and he wasn't real sure that wasn't the case.

Jody stepped to the porch. She'd slipped on a thin, pale blue dress. There was little doubt she wore anything else. Her breasts strained against the fabric, stretching it taut, the aureoles shadowed. It might be a simple dress, but she looked sexy as hell. Ah, damn, in another minute the old lady was going to see a little more of him than she might expect.

Jody's grandmother looked between the two of them, then returned her gaze solely to her granddaughter. "You found him, then. I been wonderin' if you be lettin' him slip away. The tea leaves say he coming. Now we go inside. Let the poor fella dress before he be catchin' his death."

That sounded like a good idea to him, in fact, the sooner the better. Damn, there was something very uncomfortable about standing in front of two females without any clothes on, especially when one was older than dirt.

He let out his breath when they went inside. His clothes were scattered all over the yard, and now he was paranoid. He hurried off the porch, grabbed his briefs and jerked them on before he began to relax. He slid his pants on one leg, then hopped around getting the other one in.

"Isolated, my ass," he mumbled as he tugged the zipper up and snapped the waistband. "I don't know why the hell anyone would want to live in the boonies. Friggin' alligators. Crazy old women who sneak up on unsuspecting people." He scooped up his shirt and shoes and started back toward the cabin, but stopped in his tracks before he'd taken more than two steps.

Jody leaned against the top rail of the porch. God, she was so damn beautiful she made him ache. As he walked toward her, he noticed the shadows in her eyes. He'd hoped she could forget about John Cavenaugh out here, but apparently even in the bayou, she wasn't free from this morning's events. Not that he could blame her. Crap, her own uncle had tried to kill her a few hours ago.

When her gaze strayed to his arm, he knew she'd only put it from her mind for a little while. "He won't follow us here. You said he was afraid of the swamps," he said, trying to reassure her.

Her grandmother stepped back to the porch. "You both be safe for now," she agreed. She pulled up a stool and motioned for him to sit.

His eyes narrowed. "What do you know about it?"

"The dead people they be talkin'. They tell me John Cavenaugh he come back in chains, but then he break what binds him."

Dead people talking to her. Of course, he should've known. *What the hell was he doing in the middle of the swamp about to let this crazy old woman see to his injury?*

"He won't be comin' out here none too soon. I remember the alligator almost got him once. *Capon!* Always he be the coward. Afraid of what's in de swamps." Her gaze fell on Jody. "That's why I be bringin' you here when you was shot and shocked. This be where it's safe. You stay until he crawl back to his hole." She nodded toward Logan's arm. "What happened to your fella?"

"He saved my life, *Mamere.* John Cavenaugh would've killed me." She clenched her fists.

The grandmother nodded. "They told me someone be helpin' you this time that not be me." Again she motioned for him to sit.

"She'll doctor your arm," Jody told him.

He gritted his teeth. He could do this. If nothing else because Jody didn't look overly concerned her grandmother would be seeing to his wound. *That was a good sign, right?* He stepped to the porch and took a seat.

She was surprisingly gentle as she cut away the bandage. He found himself relaxing. Odd, but a sweet fragrance lingered about her. His mother had her own herb garden, and after gathering what she needed, she would often carry the aroma whether it was sage, mint, or lavender. The old woman reminded him of her. So maybe sometimes it was best if he listened with his heart, instead of his head.

"It's good," the grandmother said as she removed the bandage.

"It's just a graze," he agreed.

"I'm not talkin' about the wound. It's good you trust *Mamere*."

He looked at Jody, who smiled back at him. Did her grandmother read minds?

"I read people," she told him as if he'd spoken his thoughts aloud. "They call me witch." She shook her head. "Foolishness. People don't pay attention to life . . . or death. It's all around, everywhere you look. Just got to listen."

She went inside. He glanced over his shoulder.

"*Mamere* is meticulous about washing her hands when she's taking care of someone. She'll dispose of your bandage and clean her hands before returning." Jody leaned her hip against the wooden rail.

Meticulous, and a mind reader. She was a little too accurate to suit him. An uncomfortable feeling rippled down his spine. "Are you sure she can't read my mind?" he whispered.

"Why?" she asked in a sultry voice. "Are you having impure thoughts?" She drew her tongue across her lips before scraping her teeth over her lower one.

A moment passed before he realized if he wanted to live, he had to breathe. He inhaled, then frowned. "That's not funny."

Their conversation was cut short when the grandmother returned. She carried a basket with her this time. He glanced inside. There were jars with powders and fat little bags. She set it on the porch before removing one of the bags and loosened the drawstring. Pinching some of the powder between her thumb and forefinger, she then sprinkled it on his wound.

"What exactly is that?" It had a foul odor.

"Healing powders. Keeps the rot away. Make it all better." She bandaged his arm again. "Keep it clean," she warned.

He wondered if she spoke about his wound or his relationship with Jody.

She went back inside, presumably to wash again. Jody grabbed his hand and tugged him to his feet, leading him away from the cabin.

"It doesn't bother you that if your grandmother had arrived an hour earlier she would've caught us making love?"

She shook her head. "But she didn't."

He ruffled the back of her hair, earning a smile. He loved the way she smiled. Out here she seemed like a different person than the one he knew in the city. She was more relaxed, less on edge.

"I love it out here," she said and for a moment he thought maybe she'd read his mind, too. "It's so different from the noise of the city." She looked up at him. "Do you feel it?"

"What?" He smiled into her face.

"Nature." She sighed. "When I was growing up she had a voice all her own and she would talk to me . . . calm me when I was scared, heal me when I was hurt."

"Your grandmother's herbs?"

She nodded. "You can't take Mother Nature for granted, or think that all this is just for you, that you don't have to take care of it. She demands respect. In return, she gifts you with the flowers and the trees, the sunshine and the rain." She glanced around, inhaling a deep, cleansing breath.

He wrapped her in his arms, pulling her back until she

leaned against his chest. It felt so right having her this close, feeling the heat of her body.

"Are you going to call your editor?"

He'd known she was going to ask, knew that she wondered why he wasn't calling his boss about the explosion. He'd seen at least two reporters arrive on scene as they left. They would've already covered the story—the prisoner's dash for freedom. His gut twisted into knots. By the time he had a chance to call, it was too late. What he could report, without involving Jody, would be old news by now.

He drew in a deep breath. "No, I'm not going to call him." A strange feeling settled over him. Maybe he was absorbing some of Jody's second sight because he couldn't see himself getting the job of assistant editor now and he could almost visualize the gloating look on Hank's face.

Andrea glared down at the mutt chewing on her new house shoe. "And just exactly what do you think you're doing?" She moved her basket of clean laundry to her other hip and bent to retrieve her shoe from the pup's jaws. A tug-of-war ensued.

"Here, let me help." Kevin took the basket before she could utter a protest.

"I don't need your help," she grumbled, letting go of her slipper. Muffin apparently took that as a sign it was hers to do with as she wanted. Andrea didn't really like the slippers *that* much.

She stood and followed Kevin. "I can carry my own clothes, you know." He'd been underfoot ever since she'd picked him up at Logan's apartment. How did one *not* think about sex with him around?

Her gaze moved to his butt. Damn, he had a great-looking butt. She was having butt envy. No man should have a butt that firm, that . . . that . . .

He stopped. She skidded to a halt before she plowed over

the very part of his anatomy she'd been admiring only moments before.

"Yeah, but now I can tell everyone I got in your underwear." He set the basket on her bed and held up a black thong by one crooked finger.

She sat on the side of the bed and crossed her legs. "You've done more than get in my underwear, cowboy," she lazily stated.

He flopped down on the side of the bed, kicked his shoes off without untying the laces, and rested against the pillows. "That seems like forever." He leaned forward and scooted her until she was snuggled in his arms. "I need lots of lovin', woman," he growled close to her ear.

She cast her gaze upward as shivers of anticipation tingled down her spine. Damn, he was cute and sexy and . . .

She sighed.

"What's the matter," he asked, brushing his fingers through her hair.

"I'm worried."

"About Logan and Jody?"

She nodded.

"Do you suppose they're okay? I don't see how anyone could survive in the swamp. I mean, I've never been there, but I think I'd rather take my chances here in the city."

"That's not the part I'm worried about. They'll be fine. Remember, Jody spent most of her life there. It's her uncle who scares the hell out of me."

She sat forward, drawing her knees up and resting her head on them. Twenty-four hours had passed and still not a damn thing on Cavenaugh. It was like he'd vanished from the face of the earth. She narrowed her eyes. She'd like to permanently vanish him from the face of the earth.

"When I brought the laundry up, I saw Tony in the hall," she said. "He said the captain's sure someone on the inside helped him. That really pisses me off. It's bad enough being a criminal, but a bad cop—the one who's there to serve and protect, really burns me up. When they discover who it was, the captain should hang him up by his balls."

"Does he have any ideas?"

"Doubtful or he'd already be behind bars. Something else happened before the explosion, though. I can't get it out of my mind. A woman was asking about Jody. I think she might have had something to do with it. She claimed to be a friend. Yeah, right. If she was a friend, I'd know, and I'd never seen her before."

"Maybe Cavenaugh has a girlfriend? Do you think they might know where Jody and Logan are hiding?"

She caught the trace of worry in his voice and glanced at him. "Even if they do, it won't do them much good. People stick together out there. They won't lead anyone to the cabin. Jody's grandmother is respected for healing people." She shook her head. "Unless he has an experienced guide, John Cavenaugh will never be able to find them. They're safe until he's caught." She just hoped like hell that would be soon, but for now, he was out there somewhere, probably laughing because he'd escaped.

Fear warred with anger. Her best friend was in danger. She'd told Jody the visions were probably nothing more than the fact Jody hated letting anyone get close to her. Damn it, she'd never been wrong before. Why had she convinced Jody the visions were nothing?

She sniffed. Because Jody had heeded her advice she'd almost been killed. Some friend she'd turned out to be.

Kevin's strong arms wrapped around her, pulling her back to lie beside him. "Shh, it'll be okay. Logan will keep her safe."

"He'd better or I'll kick his *tcheue.*"

Chapter 29

She's hiding in the swamps, Cavenaugh thought to himself. At that witch's cabin. Or maybe the more appropriate word would be bitch. He never had liked that old woman. Something spooky about the way she'd looked at him the one time they'd met.

That's where they were, though. Jody and the man who took the bullet intended for her. His instincts were rarely wrong. He'd bet his father's soul on it that they were hiding there. That is, if he hadn't already bet it a long time ago and lost. Not that he really cared. Why should he, his pa certainly never had. He'd given new meaning to the word bastard.

Paul Leger strode to the window and looked out, drawing Cavenaugh's attention. Ray had warned him to watch his back around the New Orleans cop. From what Ray had picked up from different sources, Paul would sell out his own mother if it meant he'd be living a life in the spotlight and had lots of money to support his habits.

Cavenaugh watched him. The cop had changed his position at least a dozen or so times since arriving at the shanty. He'd sit for a few minutes, then jump to his feet and pace for a while. The man was clearly nervous. Maybe he regretted helping him. If he thought for one minute Paul was going to change his mind and turn him in, he'd slit his throat right here and now.

Except he might still prove useful, so he'd wait until he was ready to leave the country, then he'd kill him. After he'd gotten rid of his darling nieces—in one way or another.

He wanted to teach Fallon a lesson. She was a real bitch; besides, she looked too much like Phillip. Her father had been a regular goddamned saint. His half brother had gotten everything he wanted from his father and their mother.

Cavenaugh's father had been the alcoholic whose drunken rages were directed more at him than anyone. He closed his eyes, refusing to let the memories overcome him. The nights his pa would stagger home, grab his fucking belt, and start beating him—at least once every damn week. He curled his hands into fists, but before his anger had time to build, he forced himself to relax.

In the end, his father had gotten what he deserved. Lesson number one: don't ever drink so much you fall asleep on the railroad tracks. He'd love to have seen the look on his father's face. At least, he'd always hoped his old man had opened his eyes at the last minute to see the train barreling down on top of him. God, that had to hurt like a son of a bitch. He grinned.

Less than a year later, his mother remarried, and Phillip was born the following year. Little bastard! The golden boy did everything right. He got all the attention, all the love. The only time his mother noticed her eldest son was if he did something wrong. In the beginning, he'd wanted her to notice him, too. Later, even before he reached twelve years of age, he decided it was a hell of a lot more fun being bad than good.

"You're not going to hang around much longer, are you?" Paul asked as he turned from the window.

Cavenaugh forced his attention back to the present. "I have a couple of things that I need to . . . eliminate before leaving. Why? Getting nervous?"

He shuffled his feet. "No, of course not, but I wouldn't

want you to stay so long that you make a mistake and get caught."

His eyes narrowed slightly. "You not be thinkin' 'bout turning old Cavenaugh in, eh?" His words were just above a whisper, but the other man heard.

Paul wiped the bead of sweat that ran down the side of his face and took a step backward. "Me? Of course not." A short, strangled noise that might have been an attempt at laughter escaped his lips. "Not when you're going to finance my political career. That would be pretty stupid since I made sure the bomb would go off at the right time. You can trust me."

Like he did one of the gators in the swamp. Before he could comment, the door opened. Cavenaugh looked up. Ray Argget, he'd done the grunt work, no matter what Paul would like him to believe. He glanced between Ray and Paul. It was apparent there was no love lost between them. It didn't matter to Ray that Paul was on the take, he was still a cop, and Ray had had too many run-ins with the law to ever like one of the men in blue.

Cavenaugh had to agree. There was something sneaky about a dirty cop. Even with bad guys there was some semblance of a code everyone lived by, even though it was real thin.

Cavenaugh nodded toward Ray. "You find out anything?"

Again, Ray cast a glance in Paul's direction.

Cavenaugh chuckled. "You can talk. Paul is okay."

Besides being incredibly stupid, he silently added. Didn't he realize when he'd agreed to help Ray plant the explosive device, he was crawling into a nest of vipers? Probably not. He was too interested in financial backing for his political career.

"The DEA agent and the sheriff have vanished." He shook his greasy mane of black hair.

"Safe house." Paul volunteered.

They both looked at him. He glanced down, shuffled his feet again.

"If she told Captain Williams what was going on," Paul explained, "then he'd put her someplace safe where you couldn't find her." He shrugged his shoulders. "That's my guess. No one's talking. Captain Williams isn't stupid. He knows you had inside help."

Cavenaugh hated to admit Fallon might be out of his reach. His one consolation was the fact that staying in a safe house had to piss her off.

"What about Jody Dupree?"

Paul's eyes widened. "Jody? What's she got to do with anything?"

"She's my niece."

Paul's smile didn't reach his eyes. "And she's always acted as if she were better than everyone."

"And now that you find out we're related you think she isn't?"

"No . . . I mean, that's not what I meant at all."

Ray frowned at Paul, then addressed Cavenaugh's question as if Paul hadn't opened his mouth. "No trace." He went to the dorm-sized refrigerator and got a beer. He twisted the cap off and tossed it toward the trash. It missed. He didn't bother to pick it up.

"She's probably at her grandmother's." Paul looked like he wished he'd kept his mouth shut . . . again.

"What do you know about her?"

"We dated for a few months."

Cavenaugh ground his teeth. The thought of this piece of shit with his hands on Jody turned his stomach. God, couldn't she see through his pretty, golden-boy persona?

But no, Angelina hadn't been able to see that Phillip was bad for her. All she'd seen was the mask he wore. Everyone thought his half brother was kind and gentle.

Look where it had gotten Angelina. Eaten up with disease. If she'd chosen him, he would've made sure she got the care she needed to make her well, but no, he wasn't good enough.

Angelina. He sighed. With her straight black hair brushing

her shoulders. Her beautiful smile. Sweet Angelina. He still remembered what it had felt like to hold her in his arms. She'd been the one good thing in his life.

His eyes clouded over. Anger rushed over him like a tidal wave.

Angelina was with her mother somewhere in that filthy swamp. But he'd save her this time. Find a way to make her love him again. And he'd take her away from this place, this country. He'd drape her in jewels and mink. His Angelina. She wouldn't even look at Phillip. She'd be all his.

All his.

Chapter 30

"Your fella has him one big appetite. That be a good thing." *Mamere* pushed the bowl toward him. But Logan shook his head.

"I can't eat another bite. It was delicious."

"Then you two be walkin' under the stars. Don't need to hang around an old woman what has one foot in the grave. Don't be forgettin' to put on my lotion what keep the skeeters away."

Jody had known her grandmother would like Logan. "*Mamere*, you'll outlive us all and we already put some lotion on." But she took her advice and motioned for Logan to follow her, grabbing a blanket as they left the cabin.

After they were a good distance away, she unfolded it under a tree with low hanging branches and spread it out. He sat down first, leaning against the tree, and motioned for her to join him. She didn't waste any time as she snuggled next to him.

The night sounds serenaded them. Crickets chirped, an owl hooted somewhere off to their right. Just being out in the fresh air made her relax. Her home here was so unlike the sights and smells of the city.

"I think I'm beginning to like your swamp, Jody Dupree."

She sighed. "I'm glad. And thank you for eating so much of the meal *Mamere* prepared. That was the best compliment you could give her. I don't think either of us has seen anyone eat that much bullfrog."

A few seconds passed before she realized something wasn't quite right. Had she said something wrong?

"Logan?"

"I thought I was eating fried chicken."

She turned until she was lying with her head in his lap, looking up at him. "Chicken?" She chuckled. It took her a bit to rein in her laughter. "It tastes a lot like chicken."

He made a face. "Frog? You're serious?"

"Sorry. We need the chickens for eggs. The bullfrogs get pretty big. We don't waste any of the meat." He was starting to look a little green himself.

"I think I could've done without that information. Could we change the subject?"

"What do you want to talk about?"

"It doesn't matter." He was thoughtful for a moment. "You've mentioned your sister before, but you never say much; tell me about her."

She closed her eyes, expecting the pain to wash over her. Odd, but it wasn't there, only a feeling of peace. She sorted through her thoughts for a moment, then began to speak. "Sometimes I think I feel her—like a twin might. That she's nearby, but it's just wishful thinking. I like to imagine she's still alive." She smiled. "She was so damn gutsy."

He brushed a leaf from her hair. Their eyes met. She took his hand and clasped it close to her.

"Once, some of the neighborhood boys dared her to climb the water tower."

"Did she?"

"Oh, she did more than that. She'd carried a black marker with her and with bold strokes, she scrawled her name and that she'd been there first. No matter who came after her, she'd been the one who climbed the tower first."

"You must have been a lot alike."

"Me? No, she was brave and daring. I just stood in her

shadow and bragged to everyone that she was my big sister. God, I loved her . . . still do. She was the one who didn't back down from anyone."

"But then you grew up. You became a cop who wasn't afraid of going into a house filled with gas and not knowing exactly what you would find. Then you stopped a burglary in progress and saved a woman's dignity and possibly her life. Daring . . . brave? Yeah, I think you and your sister are a lot alike."

"I think I like you, Logan Hart."

He squeezed her. "Tell me about what it was like, growing up in the city." He stroked her hair. "Before your uncle changed things."

She'd talked about the day her father was murdered. Andrea knew the story, and now Logan, but she'd never really spoken about her life before the tragedy. She closed her eyes and slipped back in time.

"I vaguely remember my mother. Sometimes a memory of things she used to do will flash across my mind, but I can't quite bring her into focus. I remember the love, the way she used to pull me onto her lap when she'd sit in the big old rocker." She hadn't thought about her mother in years. But as the memories came flooding back so did a sense of belonging, feeling special. "*Mamere* says I look like her. Sometimes she calls me by my mother's name. When I see my reflection in the mirror I think I catch a glimpse of what she'd looked like, but I'm not quite sure."

"You said your sister looks like your father?"

She nodded. "We both had dark hair, but that's where the resemblance ended. I always thought of her as being taller, stronger, prettier. She was fourteen, and to a seven-year-old, that seemed very mature." She smiled, wondering what their relationship would've been like had they'd grown up together.

"Yeah," Logan brought her out of her musings. "I thought the same thing about my older brothers. Gabe and Lane used to haul hay from one of our pastures to the barn. I was about eleven and I'd drive Dad's old beat-up Chevy pickup around the field while they tossed bales of hay and stacked them in the bed. They'd lift a sixty-five-pound bale above their heads and toss it up to the top row like it was baled feathers. I thought they had to be the strongest men alive."

"You miss them a lot, don't you?" She heard the wistfulness in his voice.

"I'll go back this summer on vacation. They live close to my parents."

"And you? How did you break away from ranching and become a reporter?"

He looked down at her and smiled. The sun was setting, his face shadowed, but she could still make out his features enough that her heart skipped a beat.

"I like reporting the news. I think people are interesting. Besides, with two older brothers, and two younger siblings, I had to find something that would keep me from getting lost in the shuffle. I started out on the school newspaper. At first it was a hobby, but later, it became a dream."

She heard the enthusiasm in his voice and once again a guilty tremor ran down her spine. She reached up, caressing his face. "I'm sorry."

"For what?" He turned her hand over in his and kissed the palm.

Excitement quickened her pulse. She refocused on what she wanted . . . no, needed to say. "Because you killed the story about my uncle . . . about my family. That could've landed you the job you wanted."

He shook his head. "Sometimes it's better to let go of a story if it's going to damage someone's life. If you'd been a stranger off the street, I would've done the same thing."

Conversation ceased as he continued to kiss her palm. Her thought process clogged. After a few seconds, kissing her palm no longer satisfied him.

Logan pulled her nearer to him, his warm breath fanning

her cheeks just before his mouth covered hers. She sighed, drinking in the sweetness of his lips against hers, his tongue exploring her mouth. She slipped her hand around his neck and tugged him closer.

When he ended the kiss, it was all she could do to take a deep breath. Languidness stole over her . . . until he ran his hand over her breasts. For a moment, she lost herself in the way he touched her, the small explosions of heat that coursed their way down her body to settle between her legs, but before he could go much further, she sat up, quickly straddling his hips. She moved her body over and against him and was rewarded when he groaned.

"That's nice."

She chuckled lightly. "Only nice?"

"Better than nice." She could feel his smile even if she couldn't see it as darkness closed itself around them.

He was right, though. This was nice. Logan was already hard. Spasms of pleasure swept over her. He unbuttoned the front of her dress, gathering her breasts in his hands, testing the weight, rubbing his thumbs across the nipples. She gasped. He moved his hands to her thighs, grabbing her bottom and massaging the cheeks of her butt.

In one swift movement, she scooted back and quickly found the zipper of his pants. She tugged it down and freed him. Even though it was dark, she closed her eyes, relishing the feel of him in her hands. Knowing that she had full control of his body as he arched upward, straining for more. She didn't make him wait long but retrieved a condom from his pocket and quickly slipped it on him, marveling at how good she was getting at putting a condom on him. As soon as it was done, she nudged him toward the heat of her body.

He filled her, making her gasp with delight. "God, this is so damn good."

He didn't comment, only raised his hips. He sank farther inside her. She looked up. The stars twinkled down on them, as if casting their approval. She drew in a deep breath of air and began to move her body faster over his.

"Yes, that's it," he told her, his words passion-filled, raspy, scraping across her nerve endings with a sensuous touch all their own.

The friction inside her built—taking her higher and higher. She felt as if she rode the crest of a wave, and when it came crashing over her, she drew in a deep breath and rode it until the end. Only then could she draw air into her lungs.

Logan clenched her buttocks and cried out as his release followed seconds later. She vaguely heard his labored breathing as she collapsed against his chest.

After a moment, he kissed the top of her head. "I've never felt this way with another woman," he whispered.

She bit her bottom lip. Finally, something right was happening in her life. Her feelings for Logan were beautiful and pure and decent.

Would her uncle manage to take something she loved once more? Would he, could he, steal it all away from her? Determination burned inside her. No, she wouldn't let that happen. Not again.

Andrea watched Kevin; he didn't look excited with his first trip to the swamp. He gripped both sides of the pirogue as if he'd never been in a boat before. When he looked up, she nodded toward his hands. "You might want to bring in your hands, *cher.*"

He looked momentarily confused. "Why, all I see are a bunch of logs and green scum. If you're trying to scare me, it won't work. I've already heard all the local legends about the swamps."

"Suit yourself, *cher.*" He looked pretty sure of himself. She had to admit, she liked showing the swamp to people who liked to pretend they weren't nervous being there. And right now, Kevin seemed pretty cool with his surroundings. Time to burst his bubble. "But, *cher,* one of your logs be swimming toward your pretty hands. Make sure that gator don't want to have a snack."

Kevin frowned, but stared at one of the objects he'd called a log. She waited patiently for realization to sink in. It only took a moment.

"Shit!" He whipped his hands inside the boat. "That log is an alligator. What the hell are we doing out here in the first place? Normal people don't live this close to nature."

"Are you saying I'm not normal? I did grow up not far from here, *cher.*"

"Okay, maybe you're normal, but why the hell would anyone live where there were alligators? It isn't safe."

"And rattlesnakes are?"

"At least they warn you before they strike," he said as he eyed an alligator sliding silently into the water.

She couldn't blame him for feeling the way he did. There was no love lost between her and where she'd grown up. She much preferred the bright lights of New Orleans.

"How much farther?"

"We're here." She pushed with the pole until they were close to the bank. After jumping out of the boat, she tied it off. As she straightened, she glanced around. All was quiet.

"I think I'll just wait in the boat."

She shrugged. "Whatever. Just be careful a gator don't be deciding on keeping you company and crawl in there with you, *cher.*"

She hid her smile as he came to his feet, wobbled slightly, grabbed the side of the boat, then launched himself onto land.

"*Fie,* Andrea. You shouldn't tease," Jody admonished as she stepped from behind a tree.

"But he made it too easy." She surveyed her friend. Jody looked rested . . . and happy. Logan stepped to her side. Andrea noticed everything about the way he stood, seemed protective of Jody, as it should be. There was no jealousy on her part. She knew her friendship with Jody was strong.

Jody watched as Andrea's gaze went between her and Logan. When Andrea smiled, she released her breath. For a minute she was worried about how Andrea would take Logan's presence in her life. She shouldn't have. There was room in Andrea's heart for more than one person.

"Has he been captured?" Jody asked, unable to take the suspense of not knowing a second longer.

Andrea shook her head. "I'm sorry, *chere.*"

She tensed. Damn it, why wasn't she out there searching? But when her glance fell on Logan, and the bandage on his arm, she had her reason. "It hasn't been that long. They'll catch him," she stated with more confidence than she felt.

"They have roadblocks set up, they put his name and description over the radio and TV, and it made the front page of the newspaper," Kevin said.

Andrea nodded her agreement. "There wasn't any mention of your father, Jody. They don't know you're related."

Her friend's words didn't register, only Kevin's. Jody cringed. The front page. That should've been Logan's story.

"It's only a matter of time before he's behind bars," Andrea told her.

"Yeah, only a matter of time." She once thought she had plenty of time if she didn't make any ripples in the water. Look where it had gotten her. Her uncle had still found out she was alive no matter how well she had tried to keep her personal life to herself.

Logan squeezed her shoulder reassuringly, but it didn't bring her much comfort. She'd cost him the job he wanted. That knowledge knotted her stomach.

Chapter 31

One of Cavenaugh's rules was *silence*. Let the other person stumble around for words. People usually told him more than they wanted to reveal. It worked nearly every time.

Paul had been babbling since his arrival a few minutes ago. Fool! He still didn't realize who he was dealing with.

"You have to leave," Paul warned. "It's too risky. Captain Williams is starting to ask questions. I don't like it." Paul stopped pacing long enough to glare at Cavenaugh, but only for a few seconds before looking away.

Coward! He should've slit his throat long ago. He'd become a liability—he just didn't know it yet. He inwardly sneered. Him with his pretty white teeth. Cavenaugh's hands curled into fists.

He wouldn't have Angelina running back to his half brother. Why couldn't she see he wasn't a man, but a worm? A slimy little worm he could crush beneath his boot. But not yet. No, he still might be of some use.

Cavenaugh smiled. "Soon, then you can move on with your life. Go into politics." He couldn't remember Phillip wanting to run for office. He shook his head to clear it. Not Phillip, his half brother, but Paul, stood before him.

This place was casting an evil spell over him. He ran a hand through his thinning hair and settled back against the sofa cushions. Phillip was dead. His Angelina was dead. He grimaced, and this maggot stood before him.

"Yeah, well, sometimes I wonder if it's worth all this trouble," Paul mumbled.

"Having second thoughts?"

Apparently realizing he'd crossed over the line, his face paled and he began to stutter. "No, it's . . . uh . . . not that. Of course I'll help as long as you need me."

Maybe he would let him live a while longer—if he had the right information. "What about this friend of Jody's?"

"Andrea. They're real tight. Like sisters. There was a man . with her, and they went into the swamp together. Probably to meet Jody."

Cavenaugh took a few deep breaths to keep from losing his temper. He was surrounded by idiots. Paul was right, he *would* make a good politician.

"Did you follow them?"

Paul ran his hand over his dark blue suit as if it might have a speck of dust on it. That was another thing he didn't like about the cop, he was spending a lot of money on his wardrobe. He looked like he'd maxed out his credit cards on tailored suits and Italian loafers. He even sported a small diamond ring on his pinkie.

"I wouldn't go into the swamp if you paid me." A delicate shudder swept over him.

"But that's exactly what I am doing," Cavenaugh scornfully reminded. "Paying you."

"Well . . . of course." He cleared his throat. "I only meant that I didn't see any reason to follow them. I'd just get lost. I'm not familiar with that area."

He didn't have to finish his sentence, Cavenaugh easily filled in the blanks. Nor did he intend to follow anyone into the swamp. Maybe he'd make a liar out of him. One push over the side of the boat and there would be no evidence he'd had any dealings with the man. The alligators would take care of that.

"Next time this friend of Jody's decides to go into the swamp, I want to know immediately."

"Yeah, sure. Whatever you say. You're the boss." He cleared his throat. "I'd better be going. I don't want anyone to get suspicious." He waited all of two seconds before leaving.

"You want me to get rid of him?" Ray asked, stepping from the other room.

"No, he might come in handy."

"Say the word and I'll slit his throat." His face split into a wide grin. "Might be kind of fun watching him bleed all over that pretty suit."

Cavenaugh began to laugh, the sound echoing through the small shanty. He could see Paul now, the look of shock on his face.

Damn, he'd been here too long. Ray was starting to grow on him.

"No, we wait a bit. See if he still has some use. Then maybe I let you slit his throat, *mon ami.*"

Chapter 32

"I can't wait any longer." Fallon went to the coffeepot and poured herself another cup. "I want to see my sister. For all we know, Cavenaugh could've left the country." Damn it, she felt about as useless as an empty gun. She'd let Wade talk her into staying longer in the safe house Captain Williams had acquired just for them. Only a handful of people knew it existed.

He came up behind her and wrapped her in his arms. "I know, and I understand how hard this is for you."

Yes, he would. He seemed to know her so well. How her mind worked . . . the exact place to touch when they made love.

She turned in his arms, raising her lips to his. He met her halfway. At first the kiss was gentle—a brushing of lips, but soon that wasn't enough. She scraped her tongue across his lower lip before dipping inside his mouth . . . tasting him.

Before the kiss could go any further, she pulled away, resting her head against his chest. "I love you, Wade Tanner."

He drew in a deep breath.

"What?" She looked up at him.

He shook his head. "You don't say the words very often out loud. I like hearing you say them."

"But I've said I love you all along." She touched her chest. "I've spoken it for a long time here." Damn, what if he hadn't wanted to hear her declaration? "Not that I'm wanting a commitment or anything."

"Oh, you don't?"

She pulled out of his arms and went to the counter, taking a drink of her coffee. She grimaced. It had been the last cup, and barely lukewarm. She dumped it in the sink.

All the while, she tried not to imagine a world without Wade Tanner at her side. It didn't work. The thought of going their separate ways put a very big dent in her heart. That's okay, she wouldn't put any pressure on him, or make him feel obligated.

Stiff upper lip. She squared her shoulders. "Nope, I don't need a ring or—"

"Maybe I do," he spoke quietly.

Slowly, she turned and faced him. "What?"

He went to her, caressing the side of her face with the back of his hand. "I love you more than life itself. Fallon Hargis Brigitte Dupree, and any other name you've used, will you marry me?"

Tears welled in her eyes.

Damn, she *was* becoming a wuss. Somehow it didn't really matter. She nodded. "Yeah, I'll marry you, Wade Tanner."

He kissed her again, taking her breath away and giving her all the love she hadn't let herself feel for so long. God, she loved him so much.

He pulled her close, hugging her tight after the kiss ended. "Let's go find that friend of your sister's. Hell, it's not like either one of us has ever played by the rules. Why start now?"

She grinned. "You're right. I'd hate to mess up my splotchy record now."

It took them longer to convince Captain Williams they were doing the right thing, but Fallon had always been known for her skills of persuasion and it wasn't long before they were driving through the entrance of Andrea's apartment complex.

Wade pulled into one of the parking spaces and cut the engine. Taking a deep breath, she got out of the car, giving the apartment complex a cursory glance: well-manicured grounds, a few flowers here and there, low bushes. The buildings were nice enough. Each one had a small balcony.

"You sure this is what you want to do?" Wade asked as he locked the car.

She nodded. "Positive."

Captain Williams had wanted to send a uniform along with them, but she'd refused. Hell, if a DEA agent and sheriff couldn't protect themselves then they needed to get shot.

An officer stepped out of the building and she wondered briefly if the captain had changed his mind, but then another emerged. Well, you couldn't get any safer than living in a complex with a bunch of your coworkers, especially if they were cops.

They went inside and took the stairs to the fourth floor. Before pushing the doorbell, she squeezed Wade's hand and took a deep breath.

A few seconds later, there was the sound of a lock turning. The blonde from the other day opened the door. She took one look at Fallon and started to slam the door shut, but Fallon caught it and pushed her way inside.

"You know, you're not the friendliest person I've ever met."

"If you don't leave right now I'll scream and you'll have more cops in here than you can handle." There was a slight quiver in her voice.

A man stepped from a back room. "Is there a problem?" The tone of his voice said there better not be.

Fallon's gaze ran over him. Not bad. Six-four or thereabout, dark hair, sexy. Jody's friend had good taste in men.

"No problem," Fallon told him. "I just need to talk to Andrea."

The woman's eyes narrowed. "How do you know my name?" Before Fallon could speak, Andrea began explaining to the man behind her. "This is the woman that asked me about Jody the other day. You know," she emphasized. "The

woman claiming to be Jody's *friend*." Andrea's expression
dared her to deny her declaration from a few days ago.

"I lied," Fallon calmly stated.

"Ha! I knew it!"

"I'm not her friend. I'm her sister."

If Fallon hadn't been so worried about her little sister, the
look of astonishment on Andrea's face would almost be com-
ical.

Chapter 33

"You're not Jody's sister," Andrea told her, crossing her arms belligerently in front of her.

"Sorry to disappoint you, but I am." What did she want—a sample of her DNA?

"If you're her sister, then where have you been all these years? I know everything about Jody. You're going to have to prove to me that you are her sister." She eyed her with distrust. "And it's awful strange you just happened to be at the station right before someone set off an explosive device."

The man behind her walked closer, casually placing his arm around her shoulders. Hmm, protective. Lover? Husband? Whatever, he didn't look happy she was getting agitated.

Wade had even stepped closer to her. Sheesh, testosterone. Before the two men decided to battle it out, she gave Andrea a little more explanation.

"My name was Brigitte Dupree, but I go by Fallon now. Jody is my sister; John Cavenaugh murdered our father." She swallowed past the lump in her throat. Her heart ached again for such a senseless loss. Drawing in a ragged breath, she continued. "I'd gone to the store. When I came back, I saw our uncle driving away. I went inside and . . . and our father and Jody were crumpled on the floor, lying close to each other in a pool of blood. Until recently, I thought she was dead."

Andrea still looked doubtful, but apparently she was ready to hear more. "Come inside." She moved away from the doorway.

She and Wade walked the rest of the way into the apartment, Fallon's back rigid as she kept her emotions checked. She drew in a deep breath and looked around. The place reminded her of a picked-over garage sale. Not dirty, but definitely lived in. There were also three puppies and the mother dog. Funny, she didn't look like the type to have an animal.

Andrea scooped up a pile of clothes from the sofa and tossed them on top of a desk. "Have a seat. This is my . . . friend, Kevin."

Lover. Okay, she'd assumed as much. Apparently it was a new relationship, still in the fragile stage where she didn't know quite how to introduce him.

"This is my . . . friend, Wade."

The two men shook hands. "I have beer in the fridge."

"Sounds good." Wade looked at Fallon.

"I'll be fine." She let him know with her eyes it was okay for her to be alone with the other woman. She sensed his curiosity about her sister, but she needed to hear about Jody alone so she could digest everything. And maybe Andrea would tell her more if it were just the two of them.

"I'm still not sure I want to tell you much. It doesn't feel quite right," Andrea spoke up after the two men had left.

Fallon wanted to shake her until her teeth rattled, but instead, she quickly counted to ten. She wasn't sure if their positions were reversed that she wouldn't be just as cautious.

"Please, understand that up until a few weeks ago I thought Jody was dead. Then I find out she's alive. Can you imagine what I've been going through?"

Andrea studied her for a few seconds. "What do you want to know?"

"What does she look like? Why did she become a cop?

Anything and everything that you feel comfortable sharing." She still didn't quite believe Jody was alive. The pain had been with her so many years it was hard to switch it off.

"Just a minute."

She didn't sound too sure as she stood. Fallon wondered if she was going to tell her boyfriend to throw them out because she wasn't budging until she had more information about Jody. Apparently, she saw something on Fallon's face that convinced her it would be okay.

She went to a bookshelf. Scattered amongst stacks and stacks of romances was a fat photo album.

When she'd once again sat next to Fallon on the sofa, she opened the album and thumbed through, stopping in the middle. She paused before turning the album around for her to see.

Fallon's hands trembled as she brought the album closer. She clamped her lips and stared at the picture. It was all she could do to swallow, to breathe, to keep the tears from falling.

"She looks just like Momma," she whispered. Her gaze devoured the picture. Then the tears did start. Oh, God, her sister *was* alive. She very softly ran a finger over the image. Baby sister was all grown up.

"Jody is beautiful," Andrea told her, apparently accepting that Fallon was Jody's sister.

"Tell me more."

"She's kind, she's a good cop, and she's the best friend I've ever had."

"What happened after our father was killed?"

"Her grandmother raised her. We didn't meet until she came to work at the police station."

Fallon looked at the picture. They had the same color hair, but Jody was smaller, built more like their mother. She had the same features. There was almost an ethereal look about her. Almost as if she knew more than everyone else . . . just like Momma.

"She has the second sight, doesn't she?"

Andrea stiffened. "Jody doesn't talk about that much. I think it scares her."

It had their mother, too. If suppressed, the receiver only had partial visions. She remembered her mother telling her about it one day. She'd thought her firstborn would also be cursed, but Jody had been the one who saw things. Their mother had been dead for three years by then. Fallon hadn't paid attention enough to explain what she should do, and back then, they rarely visited their grandmother—thank goodness. The old woman was more than a little spooky.

"I'm surprised our grandmother didn't help her develop her visions."

Andrea shifted on the sofa. "I think it had something to do with that day her father died. She didn't want to see anything else, but sometimes it comes and she can't do anything to stop it."

"And what does she think about me?" The question she'd been dreading asking. Would she feel like her elder sister had abandoned her? Damn it, she hadn't known! If she had . . . if she . . . Nothing would change the fact she hadn't been there for Jody.

When she looked up, it wasn't disgust she saw. Andrea wore a gentle, almost motherly smile on her young face.

"She loves you so much," Andrea told her. "She often talks about how she'd tag along after her big sister. She thought you were the bravest, smartest person she knew.

Something in Fallon began to melt. Maybe it was the last chunk of ice around her heart.

"She even searched for you when she was older, but it was like you'd vanished from the face of the earth."

"I changed my name." Just talking about Jody wasn't enough. Fallon squared her shoulders. "Take me to her."

"I can't."

After all this and Andrea still didn't trust her? She'd make her. If she had to hold her at gunpoint . . .

"I can take you tomorrow. I'm so sorry, but we're not

scheduled to meet until then." She brightened. "Unless you know the way to her grandmother's. That's where she's staying."

Fallon shook her head. "I'd never find her. I always hated the swamps. Jody loved them, though."

Andrea grinned. "You and me both. We've been meeting her in a small cove that I can get to without losing myself. I grew up there but I still have no sense of direction." Something passed between the two women. "Hey, you want a cold beer or something?"

Fallon decided she liked Andrea. "I thought you'd never ask."

Fallon was lost in thought on the drive back so was surprised when Wade pulled into the driveway and turned off the engine.

"You okay?" he asked, facing her.

Night had fallen, but the full moon cast enough light she could make out his face. "Sure, why wouldn't I be okay?" She felt perfectly fine. Why wouldn't she feel fine? She was going to see the sister she'd thought dead for . . . oh, almost twenty years. She felt great, she felt wonderful . . .

She cast a glare in his direction. "I feel super. How the fuck do you think I feel?"

He pulled her across the seat and into his arms. Her body was stiff at first, but as soon as she felt his strength, and the way her face seemed to fit perfectly in the crook of his neck, she relaxed.

"I think you've faced some pretty bad people since you became a DEA agent. Never once did you show fear about going into The Pit. But yet, when it comes to meeting your baby sister, you're terrified."

She swallowed past the lump in her throat. He'd nailed exactly how she felt. No matter what Andrea had told her about Jody looking up to her big sister, it still didn't change the fact that she hadn't listened when Jody told her something bad was going to happen that day. Her little sister had had a vision, and Fallon told her it was nothing.

Terrified? No, she was scared shitless. Except for a crazy old grandmother who she barely knew, Jody was the only family she had.

She drew in a deep breath. "When we were little I used to get such a kick out of her tagging along. She treated me like I was a queen or something. But it was more than feeling important. Jody was really sweet, and so damn brave for a little squirt. Once, we had a cocker spaniel and some older boys started throwing rocks at the dog. She picked up a stick that was bigger than her and took off down the sidewalk after them. She couldn't have been more than six at the time, but they ran down the street like the gates of hell had opened and released a demon. They didn't come back, either."

He laughed. "Sounds like you were both a lot alike."

"Maybe we were."

"Maybe you still are."

She nuzzled his neck. Wade was definitely good for her. Thoughts of her sister vanished momentarily as she absorbed his scent—musky and spicy all at the same time. A different sensation swept over her, leaving a sweet yearning in its wake.

"Ever made out in a car, Tanner?" With her head lying on his chest, she could hear his heart speed up. She smiled. Damn, she needed this, she needed him.

"Not since high school." He cleared his throat.

She moved away from him and pulled her top over her head, then unsnapped her bra and tossed it to the floorboard. "Want to reminisce?"

When he fondled her breasts, tugging on the pebbled nipples, she took that as a yes and massaged between his legs. He was already hard and straining against his jeans.

"Ever get lucky and get a blow job in your car?"

"Damn, woman, if you don't quit putting images in my

head all I'm going to have is embarrassment and a horny female in my vehicle."

"Then let's get naked, sugar, because I want to do that and a lot more."

Before she could finish another sentence, he'd swiftly undone his clothes and was tossing them on the floorboard as she tugged off her slacks and thong.

He leaned toward her, his mouth closed over her breast, tugging on the nipple with his teeth, swirling his tongue over the tip. She gasped, a thrill of pleasure cascading over her to settle between her legs.

She fondled him, not about to let Wade have all the fun. "Damn, I like the way you feel," she said, arching toward him, rubbing herself against his penis, massaging her clit against his hard length. The smooth tip was velvety soft against her sex.

"I don't think I can wait for a blow job." He grunted. "I'm still trying to figure out how you can turn me on so damned fast with just a couple of sultry words. I feel like I'm on fire."

"Then fuck me," she whispered close to his ear, intentionally letting her heated breath tickle him.

He growled low in his throat and pulled her onto his lap. She straddled him, letting his penis slide into her. He filled her, sending spasms of satisfaction curling around her. She tightened her inner muscles. He gasped. She plunged downward and rose again. Their gazes met in the dim interior. He kissed her as she continued to rock her body against his. Heat spread over her. She clung to him when the pressure inside released, sending spasms of pleasure through her. His body jerked upward and he cried out.

When he finally caught his breath, Wade cuddled her close. "Remind me to show you a pond we have back home on my uncle's place."

"We just had sex and you want to go swimming?"

"Apparently, you've never been skinny-dipping."

"Do you think we'd make it into the water?"

"If we had sex first, we might." He chuckled.

She smiled at the idea. "One thing I can say about you, Tanner, life will always be interesting." She met his lips, drinking in his kiss and knowing this man was right for her. She wished everyone could find their perfect mate. She sighed, knowing she could lie in his arms, right here in the car, for the rest of the night. She closed her eyes, felt his deep sigh against her cheek.

It was much later when they stirred enough to pull their clothes on and slip inside the house. Fallon curled next to Wade's body heat and for the first time since discovering her sister was still alive, she fell asleep with feelings of peace.

Tomorrow, she would see Jody again, and she knew everything would be all right. This time she would protect her and keep her safe.

The night slipped away with memories of her sister filling her dreams.

The first one up, Jody sat on a large, flat rock near the swamp, curling her legs close to her body. She loved this time of day best of all. A thin layer of fog hovered close to the water giving the area an ethereal quality. She could almost believe the folklore, the legends, on a day like today. Instead of letting her mind wander to the unknown, she closed her eyes and listened, absorbing the sounds of morning as it awakened those around her.

Something intruded on her thoughts. It wasn't like the suffocating feeling when her visions came. She opened her eyes, but rather than going away the feeling grew in intensity. Tingles skittered up and down her arms. She looked around. Was that a movement at the edge of the water? An alligator maybe?

I'm here, Jody. I'll help you this time.

The voice reached out to her. "Who's there?" She stood,

but the mist wavered and began to fade. Her heartbeat accelerated. She took a step forward, then another, searching past the thick layer of fog.

"You okay?" Logan put his arm on Jody's.

She stared at him, but it took a moment for recognition to filter in. She quickly scanned the fog, regret filling her. "I thought I heard her," she whispered.

"Who?"

"My sister. I thought I heard her calling to me. Telling me everything would be okay, that she would protect me." Her voice wobbled. "Do you think it was her spirit? Maybe she is . . . dead."

He gathered her in his arms and some of the cold she felt vanished as he wrapped her in his warmth.

"I don't know. I wish I had the answers."

He ran his hand lightly up and down her back. She sensed his own frustration that he couldn't help her.

"Don't mind me, I'm just anxious about everything that's happened. Maybe Andrea will bring news. Surely they have some word on where Cavenaugh is hiding. Someone will have to know something."

"He'll resurface sooner or later. Andrea and Kevin said they have a wide net thrown over the area. As soon as he shows himself, they'll nab him."

"I hope you're right."

She bit her bottom lip knowing without a doubt it would soon be over. Maybe that was what the spirit was trying to tell her.

"I didn't see your grandmother this morning," Logan told her, changing the subject.

"She must have left after I got up."

"There was this god-awful-smelling bag hung above our bed, though."

"*Mamere*'s charm. It's meant to ward off evil."

"I don't doubt that. I would imagine it could get rid of just about anything." He glanced around. "She's not going to show up dragging an alligator behind her for breakfast or anything, is she?"

Her mood considerably lighter, Jody chuckled. "She's probably gone into the swamps again to collect herbs and berries."

He frowned. "Did she do that a lot when you were little?"

She cocked an eyebrow. "I wasn't left alone to fend for myself if that's what you're asking. Most of the time I went with her. She taught me a lot, like what plants are safe to eat, which ones will speed up or slow down your heart. Lots of stuff."

She looked into his face. "Are you laughing at me?"

He shook his head. "I'd never do that. I just wondered if you'd slipped me something because every time I'm around you my heart beats a little faster."

"If I didn't know better, Logan Hart, I'd think you were flirting with me."

"I think you'd be right, Jody Dupree." He nuzzled the side of her neck, tickling the sensitive area just below her ear and making her laugh and pull away.

"Come on," she said, tugging on his hand.

"Sounds like you have something in mind that I might enjoy."

"Breakfast. I'm hungry."

"That's not exactly what I was thinking about." Disappointment laced his words.

"Don't forget, we're meeting Andrea and Kevin this morning."

He sidled next to her and scooped her in his arms. "They won't mind waiting, I'm sure."

Before she could protest, he carried her into the cabin, not putting her down until he laid her on the bed. When he lay beside her, his hand snaking its way between her legs, any protest she might have been about to utter died away.

So maybe it wouldn't hurt that much for Kevin and Andrea to wait.

She arched against Logan's hand, trying to ease the pressure between her legs.

He didn't take the time to remove her dress, but teased her hard nipples through the fabric. "You taste so damn good," he murmured as his mouth covered her breast. The sensation of having something between them only heightened her enjoyment.

She almost regretted when he moved his mouth away, but when he scooted down in the bed while drawing her dress above her hips, a different fantasy began to form in her mind. He didn't disappoint as his tongue scraped along her sex.

Her body pulsed as sweet sensations trembled over her. She wadded the covers in her fists, biting back her moan as he caressed her with his tongue.

He slid back next to her, reaching for a condom. After ripping open the foil packet with his teeth, he quickly put it on and entered her.

"I love tasting you," he told her. "I love touching you. I love when you moan and spread your legs." He entered her. "I love making love with you." He gasped when she wrapped her legs around his waist and drew him deeper inside her body.

She met his gaze, staring into his passion-filled eyes. "It feels so good having you inside me," she gasped. She met his thrust again and again, giving of herself, receiving what he offered. When she came, she knew Cavenaugh could do his worst, but he would never be able to take this moment in time from her. This was hers, to cherish for the rest of her life—no matter how long or short that would be.

Chapter 34

Cavenaugh hated the fucking swamp. Almost as much as he hated the man who was at the helm of the small boat, guiding them through the mazes of the green, filthy-looking water.

Paul had seen Fallon and her boyfriend meet up with Andrea and her man. They were going to contact Jody. Why else would they be going into the swamp?

"What if they hear us?"

"They're using an outboard, too. They won't hear us over their own motor." The man was an idiot. He swatted at a mosquito as big as his arm. Why hadn't he thought to use repellent?

Paul brushed his hand over his pants. "I'm going to ruin my suit. I still don't know why I couldn't have taken the time to change."

"Just keep your eyes peeled, and go slow so they don't spot us." Before this day was over, he was going to throw Paul to the gators—along with the rest of the dead bodies he planned to stack up.

A movement to the left drew his attention. A large alligator rose to the surface and captured his gaze. A shiver of fear ran down his spine. Phillip had talked him into going to the swamps once. He had the mistaken idea they could be friends.

That was the day he'd met Angelina's mother. He could tell the old woman saw right through him. That he lusted after her daughter.

It was also the day he'd fallen into the swamp. He closed his eyes tight against the memory. The gator had caught his jacket, latching on to it, ripping the material with its sharp teeth.

He didn't care that Phillip had risked his life to help him by jumping into the water and pulling him free of the monster's jaws. If not for him, he wouldn't have been there in the first place.

Why the hell had he returned?

His vision clouded. Now he remembered. He had to save Angelina from making a mistake. She thought she was in love with Phillip. He eyed the man steering the boat through the swamp. Disgust filled him. His oh, so perfect little brother. He'd make damn sure his body rotted in the swamps. This time, he would have his beautiful Angelina.

"You okay?"

"I'm fine," he answered him. Better be careful or Phillip would catch on to the fact he intended to kill him. "Why do you ask, *mon ami?*"

He shrugged. "I don't know, you had a strange look on your face." He killed the motor and nodded. "They're moving toward that small cove. We'd better switch to the oars. If we come around from the other side, we can slide close to the bank before they realize we're here."

He nodded. His heart caught in his throat as he watched the little group getting out of the boat and going onshore. Angelina stepped from behind a tree. His heart beat faster.

Angelina. His sweet Angelina. Soon, *mi amour.* Soon and we will be together again.

Paul aimed the boat in the other direction. Cavenaugh felt a spurt of energy. By the end of the day, Angelina would be lying naked in his arms moaning and thrashing as she begged him to take her.

He dug the oar into the water and the small boat shot forward.

Soon.

Chapter 35

Jody warily eyed the small group getting out of the boat. Who had Andrea brought with her? The woman looked vaguely familiar, but she couldn't place her, and she knew she'd never seen the man before today. Andrea shouldn't have brought two strangers.

"Andrea?"

The woman was staring. An odd feeling swept over her. As if she should know her.

Andrea looked around. "I think you two are going to want some privacy. We'll just kind of . . . uh . . . move over here a ways." She blushed; then motioned for the three men to follow her. Logan hesitated but Kevin grabbed him by the arm and dragged him along with them.

The woman cleared her throat. Jody could see she was nervous, but trying not to show it. And she was still staring. How rude of her.

"I should have listened to you when you told me something was going to happen, but I didn't."

Cold chills ran up and down Jody's arms. Her voice was vaguely familiar. She put her hand on the tree to steady herself. The woman continued.

"Besides, I really wanted to go to the store that morning. I knew Johnny Vallier would be helping his father unload the delivery truck. I had such a crush on him."

Jody squeezed her eyes closed. This wasn't happening. A dream . . . a vision. That's all this was. But when she opened her eyes, the woman was still there, still talking, her voice thick with emotion.

"When . . . when I returned home I saw John Cavenaugh leaving the house. I went inside." Tears filled her eyes and began to run down her cheeks. "Daddy was lying in a pool of blood. You were next to him."

"Oh, my God," she whispered, reaching a hand toward her sister. "You're real? Not a vision?" They stepped toward each other at the same time, arms hugging the other close.

"Jody, if I had known you were still alive I wouldn't have left. I went to the police station, but Cavenaugh showed up and I knew they wouldn't arrest him. I ran away, stole a name from a grave. Fallon. Fallon Hargis."

"It's a wonderful name," she said, choking back her tears.

Jody felt herself running through the streets of New Orleans, stumbling into an alley, crawling inside a cardboard box to spend the night. She'd thought it had been a hallucination from the fever she had after her uncle shot her, but she'd been with her sister that night—not in body, but in mind. She'd felt her fear, her pain . . . her loneliness.

"You're really my sister?" Please don't let it be a cruel joke. And if it was, she hoped she never learned the truth.

Fallon nodded.

All the years of separation fell away. "Nothing will come between us ever again."

This was really happening. Her heart pounded inside her chest. She wanted to shout her excitement to the world, but she couldn't stop hugging her.

They finally pulled away so they could look at each other. Fallon laughed.

"You look just like Momma," Fallon said.

"And you favor Daddy." She was even more beautiful than Jody remembered. She memorized every detail of her features. "We have a lot of catching up to do."

"That we do."

The last twenty years began fading away. . . . "Oh, my God, I forgot." Jody's heart skipped a beat. "Uncle John is back. You'll have to stay with me. I won't let him hurt you. It can't happen again . . ."

"Shh, it's okay, little sister. I'm the one who brought him in." She looked toward the man who came with her. "Me and Wade, that is. I'm an agent with the DEA, Wade is a sheriff. We captured Cavenaugh in Texas and he was extradited to New Orleans. I know all about his escape."

"What if he comes after us?"

She brushed Jody's hair behind her ear. Her touch brought back a flash of memory. The years slipped away.

"Don't worry, Jody. I'll take care of you." She brushed Jody's hair behind her ear.

Jody barely remembered her mother's funeral, but her sister had kept her arm protectively around Jody's shoulders. Their father was lost in his own world of pain and misery, but her big sister had taken care of her.

Until Uncle John had murdered their father, Fallon had kept her promise. She'd taken their mother's place and saw to it that Jody had plenty of love.

But who had taken care of her?

Jody had never realized the burden her older sister had shouldered. What she must have felt when their mother passed. That was all behind them now. Together, they would take care of each other.

"Now isn't this a touching scene." John Cavenaugh spoke from his boat. "Am I interrupting a family reunion?"

The blood froze in Jody's veins. Logan stepped forward, but Cavenaugh raised his gun.

"I don't think there are going to be any heroes today. Toss your guns in the swamp." A hard glitter entered his eyes. "Now!"

Fallon squeezed Jody's hand, their gazes met. No! There should've been something to warn her. To know that he'd been waiting and watching. That he planned to kill them.

Fallon angled herself in front of Jody.

Always the protector. Jody was safe. She could slip between the trees, make her way to safety before her uncle even knew she was gone.

But baby sister was all grown up and she could be a real mean bitch.

She stepped from behind Fallon. "What are you going to do? Kill us all?" She squared her shoulders and jutted her chin forward.

"Don't," Fallon hissed.

Jody ignored her as she continued to walk closer to the edge of the swamp. She didn't bother to acknowledge Paul. Damn, she should've guessed he was the dirty cop. He'd always tried to better himself by taking shortcuts. She'd never realized he would be stupid enough to betray his badge.

"Angelina," Cavenaugh breathed. "I wouldn't hurt you. Never you."

She stumbled, caught her balance. He thought she was her mother. Just like he had after the explosion. That might work to her advantage. "But I'll come with you," she spoke softly. "I've been waiting for you for so long now. You don't have to kill them."

Confusion crossed his face. She only hoped the others would continue to stay quiet and not move. They might survive this day after all.

"What the hell are you doing?" Paul spoke up. "Her name isn't Angelina. That's Jody. You lost your mind or what?"

Damn! Her uncle's face registered uncertainty as the past warred with the present. She knew the moment the present won.

His eyes narrowed, his gaze locked on hers. "Angelina was in love with me first. Then she saw Phillip. I no longer existed. She should've been mine. He always got whatever he wanted."

"Is that why you killed him?" Fallon moved to stand beside Jody.

"He flushed thousands of dollars' worth of drugs down the toilet. When I went to get them, they were gone. Sanctimonious bastard. He had the gall to tell me he wouldn't have drugs around his daughters."

"So you killed him." A deep sense of loss filled her.

Cavenaugh shrugged. "I had no choice. He'd put my life in jeopardy. The man who gave me the drugs to sell would've killed me. I had to leave the state and lay low."

"But why Jody?" Logan demanded.

"Phillip grabbed the gun. It fired." He grinned. "You might say she was in the wrong place at the wrong time."

"You going to kill them or talk all day. Goddamned mosquitoes are about to eat me alive." Paul swatted at his neck.

"My friend is anxious." Cavenaugh chuckled.

"Your friend is an idiot." Jody told Cavenaugh, then glared at Paul. "Don't you realize you'll be the only witness to our murders? Do you really think he's going to let you live?"

Paul glanced at Cavenaugh, then back to Jody. "He's my financial backer. I'm going into politics." He didn't sound or look quite so sure of himself.

"She's trying to rattle you, *mon ami.*"

He grinned at Jody and she knew Paul wouldn't live to see another sunrise. Not if Cavenaugh had anything to do about it.

A movement to her left caught her eye. Her breath stopped. Logan was inching forward. Wade was close beside him. Kevin had moved to angle himself in front of Andrea. What were they going to do? Please, God, don't let them be heroes.

Somehow she would convince Cavenaugh they should live. She would promise him anything. He seemed obsessed with her. Maybe she could play off his feelings. Bile rose in her throat, but she forced it back down.

"I'll go with you," she blurted. "Let them go free and I'll willingly go with you."

Fallon grabbed her hand. She squeezed it before pulling hers free, taking a step closer to the water.

"You would come with me, *chere*? Do anything I wanted?"

She closed her eyes for a second. She could feel the color drain from her face, but then she opened them and met his gaze head-on; she wouldn't back down from his lecherous gaze.

"Yes." Then stronger. "Yes. Anything." She held her hand toward his boat.

"No!" Fallon grabbed her arm. "I won't let you sacrifice yourself for us. Don't you see, as soon as he gets you into his boat, he'll still kill us. He knows damn well I'd hunt him down until I found you."

"She's right, *chere*." Cavenaugh grinned. "But she doesn't realize I'll kill them anyway and still take you. Phillip stopped me from having Angelina, but he can't stop me from having you."

"You sick bastard," Logan growled, taking a step forward.

Cavenaugh raised his gun. Jody threw herself into Logan's arms. The blast reverberated through the swamp. She flinched, expecting to feel her uncle's bullet slamming into her back, but she felt nothing.

Logan hugged her close. "Oh, my God, are you all right?" He ran his hands over her back.

"Yes, I think so."

They both looked at Cavenaugh. The sleeve of his white suit was turning a deep crimson. He looked at the blood as if it hadn't registered yet he'd been shot.

"My Angelina never loved you," *Mamere* spat, holding the shotgun close to her side. "She always loved Phillip. He be a good man and he be raisin' my grandbabies good, but then you killed him dead. Bastard!"

"You shot me." Cavenaugh grabbed his arm. His gun splashed when it landed in the water. Blood ran down his hand, dripping into the murky water of the Louisiana swamp.

He came to his feet, but he'd been sitting too long. He wobbled, screaming just before he lost his balance and fell over the side.

With the stealth of a skilled predator, the big gator sliced across the shadowy surface. Cavenaugh saw it and screamed again, furiously splashing the water as he grabbed the side of the boat. Paul cringed away from him rather than pulling him back to safety.

Even though Cavenaugh would've killed them without a thought, Wade and Logan jumped into their boat in an attempt to save him.

To Jody, the world around her slowed. She met her grandmother's gaze. It told her what she already knew.

She looked at Cavenaugh, at the alligator bearing down on him.

Logan jerked the rope on the boat's motor, she saw the whisper of smoke as it roared to life, smelled the fuel.

Saw death.

Kevin grabbed Andrea close to him. She buried her face in his shirt.

Fallon swallowed hard. Despising the man who killed her father, who stole her life, but not wanting to see anyone die the way he was about to die.

Jody watched him, unable to pull her gaze away from what was about to happen.

He mouthed Angelina's name, reached a hand toward Jody.

The thunder inside her head blocked his scream just before he vanished beneath the water.

Cavenaugh had been right about one thing. There would be no heroes today. At least none to pull him from the gator's jaws. Tonight, he would dine with the devil.

"Where is he?" Wade shouted.

"The *caimon* done be gots him," *Mamere* spoke. "No use you be searchin' for him now. Dat gator done have him in a death roll. Then he stuff him in some hole way down deeplike till he be ready to eat. Now we don' have to worry 'bout John Cavenaugh ever again." She looked at Fallon. "Glad you come home, granddaughter. I be missin' my other baby, but I be knowin' you have to be gone so to keep you both safe. You two come see me after you take care of other stuff. I be waitin', *chere*." She turned. A swish of skirt, a speck of colorful red scarf and she left as silently as she'd appeared.

"That old woman always was spooky," Fallon murmured.

And she'd known all along her other granddaughter was alive, Jody thought. But then, she'd said everything had to unfold like it had so they would be safe. It had to play out exactly like it did.

Silence fell over the group in the swamp. Then, as if they had all just remembered something, they each turned and looked at Paul who still sat in the boat trying to assimilate what had happened in the space of a very few moments.

Realization was slow to come. When it did, his gaze went from one person to the next.

"I'm fucked," he muttered.

Chapter 36

"I have to check in with Bradley," Logan told Jody. "Will you be okay?" His gaze skimmed over her. She seemed okay to him, but he knew how someone looked on the outside could be deceiving.

She smiled. "I'm fine. Really, I am. Fallon and I are going to get reacquainted." Her expression turned serious. "We have a lot to talk about."

He kissed her. The warmth of her lips invaded his senses and for a second he couldn't breathe. When he ended the kiss, he was light-headed. He hugged her, knowing how close he'd come to losing Jody when she'd put herself between him and Cavenaugh.

"Go be with your sister."

She stepped out of his arms. "Write your story," she told him. "Then find me . . . it's okay." She ran the back of her hand down the side of his face. She hurried away, back into the police station.

Had that been regret . . . pain . . . he saw reflected in her eyes?

He started up the steps to follow, but at the last minute changed his mind. Of course it hadn't been anything, except maybe the aftershock of all that had happened. They'd almost lost each other, faced death, and survived.

Logan whirled around and hurried to his car. He had a lot

to go over with Bradley, but it wouldn't be about Jody's story. He wouldn't risk anyone hurting her again.

After unlocking his car, he climbed in the front seat. On the drive to the newspaper office he thought about how much his life had changed since meeting her. Hell, her own life had been turned around. He was happy for her that her sister was alive. A tender smile tugged at his lips. For as long as he would live, he'd never forget the look on her face when she saw Fallon.

He put his turn signal on and went right at the light. But it could have all ended when Cavenaugh threatened them. Cold chills ran up and down his spine. It had been a close call. One he didn't want to repeat. Now he only had one goal—to spend the rest of his life making Jody happy.

But how could he ask her to share his life if he wasn't even sure he had a job? He guessed they could survive on a re-porter's pay with Jody's income, too.

As he pulled into a parking space in front of the newspa-per office he realized he hadn't asked her if she even wanted to marry him. Not that he had any doubts she wouldn't. He threw the gearshift into park and turned the key.

Of course she'd say yes. He got out of the car and locked it. Wouldn't she? Something bothered him, but he couldn't quite figure out exactly what. Nerves, that's probably all it was.

He took the steps two at a time and pushed on the glass door. He went straight to Bradley's office, rapping lightly be-fore entering.

"Come in."

Logan only hoped he still had a job as a reporter. He went inside the office, shutting the door behind him. Bradley glanced up, his eyebrows rose.

"Logan, good to see you. How was your vacation?" He folded his arms in front of him. "But wait, you weren't on va-cation, were you? Let's see, we've had an explosion and a jailbreak and I've been short a reporter who just a few days ago professed a desire to be the next assistant editor." He leaned forward, placing both hands on his desk. "Would you care to explain where you've been?"

He'd known his boss wouldn't be happy, but his calm attitude kind of bothered him.

"Well . . . ?" Bradley prodded.

"It's rather a long story."

He looked at his watch. "Funny, but I have plenty of time."

An hour later, Logan had related all the events that had taken place after he met Jody. At least, most of them.

"You're leaving something out." Bradley guessed.

"Yes, sir." He really had liked this job . . . and Bradley. That's why he felt his boss deserved an explanation. "I'm not going to write the article, sir. At least not about Jody's uncle killing her father and leaving her for dead. Or that he was the one who escaped from jail by setting off a bomb at the police station. Jody's been through a hell of a lot. She doesn't deserve to have her life story splashed across the front page."

He drew in a deep breath, wondering if he could get his old job back in his hometown. It would mean moving to Texas. Would Jody be receptive to leaving? He wasn't about to go without her.

"And what would you say if I told you not writing the articles means you'd stay a reporter."

Okay, he wasn't fired . . . yet. He squared his shoulders. "Sometimes you have to walk away from the story."

"You're right."

Had he heard correctly? "Sir?"

"You've got the job."

Great. He'd at least get to stay on as a reporter. He could probably even stomach working under Hank. If it meant being here with Jody, he could do just about anything.

"Thank you, sir. I'll do my best not to disappoint you. If you want me to work extra shifts . . ."

"Son, I don't think you understand. I don't want you as a reporter. I'm giving you the job of assistant editor."

Now he knew he hadn't heard him just say he had the job he wanted. Had he? "Sir?"

"It seems Hank has been stealing stories."

"I don't follow you."

"It was brought to my attention Hank was stealing stories from some of the younger reporters. He had them believing it was part of their job description. Fresh out of college, they assumed he was telling them the truth. Until one of them asked me when they could have their name on the stuff they were writing. I fired Hank yesterday. The job of assistant editor is yours—unless you've changed your mind."

"No, sir. Not at all." A rush of adrenaline sped through him. This was exactly what he wanted.

"Then take a couple of days off. I'm supposing you want to marry this girl." He raised his eyebrows.

Logan stood. "As soon as I ask her."

"For your sake, I hope she puts you out of your misery and says yes."

He hurried to the door, but before he opened it, Bradley spoke again.

"Being a reporter means more than getting a story, Logan. We're here to inform the public. It's always been my intention that no one is ever hurt by anything that I run in my paper. Like I said once before, you remind me a lot of myself at your age. Keep up the good work."

"Yes, sir."

Logan grinned all the way to his car. He had one stop to make, then he was going to find Jody and ask her to marry him. His day couldn't get any better than this—except when he had a ring on her finger and a yes from her sweet lips. She was his life, his love forever.

Jody shook her head as they led Paul toward lockup. He bawled and begged for leniency.

Andrea rolled her eyes. "Some people just don't learn you

have to play by the rules." She turned her attention back to Jody. "What about Logan?"

Jody's heart sank, but she knew she couldn't beg him not to write her story. Really, what did it matter now? Cavenaugh would never be able to hurt them again. Something else would come along before she knew it and her story would be old news. Maybe it was time she stopped being so private.

She straightened. "He's writing his article."

Andrea raised her eyebrows. "And you're okay with that?"

"He more than deserves to be assistant editor. He'll do a good job." She didn't want to think about when her story would come out, and what it would do to her life. She had never liked being in the spotlight. But Logan deserved this chance. He deserved his dream.

"What about you and Kevin?" she asked, changing the subject.

Andrea blushed. "He's meeting me at the apartment in . . . " She looked at her watch. "Ten minutes. He had to run pick up something at his place."

Jody didn't think she'd ever seen Andrea look this ex-cited—or happy. She almost glowed. It would seem the Hart men had stolen both *their* hearts.

"You really like him, don't you?"

"He's the best thing that's ever happened to me." Andrea smiled.

"And all this time I thought I was." She feigned disappointment.

Andrea squeezed her hand. "I love the both of you so much, sometimes I ache."

Jody smiled. "Then go be with your man." They hugged and Andrea left. As she was leaving, Fallon rejoined her.

"Wade is going back to the hotel room. He said he could sleep for a month, then he asked me if our life was always going to be this bizarre." She grinned. "Funny man, of course it is."

Jody still couldn't believe Fallon was in the same room with her, that they were talking like they'd never been apart. She doubted she would ever believe her sister was finally home.

"And Wade is okay that you're going to spend some time with me at *Mamere*'s? He's welcome to come along."

Fallon chuckled. "I think he got his fill of the swamp."

"And you? Would you rather not go there?"

"I can think of a few places I'd rather be, but I did kind of miss it. Never thought I'd hear myself say those words." She brushed her hair behind her ear. "But what about Logan. Will he be able to survive a few days without being in your presence? He looked pretty taken with you."

"He has to meet with his editor and . . . and write his article." Bittersweet regret filled her. She tried to tamp it down, but the feeling persisted.

"Then let's go."

They left the police station and drove to Jody's boat.

"I'm surprised our grandmother is still alive. Damn, she has to be close to . . . what, a hundred?"

"I think she's seventy-eight. I wouldn't mention her age. She gets a little touchy on the subject."

"I didn't think anything bothered her," Fallon grumbled. "She used to scare the hell out of me."

"But she always loved you. She kept your memory alive by telling me stories: about the day you were born, the times you would stay at the cabin." She paused. "Don't look at what's on the outside. Look at what's in her heart."

"My little sister has grown into a wise woman."

"I'm not sure wise is the word I'd use."

She pulled into a space and they got out. She only looked over her shoulder once, like she expected to see Logan chasing after her, but no, she knew he would already be writing. He probably wouldn't surface for at least a couple of days. Plenty of time for her and Fallon to visit with each other and *Mamere*.

"One thing I haven't missed are these blasted boats. You're just like our grandmother when it comes to them. Why not just use one with a motor?"

"It's the ecological system. *Mamere* likes to keep the swamp pure. A motor would have fumes, sometimes they leak gas. Besides, you miss the most important stuff if you travel too fast."

They talked about everything under the sun on the way to the cabin. Jody couldn't seem to get her fill of listening to her sister.

How she'd taken her name off a grave marker and become Fallon Hargis. That she was caught delivering drugs about a year later and adopted by a man who worked for the DEA.

She told Fallon about being raised in the swamp by their grandmother. How she could see things, just like their mother, but she hadn't wanted to develop the skill.

Before either realized it, they were tying off the boat and walking toward the cabin.

"Both my girls done come home," *Mamere* said as she slowed the rocker with the toe of her soft leather shoe. "It be doin' my body good to see you two together." She stood, holding out her arms.

Jody readily went into them, Fallon held back for just a second before she let their grandmother enfold her in a tight embrace.

Then she set the two girls away from her, studying Fallon's features. "You look like your daddy. He was a fine man. You two wait here." She went inside the cabin and after a few minutes brought out a tin box, sat down in the rocker and removed the lid. "This be his, but I 'spect it be you girls' now."

"*Mamere*, I didn't know you had this." Jody looked at the trinkets and things. Her father's wallet, a broach she vaguely remembered her mother wearing. The tin box was full of treasures.

"I saved it for when you both could be lookin' together. That's as it should be, *chere*."

Fallon gingerly picked up a silver heart. She opened it, revealing pictures of their parents. Pulling a stool close to the rocker, she sat down, still staring at the pictures. When she looked between Jody and *Mamere,* there were tears in her eyes.

"I thought I had no one. Then Wade came into my life. Now I have the both of you. I think I'm pretty damned lucky." She sniffed.

Mamere smiled, Jody felt a rush of love flow through her.

"And you have dem babies, too." *Mamere* patted Fallon's hand.

Jody was confused. By the look on Fallon's face, Jody knew her sister was, too.

"Babies? What babies?" Fallon asked.

Mamere brushed the hair from Fallon's face. "Why, dem two little girls what be inside your belly. Beautiful little girls." She grinned. "It do my old heart good to know there be little ones running underfoot again. Dis be the way it supposed to be. Dis be the circle of life."

Tentatively, Fallon touched her fingertips to her stomach. "Babies. Oh, my." She looked up. Their gazes met. They both smiled.

As the day passed, Jody would catch a tender look on Fallon's face as she glanced down at her stomach.

Twins.

A longing inside her grew. How did Logan feel about their relationship? Did he even see marriage or a family in his future?

She slipped outside to the porch, and watched as the sun dipped low in the sky. Where was he? What was he doing right now?

"You okay?" Fallon asked, putting an arm around Jody.

"Yeah." She rested her head on Fallon's shoulder. "I've missed you so much."

"I've missed you, too, but I don't think it was me you were thinking about."

Heat rose up her neck as she straightened. "But . . . I . . . uh . . ." She gave up and laughed. "And they say I'm the one with the gift. You're pretty good at reading minds."

Fallon chuckled. "Not really, but anyone can see you love Logan."

"That obvious, huh?"

"Yep."

"Eeea-ay-eeeee"

Fallon jumped. "What the hell was that?"

Jody's brow furrowed. "Maybe someone needing a doctor. They'd warn before coming up to the house." She looked toward the door as *Mamere* stepped out, drying her hands on a towel.

A few seconds passed before a man stepped from the trees. He wore a black, floppy hat and baggy britches held up by a pair of red suspenders.

"Your woman ready to deliver, Clifford?" *Mamere* asked.

He shook his head, then apparently remembered he was in the company of women and took off his hat, crushing it in his hands. "There be dat fella of Jody's down in da lower part of de bayou." He frowned. "He be lost."

"My fella?" Jody looked at *Mamere*.

Clifford vigorously nodded. "Jean done saw him feedin' the gators, and told Remy and he be tellin' me. The sun gettin' low and I thought you be wantin' to know."

Why would Logan be coming all the way out here? By himself? And why in the world would he be feeding the gators?

Chapter 37

This was great. *Just damn great,* Logan thought. How could all the boats with motors be in use when he was so desperate for something with a little speed? The man on the dock had shrugged and told him tourists. He'd taken what he could get.

And had been using the oars ever since his pole disappeared beneath the water. Maybe that hadn't been such a bad deal, he'd discovered a couple bags of marshmallows in the bottom of the boat. At least he wouldn't die of starvation. He ripped open the last bag, and popped one of the large, fluffy marshmallows in his mouth. Damn tasty since he hadn't eaten lunch.

He'd found another use for them, though. The water wasn't really moving. If he tossed out a marshmallow occasionally, he'd be able to keep track where he turned.

He'd stop rowing occasionally and chuck one into the water. They floated and the white showed up great against the dark green water. At least he shouldn't get too lost.

Logan rowed the boat, going around another bend, dropping marshmallows over the side like a trail of bread crumbs.

Exactly how hard could it be to find her? Hell, they'd only made a couple of turns.

As creepy as this place was, it was worth going into the

swamp to know he would soon see Jody. He brushed his
hand over his pants pocket just to reassure himself the ring
box was still there.

He'd purchased the ring, then hurried to her house, thinking she and Fallon would be there. They weren't. He went to
his apartment hoping to at least run into his brother. No one
there, either. Nor at the police station. He finally found where
Andrea lived and she told him they'd gone to Jody's grandmother's. He felt as if he'd been running up against a brick
wall for the last several hours.

Something splashed to his left.

He glanced on either side of the boat. A tingle of trepidation tripped up and down his spine. So maybe this hadn't
been the most brilliant plan he'd ever come up with, but he
couldn't wait a couple of days for Jody to return home.

The sun had started sinking. How long before it grew
dark? He didn't even want to think about being here after the
sun went down.

He glanced around. There seemed to be an awful lot of alligators. At first there'd only been one, then four or five. Now
it seemed everywhere he looked there was a damned scaly
monster, big eyes staring at him like he was going to be its
next meal.

Now he didn't have anything to eat, either. He'd tossed
out all the marshmallows. He guessed he could return the
way he'd come and start over again. He was almost certain if
he went in the opposite direction from that first turn he'd
made he would be able to find the cabin. He looked over his
shoulder.

Nothing.

He frowned. What the hell had happened to his marshmallow trail?

"You lost, Texan?" Jody's soft voice floated to him as she
came around the bend.

His heart almost stopped beating. He wasn't sure if it was

from fear because someone had spoken, or relief that Jody had found him. As soon as his heart slowed, he grinned, knowing heat traveled up his face.

"Yeah, I think I am. How'd you find me?" He held up a hand. "Wait, don't tell me. You had a vision, right?"

She angled the boat next to his and sat down. Pulling the pole into the boat with her. "Not exactly. A neighbor dropped by to let *Mamere* know there was a crazy foreigner lost in the swamps feeding the alligators." Her eyes laughed at him.

It took a moment for her words to sink in. He was caught up in staring at her. God, she was the most beautiful woman he'd ever seen, and he was so hopelessly in love with her.

Then her words did sink into his muddled brain. "I might have been lost, but I certainly wasn't feeding the alligators."

She leaned slightly and reached inside his boat, latching on to the empty marshmallow bag. "You say you *haven't* been feeding the gators?"

His frown deepened. "No, I was just leaving . . ." Damn, now he did feel stupid. She'd only laugh if he told her something straight out of a fairy tale.

"You were just what?" she prodded.

He squared his shoulders. "I was leaving a bread crumb trail but all I had were marshmallows."

She chuckled. The sound echoed like sweet music, touching him, washing over him. Right now, he really didn't care if she did laugh. He liked the sound.

She reached into the bottom of her boat and ripped open a bag of marshmallows. "Watch this." She glanced around, then smiled. "Here, big boy." She tossed the marshmallow into the water.

Logan watched as the alligator went straight for the marshmallow. In only a few seconds, the sugary treat was gone.

"They love marshmallows. Because it's white the gators can see it really well and apparently they love the taste."

He was thoughtful for a moment. "That's why they made a beeline for Cavenaugh. He was wearing a white suit."

"That, and the blood from his wound. He didn't stand much of a chance." She was silent for a moment. "So, Logan Hart, you going to tell me why you were looking for me? I would've thought you'd still be writing your article."

"I'm not going to write the article."

"No, you have to." Her forehead wrinkled. "Please, I know how much getting this job has meant to you."

"I spoke with Bradley and told him I couldn't write the article if it meant hurting you."

Her shoulders slumped.

"He gave me the job of assistant editor anyway."

"He what?"

"It seems Hank hasn't been playing fair. He was stealing stories from the younger reporters, feeding them a bunch of bull about how they'd have to wait to get their own byline. Bradley fired Hank."

"Good for him!"

"Yeah, I didn't relish calling the weasel boss."

"But what about my uncle? The story of how Fallon and I found each other? That would sell a lot of papers."

"He told me the paper wasn't out to hurt people, only inform them. I think I'm going to like training under him."

"I think he could learn from you as well."

He took her hand in his. "I love you. I won't let anyone ever hurt you again."

"It still doesn't explain why you came into the swamp looking for me."

He let go of her hand and reached into his pocket. The boat rocked as he brought out the white velvet box. He juggled it for a moment before it plopped into the water. White! Damn! He scooped it out, feeling slightly ill as a green head popped to the surface.

"Logan, be careful!"

He closed his eyes and swallowed hard. After taking a few deep breaths, he relaxed.

"Jody Dupree, will you do me the honor of becoming my wife?" He opened the box. The small diamond winked back.

Tears filled her eyes. She nodded her head. "Yes. Yes. Yes!"

And the circle of life was complete.

Please turn the page for a sneak peek at
Lori Foster's enchanting new fantasy
"Once in a Blue Moon"
in the STAR QUALITY anthology
coming in May 2005 from Brava . . .

Stan's gaze lifted and locked with hers. Sensation crackled between them. His awareness of Jenna as a sexual woman ratcheted up another notch. Even without hearing her thoughts, what she wanted from him, with him, was obvious to any red-blooded male. Heat blazed in her eyes and flushed her cheeks. A pulse fluttered in her pale throat. Her lips parted . . .

Amazing. A mom of two, a quiet bookworm, a woman who remained circumspect in every aspect of her life—and she lusted after him with all the wonton creativity.

Not since the skill had first come to him when he was a kid of twelve, twenty-eight years ago, had Stan so appreciated the strange effect a blue moon had on him. It started with the waxing gibbous, then expanded and increased as the moon became full, and began to abate with the waning gibbous. But at midnight, when the moon was most full, the ability was so clean, so acute, that it used to scare him.

His parents didn't know. The one time he'd tried to tell them they'd freaked out, thinking he was mental or miserable or having some kind of psychosis. He'd retrenched and never mentioned it to them again.

When he was twenty and away at college, he signed up for a course on parapsychology. One classmate who specialized in the effects of the moon gave him an explanation that made sense. At least in part.

According to his friend, wavelengths of light came from a full moon and that affected his inner pathogens. With further studies, Stan had learned that different colors of lights caused varying emotional reaction in people. It made sense that the light of a full moon, twice in the same month, could cause effects.

In him, it heightened his sixth sense to the level that he could hear other people's tedious inner musings.

Now, he could hear, *feel,* Jenna's most private yearnings, and for once he appreciated his gift. Nothing tedious in being wanted sexually. Especially when the level of want bordered on desperate.

She needed a good lay. She needed him.

He wanted to oblige her. Damn, did he want to oblige her.

Casually, Stan moved closer to her until he invaded her space and her alarm thumped louder with every beat of her heart. He left himself wide open to her, relishing each tingle she felt, absorbing each small shiver of excitement—and letting it excite him in return. He no longer cared that he had a near-lethal erection.

Reaching out, he brushed the side of his thumb along her jawline, up and over her downy cheek, tickling the dangling earrings that suddenly seemed damn sexy. "Maybe you need the iced tea," he murmured, his attention dipping to her naked mouth. Jenna never wore lipstick, and he liked the look of her soft full lips, glistening from the glide of her tongue. Oh yeah, he liked that a lot. "You feel . . . warm, Jenna."

Her breaths came fast and uneven. "I've been . . . working."

And fantasizing. About him.

Lazily, Stan continued to touch her. "Me, too. Out in the sun all day. It's so damn humid, I know I'm sweaty." His thumb stroked lower, near the corner of her mouth. "But I didn't have time to change."

Her eyelids got heavy, drooping over her green eyes. Shakily, she lifted a hand and closed it over his wrist—but she didn't push him away. "You look . . . fine." *Downright edible.* She cleared her throat. "No reason to change."

Stan's slow smile alarmed her further. "You don't mind my jeans and clumpy boots?" He used both hands now to cup her face, relishing the velvet texture of her skin. "They're such a contrast to you, all soft and pretty and fresh."

Her eyes widened, dark with confusion and curbed excitement, searching his. He leaned forward, wanting her mouth, needing to know her taste—

The bell over the door chimed.

Jenna jerked away so quickly, she left Stan holding air. Face hot, she ducked to the back of the store and into the storage room, closing the door softly behind her.

Well, hell. He'd probably rushed things, Stan realized.

Like it hot? Here's an advance look at
OUT OF CONTROL
by Shannon McKenna,
now available from Brava . . .

San Cataldo, California

A poke in the eye, that's how it felt.

Mag Callahan curled white-knuckled hands around the mug of lukewarm coffee that she kept forgetting to drink. She stared, blank-eyed, at the Ziploc bag lying on her kitchen table. It contained the evidence that she had extracted from her own unmade bed a half an hour before, with the help of a pair of tweezers.

Item number 1: Black lace thong panties. She, Mag, favored pastels that weren't such a harsh contrast to her fair skin. Item number 2: Three strands of very long, straight, dark hair. She, Mag, had short, curly, red hair.

Her mind reeled and fought the unwanted information. Craig, her boyfriend, had been uncommunicative and paranoid lately, but she'd chalked it up to that pesky Y chromosome of his, plus his job stress, and his struggle to start up his own consulting business. It never occurred to her that he would ever . . . dear God.

Her own house. Her own *bed*. That pig.

The blank shock began to tingle and go red around the edges as it transformed inevitably into fury. She'd been so nice to him. Letting him stay in her house rent-free while he bug-swept and remodeled his own place. Lending him

money, quite a bit of it. Cosigning his business loans. She'd
bent over backward to be supportive, accommodating, womanly. Trying to lighten up on her standard ball-breaker routine, which consisted of scaring boyfriend after boyfriend
into hiding because of her strong opinions. She'd wanted so
badly to make it work this time. She'd tried so hard, and this
is what she got for her pains. Shafted. Again.

She bumped the edge of the table as she got up, knocking
over her coffee. She leaped back just in time to keep it from
splattering over the cream linen outfit she'd changed into for
her lunch date with Craig.

She'd come home early from her weekend conference on
purpose to pretty herself up for their date, having fooled herself into thinking that Craig was only twitchy because he was
about to broach the subject of—drum roll, please—The Future
of Their Relationship. She'd even gone so far as to fantasize a
sappy Kodak moment: Craig, bashfully passing her a ring
box over dessert. Herself, opening it. A gasp of happy awe.
Violins swelling as she melted into tears. How stupid.

Fury roared up like gasoline dumped on a fire. She had to
do something active, right now. Like blow up his car, maybe.
Craig's favorite coffee mug was the first object to present itself, sitting smugly in the sink beside another dirty mug, from
which the mystery tart had no doubt sipped her own coffee
this morning. Why, would you look at that. A trace of coral
lipstick was smeared along the mug's edge

Mag flung them across the room. Crash, tinkle. The noise
relieved her feelings, but now she had a coffee splatter on her
kitchen wall to remind her of this glorious moment forever.
Smooth move, Mag.

She rummaged under the sink for a garbage bag, mutter-
ing. She was going to delete that lying bastard from her
house.

She started with the spare room, which Craig had com-
mandeered as his office. In the bag went his laptop, modem,
and mouse, his ergonomic keyboard. Mail, trade magazines,

floppy disks and data-storage CDs clattered in after it. A sealed box that she found in the back of one of the desk drawers hit the bottom of the bag with a rattling thud.

Onward. She dragged the bag into the hall. It had been stupid to start with the heaviest stuff first, but it was too late now. Next stop, hall closet. Costly suits, dress shirts, belts, ties, shoes, and loafers. On to the bedroom, to the drawers she'd cleared out for his casual wear. His hypoallergenic silicone pillow. His alarm clock. His special dental floss. Every item she tossed made her anger burn hotter. Scum.

That was it. Nothing left to dump. She knotted the top of the bag.

It was now too heavy to lift. She had to drag it, bumpity-thud out the door, over the deck, down the stairs, across the narrow, pebbly beach of Parson's Lake. The wooden passage-way that led to her floating dock wobbled perilously as she jerked the stone-heavy thing along.

She heaved it over the edge of the dock with a grunt. Glug, glug, some pitiful bubbles, and down it sank, out of sight. Craig could take a bracing November dip and do a salvage job if he so chose.

She could breathe a bit better now, but she knew from experience that the health benefits of childish, vindictive behavior were very short-term. She'd crash and burn again soon if she didn't stay in constant motion. Work was the only thing that could save her now. She grabbed her purse, jumped into the car and headed downtown to her office.

Dougie, her receptionist, looked up with startled eyes when she charged through the glass double doors of Callahan Web Weaving. "Wait. Hold on a second. She just walked in the door," he said into the phone. He pushed a button. "Mag? What are you doing here? I thought you were coming in this afternoon, after you had lunch with—"

"Change of plans," she said crisply. "I have better things to do."

Dougie looked bewildered. "But Craig's on line two. He

wants to know why you're late for your lunch date. Says he has to talk to you. Urgently. As soon as possible. A matter of life and death, he says."

Mag rolled her eyes as she marched into her office. "So what else is new, Dougie? Isn't everything that has to do with Craig's precious convenience a matter of life and death?"

Dougie followed her. "He, uh, sounds really flipped out, Mag."

Come to think of it, it would be more classy, dignified, and above all, final if she looked him in the eye while she dumped him. Plus, she could throw the panties bag right into his face if he had the gall to deny it. That would be satisfying. Closure and all that good stuff.

She smiled reassuringly into Dougie's anxious eyes. "Tell Craig I'm on my way. And after this, don't accept any more calls from him. Don't even bother to take messages. For Craig Caruso, I am in a meeting, for the rest of eternity. Is that clear?"

Dougie blinked through his glasses, owl-like. "You OK, Mag?"

The smile on her face was a warlike mask. "Fine. I'm great, actually. This won't take long. I'm certainly not going to eat with him."

"Want me to order in lunch for you, then? Your usual?"

She hesitated, doubting she'd have much appetite, but poor Dougie was so anxious to help. "Sure, that would be nice." She patted him on the shoulder. "You're a sweetie pie. I don't deserve you."

"I'll order carrot cake and a double skim latte, too. You're gonna need it," Dougie said, scurrying back to his beeping phone.

Mag checked the mirror inside her coat closet, freshened her lipstick and made sure her coppery red do was artfully mussed, not wisping dorkily, as it tended to do if she didn't gel the living bejesus out of it. One should try to look elegant when telling a parasitical user to go to hell and fry. She thought about mascara, and decided against it. She cried easily: when she was hurt, when she was pissed, and today she was both. Putting on mascara was like spitting in the face of the gods.

She grabbed her purse, uncomfortably aware, as always, of the automatic pistol that shared the space inside with wallet, keys, and lipstick. A gift from Craig, after she'd gotten mugged months ago. A pointless gift, since she'd never been able to bring herself to load the thing, and had no license to carry concealed. Craig had insisted that she keep it in her purse, along with a clip of ammunition. And she'd gone along with it, in her efforts to be sweet and grateful and accommodating. Hah.

If she were a different woman, she'd make him regret that gift. She'd wave it around at him, scare him out of his wits. But that kind of tantrum just wasn't her style. Neither were guns. She'd give it back to him today. It was illegal, it was scary, it made her purse too heavy, and besides, today was all about streamlining, dumping excess baggage.

Emotional feng shui. Sploosh, straight into the lake.

By the time she got to her car, the unseasonable late autumn heat made sweat trickle between her shoulder blades. She felt rumpled, flushed and emotional. Frazzled Working Girl was not the look she wanted for this encounter. Indifferent Ice Queen was more like it. She cranked up the air conditioning to chill down to Ice Queen temperatures and pulled out into traffic, the density of which gave her way too much time to think about what a painful pattern this was in her love life.

Used and shafted by charming jerks. Over and over. She was almost thirty years old, for God's sake. She should have outgrown this tedious, self-destructive crap by now. She should be hitting her stride.

Maybe she should get her head shrunk. What a joy. Pick out the most icky element of her personality, and pay someone scads of money to help her dwell on it. Bleah. Introspection had never been her thing.

She parked her car outside the newly renovated brick warehouse that housed Craig's new studio and braced herself against seeing Craig's assistant bouncing up to chirp a greeting. Mandi was her name. Probably dotted the "i" with a heart. Nothing behind those big brown eyes but bubbles and foam. She had long dark hair, too. Fancy that.

But there was no one to be seen in the studio. Odd. Maybe Craig and Mandi had been overcome with passion in the back office. She set her teeth and marched through the place. Her heels clicked loudly on the tile. The silence made the sharp sounds echo and swell.

The door to Craig's office was ajar. She clicked her heels louder. *Go for it. Burn your bridges, Mag, it's what you're best at.*

Here's a first look at
TAKE MY BREATH AWAY
by Tina Donahue,
coming from Brava in May 2005 . . .

Beyond the expanse of lush lawn, where tables and chairs had been set up, Thaddeus's Spanish-style villa hugged the hill above the sea. The sprawling compound was crowned with a red-tiled roof. Clusters of scarlet, purple, and yellow bougainvillea clung to the dwelling's startling white walls and fluttered in the persistent breeze to scent the balmy air. Coconut palms and ferns were in abundance though more widely spaced than the thick foliage of the rain forest that lay behind. There, monkeys and other wildlife played and watched. Here, the sounds of the ocean were muted as it licked a beach that looked like powdered sugar beneath the lowering sun.

Okay, Cole thought, *so this* is *nice . . . but still dangerous, given the old guy's niece.* Sort of like a Club Med Hell since there was no escape until his pilot returned tomorrow morning—unless, of course, Cole opted to swim to the next island.

His gaze drifted in that direction. From this vantage point, that island looked like a speck of dirt in an endless sea.

He looked away. Coming here hadn't been such a good idea after all, but Cole reminded himself that he had been in far worse situations. Not the marines, mind you, but dealing with the suits and creative types in Hollywood. That was enough to give nightmares to a soldier of fortune. So, this couldn't be that bad. He'd meet Ariel, whom he was going to *dearly love before this was all over,* be polite, listen to what she had to say, then cut out as quickly as he—

Cole's thoughts paused when he heard the unmistakable *whap-whap-whap* of a helicopter in the distance. As he lifted his head and looked in the direction of that noise, Cole wondered if his pilot was returning. Had the guy forgotten something? Would it be possible to actually escape this place before—

"Ah," Thaddeus said, his voice serene and filled with love as it cut into Cole's thoughts, "that must be my dear niece—Ariel."

"Yes, sir," Cole said, steeling himself for the worst as the helicopter finally came into view from behind a cluster of thickly crowned palms, then headed straight for them.

The aircraft, at least, was sexy as hell. A sleek, black Bell 407 that effortlessly cut through the air and brought to mind strains of ominous music—something classical and Wagnerian—with lots of low tones and clashing cymbals. The kind of refrain that might have opened an old Schwarzenegger or Bruce Willis action flick. Music that Cole figured he'd use, along with this scene of a helicopter coming closer, closer, closer as it opened his political–military thriller and gave a hint of what was to come once the insurgents—or in this case, Ariel—landed.

"She's quite good at that, isn't she?" Thaddeus shouted above the noise.

Cole looked at the old guy. Thaddeus was holding onto his Panama hat, while his weathered face was raised to that copter as it reached the helipad to the left of this area.

"Good at what?" Cole shouted.

"Why, flying that helicopter, of course!"

She pilots helicopters? Cole thought, then glanced to the side and saw the silhouette of only one body in that bird. *Well, what do you know.* Not only was Ariel piloting the thing, she was landing it pretty damned well, too.

Glancing up from that flawless descent, Cole tried to see details of her, but was out of luck—or maybe in luck. Who knew? The next few minutes were pure torture as the blades of that copter slowly *whap-whap-whapped* to a stop. During this, Ariel leaned down until she was completely out of sight as she fiddled with something inside the cabin.

"Patience," Thaddeus said.

Cole pretended not to hear.

"She'll join us in good time," Thaddeus added.

That's what Cole was afraid of as the door to that copter finally popped open and Ariel stepped outside.

She was immediately surrounded by Thaddeus's housekeeping staff, who had run across the lawn to the helipad. As Ariel came around the copter door and bent at the waist to lower something to the ground, she was again obstructed from view.

Cole wondered if that were a good omen . . . or maybe a bad omen of things to—

His thoughts suddenly stopped as the staff moved aside just as Ariel straightened.

Thaddeus called out, "Please be certain you get those books she's brought to me!"

The staff chorused a "Yes, sir!"

Thaddeus leaned toward Cole. "Ariel's found a simply delightful bookstore that deals in rare volumes."

Cole nodded absently to that.

Thaddeus shouted more directives to his staff, the gist of which escaped Cole. Lowering the bottle of beer from his lips, he pushed up in his chair as his gaze simply prowled over Ariel Leigh.

Patience, Thaddeus had said.

Not a chance, Cole thought. He couldn't explore every part of her quickly enough. She was a tall woman, probably five-ten, with a sleek and well-toned body that was a delicious caramel color from days spent outdoors. As she moved fully into the sun, it intensified the color of her hair. That red-dish-gold mane was worn in a thick braid, while delicate tendrils danced over her tawny cheeks with the constant breeze.

Warmth continued to flood through Cole, settling in his groin. *That's Ariel?* Not only was she nothing like what he had feared, she was exquisitely female—the real deal, not the Hollywood version of what femininity should be. From this distance it appeared she wore little, if any, makeup.

She didn't need it. Her charm was natural, her beauty unique and more stunning than anything Cole had seen in Los Angeles where plastic surgery and excess were the norm. Even Ariel's clothing was simple, yet elegant—a white, sleeveless cotton top, white shorts that revealed an amazing expanse of her sleek legs, and white moccasins on her feet.

Cole's body continued to respond as he imagined licking her long, slender toes before he worked his way up those taut calves and creamy thighs to those delicate curls between her legs. Were they auburn, too?

A man could hope. A man should really know.

Of course, to do that, he would definitely have to stay longer than just tonight, possibly several days, which wasn't out of the question if he played dumb about this survival stuff, pretending he knew absolutely *nothing* about it. That would get her to show him everything she knew for as long as was needed. That would give them time to get to know each other.